C000226330

The Innocent Infidel

The Innocent Infidel

K.V. BETTS

Aldabra Publishing

First Published 2020
by
Aldabra Publishing
Five Wishes, Stalbridge,
Dorset DT10 2PQ

This is a work of fiction. Names, characters, businesses, places, events, locales, and incidents are either the products of the author's imagination or used in a fictitious manner. Any resemblance to actual persons, living or dead, or actual events is purely coincidental.

Printed in Great Britian by

Unit 4, Barton View business Park, Sheeplands Ln. Sherborne Dorset, DT9 4FW

ISBN 978-1-9162035-1-8

For Fran

Mam, without your inspiration I could never have succeeded, so this is for you! ...
And a massive thank you to Clyde for all his untiring help with publishing.

1

Concentrating on his target, Tomos Morgan stubbornly ignored the sudden cold that made him gasp within seconds of plunging into the flood. Beyond the slow-flowing wadi, long inky shadows cast by the desert dunes smoothed the land and danced off the swirling waters around him. Directly ahead, moonlight and starlight softly reflected off the stranded silver Land Cruiser, the tragic player held in nature's spotlight.

There was no sign of movement in the vehicle; why wasn't the driver trying to escape?

The answer would have to wait. For now, he needed to put all his effort into reaching the stricken 4x4. Although the current had subsided from its earlier fury, his feet still sank into the saturated sand and had to be dragged free with every heavy step.

He refocused his attention on the driver's door until he was close enough to peer inside. The window was fully open, the white-clad figure within slumped over the steering wheel. Steadying himself, he grabbed the handle and yanked on it as hard as he could. It didn't budge. He ran his hands down the metal of the door's edge, his fingers telling him what he already suspected; it was badly buckled, probably needing a crowbar to force it open. Reaching through, he caught hold of the man's shoulder and tugged it towards him. He recoiled in horror as the driver's head rolled back revealing a rigid face, a great red gash across the forehead, mouth frozen open, the eyes staring in an unblinking gaze.

Was he dead? He certainly looked dead. Maybe there was a chance he was still alive...

The whine of a revving engine clawed its way into his consciousness as a pair of powerful headlights swept over him. A glance revealed a car pulling up to the same point where he'd entered the flood. There wasn't time to wait for help. He waded round to the other side of the Land Cruiser and wrenched open the front passenger door, barely noticing the flush of water that emptied itself out of the cabin drenching him from waist to thigh. Climbing inside he leaned across to the driver and felt for a pulse. Nothing; his fingers sensed only the cold clammy skin of the man's neck. Despairingly, he tried the wrist; still nothing. A fuzzy memory from a first aid course flashed before him - a practice dummy on the ground - the urgency of giving CPR. He needed to get the driver lying flat. One hand fumbled for the seatbelt release button, allowing the sodden belt to slither back to its set position. With growing desperation, he sought a lever to lower the back of the seat.

The newcomers were on their way. As he struggled, he spotted at least one person through the windscreen splashing towards him, guided by the headlamps from the onshore vehicle. Ahead of them two small circles of light bobbed on the water from handheld torches. He was still grappling with the stubborn seat when the grisly scene lit up as the torch bearers came up behind him.

'Out, out!' A hand gripped the back of his shirt.

He felt himself hauled from the vehicle, his arms pinioned by someone standing behind him. A second person, a man - dressed top to toe in the traditional Arabic white dishdash robe - clambered past him into the cabin. Time slowed, the only sound the quiet breathing of the man behind him and his own thumping heartbeat. Legs followed by a torso and head re-emerged, the face of an old man glared at him, grim and angry. He shook his head at his companion and growled something in Arabic. Looking at Tomos, he spoke angrily, savagely.

'You too slow ... too slow ... he is dead! Why you waste time looking through the other window? Oh yes ... I see you ... only looking ... not helping.'

'Dead, is he? That's too bad, poor bugger never stood a chance; current's too strong.' His shoulders dropped. 'Don't even know the man.'

The needless loss of a life was a shock. Energised by the anger at his failure to save the stranger he shrugged off the shackling arms and staggered away from the metallic tomb. He cast one final look back at the ghastly scene and shuddered, the white robes of the Arabs made them look like ghouls as they hunched over their dead countryman.

There was nothing more he could do, the locals would take care of the deceased. The slow shuffle of a walk back to his own 4x4 gave him time to appreciate the full darkness of the night, a darkness which enveloped him, creeping into his soul. Cold and wet, he sat shivering in the driver's seat of the Isuzu for several minutes before he had the presence of mind to switch on the engine and the heater. Could he have done more?

He remembered the gash on the man's head and imagined the terrifying moment when the driver would have realised he was going to be swept away. He must have opened his window to escape before banging his head as the car jolted its way downstream, perhaps falling unconscious only to drown as his vehicle filled with water. It was the first time he'd ever seen someone die. He stared into the darkness, trying to come to terms with it. He was aware he was trembling, but whether from cold or shock, he neither knew nor cared.

. . .

The dashboard clock was showing almost eleven by the time Tomos reached the coastal town of Sohar. For the last hour, only the mildly irritating feel of his drying trousers, gritty with silt, had helped him battle a tiredness that constantly threatened to close his eyes. Sohar's streets were deserted, the only signs of life being a restaurant where the lighted windows silhouetted the last of the diners at their table. Inside his lodgings – a rented flat - there was only depressing silence. To lighten the mood, he switched on his little transistor radio. Pure static greeted his tired ears so he switched it off and took a shower instead. Refreshed, but with little appetite, he forced himself to eat a hastily-made sandwich. With just the silent night for company, he lay back on his bed, closed his eyes, and ran over the evening's events.

The day had started typically hot and humid, a bright sun rising ever higher into a clear blue sky. The storm had brewed incredibly quickly over the nearby mountains, the sky above the bare jagged crests darkening within minutes. He had been driving home to Sohar, an ancient seaside town to the east of the great Al Hajar Mountains of northern Oman. Frequent glances over his shoulder had confirmed the storm's approach, a gathering black mass of cloud flickering with half-hidden flashes of lightning.

The real troubles had started at dusk; the moment he'd first spotted the red tail lights queuing up on the approach to the large and normally dry river bed of Wadi Bani Khalid. The events that followed tumbled ever faster through his head, blurring his thoughts to finally send him into a shallow, restless sleep.

2

Dawn. The moment self-awareness overcame the drowsy remnants of sleep, Tomos began the fight to push away yesterday's memories. Those thoughts weren't pleasant and with work to do, he needed a clear mind at the start of a new day.

The thin shutters filtered the weak morning sunshine, filling his bedroom with a soft yellow glow. Despite a head heavy with fatigue, he dressed in vest and shorts. He had been a runner since boyhood, and fortunately his slim frame for an average height was ideal for distance running. He glanced at himself in the mirror on his way out of the front door, noting the bags under his eyes from a poor night's sleep. His reflection looked back at him; grey green eyes giving away his Celtic roots as did his untidy mop of uncombed hair.

Running was his main hobby, a pastime that rarely failed to deliver a boost to morale. Today was no different, the combination of exercise, fresh sea air and hissing waves breaking softly on the sandy shore provided the best tonic possible. The tide was in, forcing him to run on the dry sand higher up the beach. The extra effort needed cleared the remaining fog between his ears; after two miles he turned around and retraced his steps.

For the drive into the office, he chose the coast road which wound its way past the dhow-making end of the beach where the traditional Arab craft had been constructed for centuries. Beyond the boats countless wavelets glinted and sparkled in the early morning sunshine, playing their part in lifting his mood.

Driving on auto-pilot, he reflected on the career path that had brought him to the Arabian Gulf. He'd left his childhood home in the village of Pontyafon in Wales, to go to university. After graduating with a top degree in geology he'd initially spent a year employed by the Ministry of Defence in London, working on the interpretation of satellite imagery and aerial photography. Many of the images he examined were from the Middle East, and after twelve months of poring over them in the office, he'd developed the motivation to search for a position that would allow him to see the desert terrain for himself.

He had applied for his current post as a hydrogeologist without any real expectation of success, but his interview went well, and the offer of work had come as a welcome relief. He'd resigned from the MoD, and so at twenty-four years of age and five months into his new job, he was experiencing the secluded mountain villages, remote beaches and deserts of Arabia he had once longed to know.

His new role found him working for the Department of Water Resources within the Ministry of Water, where he was heading a team undertaking a nation-wide well inventory. The mapping of wells in foreign lands represented the perfect job; a golden opportunity to apply his skills in a largely uncharted environment - a vocation which offered travel and adventure, as well as a good salary.

The morning run and longer drive-in meant he was late for work, the cars parked in the street outside the office telling him most others had already arrived. Inside, he was greeted by

Abdul, a recent graduate from the University of Muscat, and his right-hand man. Abdul, was invaluable. One of two supervisors under Tomos, he was both competent and dedicated.

'As salaam al akum,' Abdul cordially greeted Tomos in the traditional manner. At five feet two inches tall and stocky; his small stature was oddly offset by a surprisingly deep voice.

'Walakum salaam,' replied Tomos, before switching to English. 'Let's grab a coffee in a minute, I need to ask you something.'

He took a circuitous route to the coffee table, stopping to greet each of the staff in turn, as was his habit at the start of every working day. There were twenty employees in total; a mix of fieldworkers and data-entry clerks. The fieldworkers would soon be heading off to the outlaying houses and surrounding farmsteads where they would systematically map every well and borehole they could find. The clerks would then enter the returned data into the official records.

Abdul was waiting for him outside his office, a coffee in each small paw. Tomos pushed open the door and gratefully accepted his cup before sitting.

'Problems?' Abdul queried with a smile. 'I think things are going well so far; everyone's doing their best.'

'No, the work is fine. Something happened driving home last night, I'd like to ask what you think about it.'

Tomos unconsciously took a sip and cast his mind back. He trusted Abdul and wanted to offload yesterday's events while the facts were still clear. Reliving events he explained how, after parking his car at the rear of the queue on the approach to Wadi Bani Khalid, he'd joined the small gaggle of drivers and passengers watching the storm-water filling the channel. Another group of thirty or so people stood loitering on the other side of the wadi, about fifty metres away. The flow was rushing down from the mountains and surging onwards towards a series of mini-dunes leading to the plains. He remembered observing the flood take shape, the turbulent waters pushing powerfully downstream, eager to taste the dry sands that lay ahead. The grit and general detritus picked up by the torrent had turned the water into a dirty brown churning mass. He guessed it must have been rising at least six inches a minute.

The sun had been setting fast, the descending gloom highlighting the occasional bright flashes above the distant mountains. The air had remained relatively warm, promising another typical Arabian night to come. Apart from the underlying rumble coming from the water-laden wadi, the only sound had been the low guttural mutterings of the Omanis. He took a moment more to reflect ...

'Another vehicle arrived, a brand-new silver Land Cruiser. It drove past us all, right up to the water's edge. You know what Abdul ... at first I thought it was someone queue jumping.'

The image remained crystal clear; the land cruiser accelerating into the muddy torrent, everybody edging forwards as if about to watch a sporting spectacle.

'Whoever he was', Tomos asserted, 'he must have thought he could still cross at that time. Maybe because he was driving such a big heavy 4x4, or maybe it was just a macho thing to show off in front of a crowd.'

He too, had watched. By the time it was about a third of the way across, only the silver roof remained visible, the windows already lost in the evening gloom, the submerged headlights creating an eerie glow through the water which gradually dimmed until it too was lost in the murk.

'What happened next?' Abdul asked softly.

'When I realised he wasn't going to make it, I had to try and do something. That's when I started running, following the flood, looking for a chance to help.'

Even as he ran, he'd been dimly aware of the anxious cries from the other onlookers. He'd stopped only for the briefest pause, to witness the moment the 4x4 lost contact with the ground. Despite its heavy weight and high ground clearance, the vehicle had slowly but inexorably been lifted by the powerful waters, spun through ninety degrees and sent floating downstream, rear-end first.

'I followed the car 'til it grounded mid-stream. I waded over but got there too late, the cabin was full of water so reckon the driver probably drowned. A couple of your countrymen turned up and said he was dead. There didn't seem to be anything I could do, so I left them to it.'

He examined his colleague's face for a reaction. 'So ... what d'ya think?'

Abdul gave a long, drawn out whistle. 'What can I say? Wonder who he was? I suppose you don't even know his name? Thing is ... thinking about it ... you're a witness. You'll have to report it to the police.'

'I intend to, later this morning, after sorting things out here first.'

'Right ... My uncle's a policeman in the Sohar station. I'll give him a call, he might know something. Wadi floods are not so unusual, someone always seems to get caught.'

Alone, Tomos drained the rest of his coffee and walked over to the window. Below him lay a walled courtyard guarded by wrought iron gates which were always left open during working hours. As he watched, a white sedan with a blue stripe along its side drove boldly in, its fat tyres crunching authoritatively on the gravelled surface. A policeman in a tight-fitting khaki uniform stepped out. Tomos felt a twinge of uneasiness, an unexpected visit from the officials making him instantly apprehensive.

The policeman was shown into his office by Nazir, the other supervisor under Tomos. He introduced Tomos as *Mr Morgan the Project Manager,* before leaving the two men together.

'Inspector Al Malky,' announced the newcomer, holding out his hand.

Tomos accepted the handshake. 'Inspector, please take a seat, would you like a coffee?'

'No thank you, Mr Morgan. May I ask if you know why I'm here?'

Tomos grimaced. 'I can guess ... last night's flood in Wadi Bani Khalid?'

'Right. I believe you were there, is that correct? If so, I want you to tell me everything that happened as you saw it.'

'Yeah, of course. Saves me the trouble of going to the police station later.'

Beginning from the time he'd first spotted the doomed driver at the wadi, Tomos retold his story. The inspector did not interrupt but stared at him intensely, an occasional nod his only acknowledgement.

Report completed, Tomos leant back in his chair to await the verdict. The inspector did likewise, shaking his head slowly from side to side before speaking.

'You have my sympathy, Mr Morgan, it must have been very difficult to see such things. A shame you couldn't help, but it's God's will this has happened. We have identified the deceased but it's of no consequence to you. His father has already been informed; it will be a hard time for the family, that's for sure.'

The inspector stood and reiterated Abdul's words. 'Wadi floods are not unusual, people often get caught. Now that I've heard your story I hope I won't need to see you again. If I do, I can always contact your office.'

'Can I ask how you knew I was a witness? I hadn't told anyone about what happened 'til this morning.'

The inspector shrugged. 'Oh, your government vehicle was identified at the wadi, and a description of a westerner was provided. These two facts linked you to the Sohar office. You were also seen approaching the vehicle and the driver. I had a slightly different account of your actions from another witness, but as I have no reason to doubt your intentions, I'll leave it there.'

'Well, inspector, I did my best, just sorry I wasn't able to do more.'

'The deceased belongs to a well-known family. With such people, we need to take things very seriously. Let's hope this meeting marks the end of the matter, for all concerned.'

Tomos saw the policeman to the door before returning to his desk to consider things. It must have been the older man or his companion who'd advised the police of his presence.

Strange that the police had been told a different version of events.

He pushed the inspector's comments to the back of his mind. There was a job to do, others were relying on him. He glanced at his watch; time to check the readiness of the field teams. The inspector hadn't stayed long; everyone was still in the main office which went momentarily quiet as he walked in.

The operatives were nearly ready to leave, their routes for the day having already been drawn up. Most were last-minute checking their GPS units were charged and working. The new technology had proved a godsend in mapping remote wells and boundaries in a country where few paper maps were available. Abdul would normally chase the field staff out to start work but he was still busy on the phone.

Nazir approached Tomos, waving a GPS unit. Nazir was also proving himself a key player, his fluency in both Arabic and English a big help. Along with Abdul, they had won the team's support and allowed Tomos to put his ideas into practice.

'This one's faulty, we need a replacement - it won't even charge,' Nazir complained.

'There's enough units, use one of the spares,' replied Tomos, noticing Abdul putting the phone down and trying to catch his eye.

'I'll return it to Muscat and ask for a replacement, that's the second one this week,' Nazir moaned, returning to his own desk. As he lowered his tall stick-like body into his chair, the short, stocky figure of Abdul rose. The two supervisors occupied adjacent desks as they were obliged to work so closely together.

'I have some news. Perhaps we can talk in your office again?' Abdul suggested, stepping towards the door.

Inside, the two men sat facing each other. 'So, what's new? Get through to your uncle?'

'The policeman ... yes. It seems last night's wadi flood is big news. Uncle told me the name of the man who died. It's Ahmed Al-Hazbar.'

'Al-Hazbar? I know that name from somewhere.'

'I'm not surprised. You met Rashid Al-Hazbar about two weeks ago when he came to this office. The man you saw drown was his son.'

Tomos stared blankly at Abdul for a second before clapping his hand to his head as the name linked itself to a face. 'You're right ... Al-Hazbar. Oh no - please don't tell me we're talking about the same man who threatened us over his wells?'

The full memory came hurtling back. One of the project field teams had stumbled upon a huge area of cultivated land surrounded by high-security wire fencing, to which they'd been denied access. Agriculture so far inland implied irrigation from boreholes, there being no rivers in Oman, and the water table at that location too deep to allow the digging of hand dug wells. The denial of access was illegal as the survey had the backing of a royal decree signed by no less than the Sultan himself.

Tomos had reported the incident and the problem had escalated. Eventually the minister himself had written an order that right of access be given to the inventory project. The team had returned to complete the survey armed with the ministerial letter which had only further infuriated the landowner, identified as the rich and influential businessman Rashid Al-Hazbar. Powerless to defy a government order, Al-Hazbar had resorted to verbally abusing the team.

Entering the site, they quickly discovered the motive for Al-Hazbar's obstruction. Two recently drilled deep boreholes had been found with high capacity pumps, generators, and fields of irrigated wheat. The relevant government register confirmed the illegality of the operation, the boreholes having probably been drilled at night to avoid detection. As in all the desert Gulf states, every drop of water had to be accounted for; drilling unpermitted boreholes was a very serious offence. The adverse publicity would have caused great embarrassment to Al-Hazbar; the loss of face an intolerable shame.

It didn't take long before Al-Hazbar had burst into Tomos's office - a flowing mass of swirling white robes and pent-up fury. Tall and bony, he had leant across his desk to announce himself. For Tomos, it had been a harrowing experience. The angry businessman, his face contorted in anger, had been only inches from his own.

In his mind's eye, Tomos could still see his features reddened with unsuppressed rage, the spit landing and glistening on his grey goatee as his thin lips spouted forth a tirade of abuse. What he lacked in physical bulk he more than made up with vitriolic speech, aggressively delivered.

Al-Hazbar had hissed out his opinion of "the interfering foreigner and his useless project!" in harsh accented English. It was his final words however that stayed strongest in Tomos's mind.

"I wanted to meet you, to know your face, and now I will remember you, Mr Morgan; you and your infidel ways. You would humiliate me in my own country, the greatest insult. Your work on my land is now finished. If I ever see you there again you will be punished, and if you ever cross me again - then I promise - I will kill you."

After Al-Hazbar had stormed out, Abdul had been keen to set the record straight.

'I'm glad to say he's not from Oman, not quite sure where he's from to be honest, my uncle says he settled here a few years ago. He's well known 'cos he's rich, though no-one seems to know how he's made his money.'

Now that the link between the dead man and Al-Hazbar had been established, the memory of those previous threats was not easily dismissed. The publicly declared illegality of Al-Hazbar's boreholes was surely nothing compared to the death of a son.

Since meeting Al-Hazbar, the demands of his day-to-day work had helped Tomos put the whole episode behind him, or as much of it as he could. One annoying legacy had been that he was aware that behind his back his staff often referred to him as "the infidel", Al-Hazbar's derogative having been overheard by the entire office.

The wadi incident however was a game-changer. He couldn't help wondering what the man was capable of, should he ever discover that he was present at the time of his son's death.

3

For three weeks Tomos neither saw nor heard a whisper from Al-Hazbar. Work progressed smoothly. His team continued the field surveys while he focused his efforts on writing up the findings, something which was well received by his manager in Muscat. Eventually when he estimated ninety percent of the wells had been mapped, he decided it was time to move into the neighbouring region.

Today was a workday, and he and Abdul were driving south to the next major town along the coast for a meeting with a local dignitary, the Wali of Al Khaburah. Abdul was unusually quiet, concentrating on driving, his head only just making it above the steering wheel, eyes squinting against the sun's glare off the road. Like many locals, he disdained the wearing of sunglasses believing them to be a sign of weakness, only to be worn by westerners.

From the front passenger seat, Tomos considered he didn't really need sunglasses either; there were so few features of interest to interrupt the flat monotonous landscape of the Al-Batinah coastal plain. The deep azure blue of the Gulf of Oman held his eye for a while, but even this view was punctuated by too many roadside buildings to hold his attention for long. To the soothing drone of the engine he sat back and let his mind drift across the sea, to his roots in Wales.

Home was a nineteenth century terrace cottage, one of thousands built to house the colliery workers who'd done so much to carve out the industrial landscape of South Wales. His own house was set in the small mining village of Pontyafon.

The coal mines had long since closed but the descendants of those tough subterranean workers continued to inhabit the half dozen long ribbons of houses that hugged the contours of the hillside above the river.

It was April. Was the weather there being typically Welsh ... cold, wet and windy?

He tried to visualise the scene: valley sides cloaked with a soft-textured patchwork of newly-greening woodland, the harder ridges of the mountain peaks swathed in a coating of brown bracken, all topped with a covering of dull slate-grey sky spitting an unending drizzle. The sun seemed to enjoy playing tricks this time of year, occasionally darting into sight to chase cloudy shadows into hiding in the dark recesses of the woods or into the next valley.

Contemplating of home made him consider his folks, his mam and dad. What would they be up to right now? It was a Sunday, so probably the roast would be in the oven filling the house with wonderful aromas. His mam often said a roast chicken dinner gave the same comfort as a cwtch or Welsh hug.

The thought of food prompted a pang of hunger followed immediately by a sense of homesickness. Were things really better away in foreign lands?

'The project will be so much easier with the wali on our side,' Abdul's words snapped him back to the present.

'I suppose since the project is backed by royal decree he's got no real choice but to support us. But I agree, if we can show him the benefits then hopefully he'll be more enthusiastic and talk to his people. Can he really make such a difference?'

Abdul nodded vigorously. 'Oh yes, he's a very powerful man, I think you could describe him as something of a cross between a mayor and a magistrate in your own country. He controls an area we call a Wilayat, which I think is something like one of your English counties. We just need to explain things clearly, that's all.'

The car's a/c was on its last legs, generating more noise than cold air, and allowing the occupants to become uncomfortably warm by the time they pulled off the highway to enter the town of Al Khaburah. They passed through a new commercial zone still under construction, advertising boards informing them that M&S and McDonalds would soon be opening new premises, the encroachment of western companies a relatively new phenomenon. Abdul steered them through the old town centre, a large central souk with a labyrinth of narrow winding alleyways snaking off in different directions. The shops and stalls here were small and simple, bustling with people going about their daily business. They turned down the widest of the streets leading off the main square and parked outside a grandiose villa.

'Arrived,' Abdul grunted unnecessarily, 'and its ten o'clock; we're right on time.'

Tomos got out, stretched, and just managed to smother a yawn.

'This way,' muttered Abdul.

They passed under an archway bearing the symbol of the crossed khunjars or traditional daggers, the national emblem of the Sultanate, and into a paved courtyard dominated by a black limousine bearing government licence plates. From a pole on the perimeter wall, the national flag fluttered feebly in the weak onshore breeze. Tomos reckoned he could faintly smell the sea which he knew must be only a few streets away.

A cool air-conditioned interior welcomed them as they stepped inside to a spacious waiting room. They were greeted warmly in both Arabic and English by a bespectacled male receptionist who wasted no time in politely ushering them into the dignitary's private office.

The wali stood up from behind a large mahogany desk and strode over to meet his guests. He was a large jolly looking man, massive both in frame and height. A neatly cropped black beard edged with white, seemed to add to his status. Even after everyone was sitting, he continued to loom over his visitors.

The office was simple but comfortable. The only sound was the barely audible hum of the air conditioning, a centrally run system with ceiling vents rather than the cheaper, more common hole-in-the-wall units. There was a sofa against one side wall and a rank of filing cabinets on the other. Natural sunlight struggled in through a half-shuttered window, its efforts supported by a small ceiling chandelier. He refocused on the job in hand as the wali addressed him.

'So, the Ministry of Water wishes to operate in the wilayat of Al Khaburah? You're very welcome. I know a little of your program; perhaps you can tell me more? However, before you begin, please help yourself to dates and coffee.' A wave of a giant bejewelled hand indicated several bowls containing either fresh or dried dates and a large pot of percolating coffee sitting on one end of the desk.

‘Ah shookran,’ replied Abdul automatically in Arabic, helping himself. He switched effortlessly to English, ‘Coffee for you Mr Morgan? Allow me.’

‘Mr Morgan is too skinny, make sure you give him plenty.’ The walis’s words were contagiously spoken through a half-smile that made Tomos chuckle as he helped himself to a handful. Following Abdul’s example, he pressed out the stone before putting the flesh of the fruit into his mouth.

‘Very nice, as delicious as it looks,’ he confirmed.

‘If Mr Morgan is happy I will explain to you in Arabic the purpose of the project and what we propose to do,’ Abdul suggested. ‘It’s just that I can explain things better in Arabic.’

‘Yes, that’s fine with me,’ Tomos agreed. Not being an Arabic speaker, he immediately lost the thread of the discussion. As his concentration wavered he became aware of a vehicle pulling up outside, the unmistakable reverberation of a diesel engine.

The wali waited until Abdul completed his explanation before summing up his thoughts in English.

‘I don’t know exactly how many wells we have here in Al Khaburah; hundreds I should think. It’s going to take months to find them all. Don’t you think it better to open another field office here to reduce travel time? Also, during the day only women will be at home, and they’re unlikely to open the door to men they don’t know. Apart from that, I don’t think you’ll have any problems from the people. If you do, please come to me. I can help arrange visits on your behalf.’

‘That’s very kind sir,’ Tomos replied respectfully, ‘and I think you may be right about opening an office here. I’ll suggest it to my manager, it would be his decision.’

The telephone rang. 'Yes?' the wali asked lifting the receiver. He listened for a few seconds, then replaced it. 'Very good - now if there is nothing else, I must return to my work. I have another visitor, one even more important than the Ministry of Water.' He rose, using his height to lean across the desk to shake hands. 'Don't forget to keep eating the dates,' he advised Tomos with a wink

Outside, the courtyard trapped the heat like a furnace, the air heated from a sun now high in a steel blue sky. The gentle onshore breeze was blowing in moisture-laden air making breathing a real effort. There was a new vehicle parked close by, a white Mercedes, its diesel engine purring smoothly.

'I think that went well, don't you?' Tomos asked.

'Oh, yes, I'm sure we have his blessing. There won't be any problems from now on, Inshallah,' Abdul replied. 'Ah, wait ... maybe I spoke too soon. I suggest you leave right now,' he added under his breath.

'What?' Tomos, puzzled by his colleague's sudden warning, looked up as a car door slammed shut. Someone had just stepped down from the Mercedes, someone he recognised. He knew he should continue walking, but he simply couldn't bring himself to do so. Foolish bravado or an unwillingness to accept what he saw made him freeze. Walking towards him, grim faced, was the last person he wanted to see ... Rashid Al-Hazbar.

'Well, well, if it isn't Mr Morgan, the cursed infidel. You didn't run to my son's aid when he needed help, so you better not run away now!'

Al-Hazbar strode up to Tomos and thrust his face close up, hissing in a low harsh tone. 'I hope you remembered my words. Let me remind you: I said I would kill you, if you ever wronged me again - and what have you done? You had the chance to save my beloved son - yet you deliberately did nothing. Oh yes, I know you were there that day in the wadi, and I have vowed that you will pay for your evil deeds against me and my family. First my wells: now my son.'

Al-Hazbar's face darkened. 'Hear me now - I swear I will see you die no matter where you run - you cannot hide from me. This you will find to be true. It is only a matter of time. Revenge will be sweet, infidel. I look forward to it very much. That is all I have to say.'

Anger boiled through Tomos as he desperately fought the urge to strike out and punch the almost demonic face invading his personal space.

Hit him, and you lose your job at best, the voice of reason echoed.

'I don't run from any man, especially one as bitter as you. Don't you threaten me again, or it will be *me* who comes looking for *you*. I'm sorry about your loss, but that's down to God - not me. You should realise that.'

Al-Hazbar looked stunned, as if he could not believe anyone would dare answer him back. Before he could respond, Tomos spun on his heel and walked away to join an anxious Abdul loitering at the gate. He was still fuming inside, but intuitively knew nothing good would come about through further confrontation. Not yet, at any rate.

4

Another two weeks passed before Tomos and Abdul took their first field trip to the Khaburah region. In preparation the two of them had spent long hours poring over the few relevant aerial photographs made available to them, and the even rarer large-scale maps. The photographs were especially useful for identifying irrigated areas. Irrigation implied wells; in Khaburah, the areas of interest were clustered around the small villages either hugging the coast or high up in the mountains.

Tomos decided to subdivide the area into its major water drainage catchments and begin work in the nearest, the most northerly one. A schedule was compiled, and together with maps of the proposed survey areas, was copied to the wali. He took the request from the dignatary's office for a detailed schedule as a sign of support, so was more than happy to comply.

Today's scouting sortie was to a mountain village called Lihban. Tomos had picked himself and his two planners, Abdul and Nazir for the trip. If the three of them understood the nature of the terrain they would be better able to plan ahead for the field teams.

An early morning start saw them drive south from Sohar along the main coastal highway. A few miles before Al Khaburah they turned off and headed west along a dead straight blacktop road, towards the mountains of the interior.

This time Tomos watched the passing landscape with interest. They passed several farmsteads engaging in large-scale irrigation, numerous rotating spray guns ejecting water in great silvery arcs onto the thirsty crops. The big farms gradually petered out to be replaced by an uninhabited and featureless stony plain utterly devoid of any vegetation. The air shimmered under a pitiless sun, whilst on the horizon the formidable mass of grey mountain that concealed their destination slowly grew and took shape out of the intervening haze.

At the end of the plain and at the foot of the mountains they drove through a village of traditional stone houses with metallic doors and shuttered windows. Here, dark foliage of date palms contrasted with the sharper bright green of swathes of alfalfa grown for animal fodder. In between the alfalfa fields, thorny shrubs struggled their way up through the baked ground. A herd of scruffy goats were the only signs of animal life, no people being in sight. Litter marked both sides of the road and discarded plastic bags fluttered from the bushes of whichever thorn had snagged them. All in all, the village presented a truly forlorn picture.

'This place is called Al Ghazayn,' Abdul offered, his voice flat with disdain. 'We start going up now.

Ahead of them lay one of the great wadis of Oman - a long sinuous gorge penetrating into the heart of the high mountains. The tarmac ended at the village, so 4-wheel drive was engaged as they swung into the mouth of the wadi. Immediately the going got very rough, and a lot slower, as Abdul carefully tried to pick out a path using the traces of old tyre tracks in the gravel that lay in-between the rocks and boulders that dotted the narrow floor of the gorge. As they rumbled their way up the valley, the vehicle swayed from side to side, making the massive cliffs repeatedly loom over them as if the walls of rock were being dropped down from the heavens above. They drove past a series of pools of water lying cold and dark in the shadows of the overhanging precipices. Snaking down one side of the wadi was a stone-lined open channel, a still in-use relic of the ancient local falaj system, a network of irrigation channels built to carry water to the lower settlements from the high mountains above. The three men drove on. The falaj system disappeared underground; long ago engineers had deliberately built such subterranean channels to protect the precious water supply from both evaporation and sabotage by warring neighbours. The wadi narrowed and after another hour's drive they rounded a bend and arrived at their destination, the small settlement of Lihban.

The village was a tightly packed cluster of houses set on the mountainside. All the buildings were the same sandy colour as the outcropping rock on which they sat. By following the natural curves of the land, the whole nucleus of dwellings blended perfectly with the surrounding environment. Tomos wondered how long the village had stood there, man's sentinels guarding the anciently-formed contours of the natural landscape. In fact so well was the village camouflaged, it would have been virtually invisible to the casual eye, if it wasn't for the betrayal of the regular straight lines of the rooftops.

'Come,' breathed Abdul, breaking into Tomos's thoughts. 'Let's find the wakeel first.'

Tomos raised an eyebrow prompting more from his tiny assistant.

‘The wakeel is the name given to the man responsible for controlling where the irrigation water flows through the village. Good manners to let him know we’re here. Anyway, he’ll know where all the wells are; could save us a lot of time.’

Together they walked towards a grove of date palms marking the approach to the village. Out of the wooded shadows trotted the shape of a donkey carrying a sun-wizened old man on its back. He was urgently pushing his sturdy steed forward with a short stick and rode right up to them before dismounting and handing out a flustered flurry of handshakes.

Abdul gave a rare grin. ‘Well, that didn’t take long ... this is the wakeel ... Says he’s been waiting for us. I’ll tell him why we’re here and what we want to do.’

To Tomos, the old man seemed satisfied from the way he kept vigorously nodding his head in time to Abdul’s words.

‘Says he’ll let the sheikh know we’ve arrived,’ his colleague explained as together they watched the wakeel remount his donkey and trot away.

They continued on through the swathe of crops fronting the village which proved the impossibity of mapping the field boundaries using the car mounted GPS - the tracks were just too narrow for vehicles. It would all have to be done on foot. They also discovered the ground-hugging alfalfa was being irrigated by wells, whilst the palms were being irrigated by the falaj system. Within the alfalfa plots they found three wells, two of which were hand-dug and appeared abandoned. The third was a newish-looking borehole.

‘Maybe the borehole is more productive so it’s replaced the wells,’ Tomos observed. ‘It’s the sort of thing we need to know.’

'We can ask the local sheikh today. The wakeel said he's invited us to eat with him at midday, if we go back to the village through the palms we should get there around twelve o'clock,' Abdul added.

Walking into the cooler air and hearing the wind-rustled trees was a pleasure after the exposed heat of the open fields. The whispering palms were accompanied by every rivulet of water sparkling in time to its own gurgling song. They followed the narrow path upstream, twisting their way around the trees–and over numerous little bridges that crossed the bubbling waters. They rounded a bend and Abdul suddenly stepped sharply away without a word. Tomos and Nazir looked at one another in bemusement. There was nothing in view to explain his behaviour, only some old lady shuffling towards them on the same path. Catching up, Nazir asked Abdul if there was a problem.

'Didn't you two see that old woman? Not good to pass her ... what if she's a witch and curses us?'.

Nazir laughed out loud while Tomos masked his feelings, barely able to believe his ears. Here was an intelligent young man, well-educated but still believing absolutely in the existence of witches.

'Well, we've missed her now, so we should be safe,' was all he dared muster.

'This way,' Abdul mumbled clearly embarrassed at his colleague's reactions. 'Let's search for the sheikh's house.'

The wakeel found them again, just as they reached the village proper. He hurriedly shepherded them to a long low-ceilinged room in a building adjacent to the small village mosque.

Shoes left at the door, they entered to find four men sitting, all of whom immediately stood to offer a friendly greeting. Abdul performed the translations, introducing the leader as the Sheikh of Lihban. Two more were described as local elders, the fourth, a youth called Ali, acted as an assistant to his seniors.

Everybody was invited to sit on the carpeted floor. Lunch was served in the traditional manner with communal plates of boiled rice and roasted goat, placed strategically in the centre of all the cross-legged bodies. After washing his hands, Tomos took his cue from the others and ripped off a hunk of meat and ladled a helping of rice onto his bowl. The food was eaten by hand, which was not so easy with rice as he quickly discovered, the moist grains slipping through his clumsy fingers as he struggled to mould them into mouth-sized balls.

A selection of dates was offered after the main course. Until this point Tomos had been largely left out of the conversation; enjoying his lunch while the harsh Arabic tones washed over him. Indeed it felt like the elders and the sheikh were almost deliberately avoiding eye contact with him. Once they started on the dates however, the sheikh focused on Tomos, and with Abdul again acting as interpreter, asked him if he was enjoying his time in Oman.

'Oh, very much; I also have to say what a beautiful village you have here; very nice indeed.'

Abdul took up the conversation, addressing Tomos. 'Everyone already knows why we're here and what we're trying to do, so that's all fine, the field teams will be free to come and go as they please. Before we leave, the sheikh has suggested that Ali shows you to a viewing point above the village, while myself and Nazir stay here to pray. The sheikh would like you to see how Allah has blessed his village with magnificent scenery ... His words not mine.'

Nothing could appeal to Tomos more than the ascent of a new mountain. The challenge of a climb and the reward of a view were two things he'd always appreciated. Once the meal was over, Ali beckoned Tomos over to the door, the youth clearly unable to speak English.

Having agreed to meet the others later outside the mosque, Tomos followed Ali along the main central street. At the top end of the village the street gave way to a rough stony path which narrowed more and more the higher they went, until it eventually became just a groove in the underlying rock. Though fit, Tomos found the going tough. The surrounding exposed rock reflected the sun's heat, focusing its effect to an almost suffocating intensity.

A little way on, the path continued between two towering cliffs only metres apart. As they approached, the cliffs closed overhead to form a natural cavern some fifty metres in length. At the far end an irregular circle of sunlight hinted the path carried on beyond the natural passageway.

A brush of cool air welcomed them as they entered the dimness. They stopped to look at a series of pools of water stretching ahead of them. Ali tapped his chest and touched the nearest wall before pointing at Tomos and the other end of the cavern, which Tomos understood to mean that Ali would wait for him while he went on alone. The reason for Ali's reluctance to carry on wasn't clear, but Tomos didn't question the decision, merely nodding his understanding. He guessed it wasn't far now to the top but supposed his guide simply didn't want to get his feet wet by walking any further. This seemed a reasonable assumption as the pools turned out to be almost knee-deep, prompting Tomos to remove his trainers and roll-up his trouser legs.

He re-entered the broiling heat on the other side of the cavern, reshod, and after another five minutes of hard slog reached the end of the path. He walked out onto a rocky ledge and found himself standing above a deep boulder-filled gorge, the bottom of which he estimated to be many hundreds, if not a thousand feet below him. He could see now why the sheikh had advised him to come ... the vista across the gorge really was amazing! The other side of the valley and a little lower down was another village, tiny dolls-houses shimmering in the afternoon heat. The hot air was heavily oppressive, not a sound from anywhere. Total silence. Wishing he'd brought his camera, Tomos attempted to relate the other village to the maps he'd studied, trying to remember what it was called.

'Crack!'

The echo reverberated off the angular rocks, stunning Tomos with its sudden shattering of the silent serenity. A small shower of stones and dust cascaded down to land beside him. A second crack and something slammed into the rock face just above his left shoulder.

'What the hell!'

The sharp retort of another projectile hitting the rock even closer hammered home its message. He was being shot at!

Instinct took over, spinning him round in an instant to flee back down the path. He heard the echo of a fourth shot even as he ran, though where it landed he had no idea. One stray bullet could be an accident, but not four!

The walk from the cave up to the rocky ledge had taken five minutes; the return trip took less than one. Only after sprinting beyond the second bend did he slow down. He hadn't spotted the culprit, but line of sight told him he must have been on the opposite side of the gorge, so he was at least safe from pursuit. If he was right, that also meant he couldn't double back to track down his attacker; it would take the best part of a day to cross such a deep chasm.

Heart still pounding with adrenalin, he arrived at the top entrance to the cavern. He peered along its dark length; it looked empty. What the heck was going on? And where the hell was Ali?

He stumbled and splashed his way through the pools and puddles and out of the cavern's lower end. Still no sign of Ali. He jogged the last section of the track, all the way back down to the village.

Prayers had finished, and a small group of worshippers were loitering and talking in the street in the shade of the domed mosque. Among them Tomos first spotted Nazir, who stood out from the rest as he was wearing jeans and shirt, then Abdul - one dishdash among many. He was aware of the disapproving looks of his colleagues as he approached them, all chat hushing to a halt. He was sweating profusely from his unplanned run; his lower trouser legs were soaking wet and his trainers squelched as he walked. He wasn't looking his professional best, but he couldn't give a damn about that. Shock had turned to anger during his run back to the village, and he intended everyone to know it.

'Enjoy yourself?' inquired Nazir somewhat sarcastically, as usual getting in the first words.

'No - not really Nazir. Abdul, can you please inform the sheikh that someone has just been shooting a gun at me, and I think I was lucky to escape.'

The disapproving look dropped from Abdul's face. 'What do you mean? Are you sure? What exactly happened?'

'Let me tell you ... I reached the end of the path and someone started shooting at me. I didn't see who, thought it better to leave at that point,' he snapped angrily.

Just as he finished speaking, the sheikh himself pushed through the small throng. He and Abdul conversed in animated tones. The sheikh looked annoyed at what he was being told, but Tomos detected no trace of surprise on his craggy features.

Abdul translated what he'd learnt; telling Tomos that the sheikh was deeply apologetic but that whoever had been shooting was surely not from his village, no-one there would ever treat visitors in such a shameful manner. He'd heard that a tourist had once been fired upon at a village in the next valley, the people there not liking strangers as much as in Lihban. Even then he was sure the culprit had only meant to scare off the visitor, not actually harm him. He hoped that Tomos would not hold this terrible action against his village and its good citizens.

The apology sounded genuine enough, making Tomos hesitate before replying. He wanted to say, 'let's get a group of men together and try to catch this man', but common sense told him his assailant would be long gone. In any case, he doubted any local would be willing to hunt one of their own on behalf of an outsider.

Still smouldering, Tomos reluctantly acquiesced.

'OK Abdul, tell him I expect he's right. Anyway, as I'm unhurt no harm was done.'

Farewells were awkwardly completed before the three visitors returned to their vehicle. Tomos's mind was a whirl. Why was he walking away as if nothing had happened?

The problem was there didn't seem to be anything he could do, once the sheikh had denied any knowledge of the event. He was possibly right anyway. He'd heard that every mountain village was different, some very welcoming to outsiders, others more hostile.

Nazir and Abdul climbed into the car. On impulse Tomos took a final glance back towards the village. A slight movement caught his eye, a figure dressed in white, stepping back into the shadows. The figure had moved too late. Tomos recognised Ali and raised his hand in a quick wave which, after a moment's hesitation, was returned by the young man. With that, Tomos climbed aboard for the long drive back to Sohar.

Abdul turned the ignition and set the car in motion before speaking. 'Can you just repeat what happened again? This is not a good start to our work in this area.'

'I walked to the top of the hill and someone started firing a gun. There's no doubt they were aiming for me, I counted four shots, rifle shots I think, before I managed to get away. What do you two make of it?'

Abdul's reply was calm and measured. 'I'm sure the sheikh is right. Certainly it must have been someone from another village who didn't know about your visit. Lots of the older people don't like westerners and don't want them getting involved in their way of life, so I think he was probably only trying to scare you away. Don't forget many of the older mountain men also carry guns; we call them Jebali's. These people still hold onto their tribal values so like to carry arms; others have guns for hunting. These days guns are part of the traditional costume.'

'Yeah, that must be it. Just some unfriendly villager, nothing to worry about boss,' Nazir agreed. 'I mean, nothing to worry about now that you're safe.'

Tomos silently disagreed, the shots had been too close making him believe the antagonist had been aiming for a kill. Besides which, he had only recently been threatened. Could there be a link between the shooting and the threats made by Al-Hazbar?

He remembered the wali's late request that they post him their schedule. He'd taken a very keen interest in the project, much more than might have been expected from such a high-ranking official. He'd even arranged for them to be met, all of which had taken place after Tomos had bumped into Al-Hazbar at the wali's office. Anxiety knifed through him. Doubtless Al-Hazbar would have asked the wali what Tomos was planning. It was not impossible that Al-Hazbar had requested the wali to send him Tomos's schedule and therefore he would have known in advance of the planned visit.

He considered the sheikh's reaction, his total lack of surprise at being told of the attempted shooting.

Was it all pre-planned? His thoughts turned to the guide, Ali; he had lots of questions about him, too. Why hadn't Ali come with him all the way to the top of the path? Had he been told to stop at the cavern to avoid being accidentally shot by the would-be assassin? And why had he followed him back to the car but not approached? Had he been spying?

He wondered if Ali had wanted to explain himself but lacked the courage to step forward. It was all conjecture, nothing seemed that significant on its own, but when everything was put together it didn't look good. The basic facts were Al-Hazbar had threatened to kill him and now someone had tried to shoot him.

A chill ran down his spine. Was he being hunted? If so, he hadn't a clue what to do about it.

5

Tomos lay back on the sofa, closed his eyes and tried to relax. His efforts were in vain, as he knew they would be. Inevitably he gave in to the temptation to reflect on the course of events over the last few weeks.

Following the incident in Lihban village, he'd tried to make some improvements to his life. Firstly, he'd talked to Hassan, his manager, who'd accepted his request for a transfer away from Sohar. James, another British expat who had been covering the Muscat Capital area, had happily swopped positions with him. Secondly, he'd taken two weeks leave. This, he reasoned, would give him time to decide if he wanted to continue working in Oman.

His leave had been good, staying in the family home in Pontyafon with his parents and Oscar, their fat old golden labrador. Most of his time had been spent either catching up with friends or out running the surrounding hills, something he'd done throughout his teenage years; normal things.

He'd spent ages mulling over whether or not it was in his best interest to return to the Gulf, a straightforward choice of common sense safety versus ambition and money. It was an argument he inwardly knew the answer to, even as he'd undertaken a perfunctory job search, just to see what else was available. An over-riding need for ready money and a reluctance to run away from his problem were always going to win the day. In any case, there wasn't much on offer. The two most promising overseas posts were for a geologist in the

Ashanti gold mines of Ghana and a hydrogeologist working in Libya. He hadn't pursued either.

Anyway, once back in the Welsh valleys the events in Oman appeared less serious and completing his one-year contract would look good on his CV. So he'd returned to Oman and relocated to a rented flat in Muscat.

One month in, and the new day job consisted of working in the main ministerial office where he concentrated on analysing the results of field surveys as they came in from the various regions. And working in Muscat had brought other benefits. He'd seized the opportunity to get into a routine of running every evening on many wonderful new routes. Beach and wadi runs, and even mountain trails were all possible after work. There was even an ex-pat league with organised races mid-week which he'd started participating in. He'd won both his first two races, but more satisfying was meeting other runners of different nationalities, sharing stories and socialising with after-run barbecues and drinks.

Another advantage to his move to the capital was having time to go camping. The last few weekends had provided memorable trips out. He now looked forward to these all week. Invariably they took place along one of the numerous small sandy coves to the south of Muscat reached by a jarring two-hour cross-country drive. He had also become good friends with Simon, a work colleague who shared a similar love of an active outdoor life.

The first of July was a weekend, and Tomos was lounging around in shorts and t-shirt, relaxing and waiting for Simon to call. The doorbell chimed. Padding barefoot across the tiled floor, he opened the door to greet his pal.

'Coming out to play?' Simon greeted him with impatient enthusiasm.

Six feet tall, blonde and heavily built, he was physically very different to Tomos, but his psyche was similar; both sharing an almost nervous excitement about whatever life was about to throw at them. Finding in Simon the echo of his own spirit had helped Tomos develop their friendship over the last few weeks.

'Just change my shorts, don't want any funny looks. Coming in for a drink?'

'Nah, I'll wait in the jeep,' replied Simon, his West Country drawl very pronounced. 'Trust the Welsh not to be ready.'

Simon hailed from Bristol, and the long tradition of poking fun at their neighbours across the Severn Estuary was faithfully upheld by both parties. He had been taken on through the same recruitment drive as Tomos. Based in Muscat, in the newly founded labs, he worked as a hydro-geochemist, analysing water samples from wells and boreholes taken from all over the country.

Shorts changed for jeans, Tomos jumped into the passenger seat of Simon's Jeep Cherokee, and they set off with an accelerated roar from the 4-litre engine. Once on the main road, Simon headed towards Mutrah, the old town of Muscat.

He glanced at his passenger. 'Remind me again, who recommended this little sortie to you? I'm blaming you if it's any less fun than sea fishing in the company of a crate of lager for the day.'

'That's what I like about you, so culturally inquisitive. Hassan, my manager, suggested it. It's supposed to be quite a sight, traditional dancing and so on. Can't remember what it's in aid of ... to celebrate some battle I think.'

'Well, I'm sure the trip'll be even better with some music, a bit of Phil Collins should help pass the time,' Simon added, slipping a tape into the deck.

To the tune of *There's something in the air tonight,* they zig-zagged up over the hills that rose high above the eastern flank of the city. From there they hit the road that snaked southwards through the exposed grey and black geology, the same road that led them towards their destination, the small town of Quriyat.

The journey took a little under two hours, by which time the series of sun-bleached hills of the lunar-looking landscape had merged in the mind's eye into one long blur. The tape, played through once only, had long since finished by the time they closed in on their destination. Negotiating the first of many downhill bends of the final descent, Quriyat made its first appearance, the houses a necklace of white pearls set on a band of black tarmac that arched along a concave sandy bay; at its centre a jumble of clustered diamonds guarding the jewel of a tall minaret. They s-bended to sea level and the final run along the beach to the edge of town.

'Looks like the end of the road,' Simon remarked as they drew up behind ranks of parked vehicles blocking the way ahead.

'Yeah, we'll leave the jeep here and walk in. Let's hope there's something worth seeing'.

They threaded their way on foot through the jumble of stationary cars to the rhythmic sound of human chanting. Ahead Tomos could see people congregating at the end of the road. A picturesque arc of small villas fronted the right-hand side of the street; the left side offering a panoramic view of a wide bay. The road surface was flush with the top of a broad white sandy beach which swept down to the gentle expanse of blue sea some four hundred metres away, where a small flotilla of brightly-coloured canvas-awned fishing craft bobbed up and down on the gentlest of swells. Every hull was painted: yellows, reds, greens and whites being the most popular. Together the colours added just the right amount of contrast against the subtly different blues of ocean and sky to satisfy even the most perfectionist of artists. Watching them, he found he could easily envisage the local fishermen loading their catch onto trucks for the short drive up the beach.

The chanting levelled off in volume when they melted into the rearmost rank of spectators, composed mostly of Omani's interspersed with the occasional foreign tourist. Immediately in front of them the road curved away from the sea, heading inland towards the town. The bend had been widened out to form an open square, an ideal arena for a festival. The performers occupied the centre and were ringed by the spectators, three or four deep. On the adjacent beach adolescent boys were playing football, their high-pitched shouts occasionally rising above the rumble of their seniors.

Peering through the throng Tomos could see a dance in progress. All-male, the performers were in a huddle hopping up and down in rough time to their own singing. He'd seen enough acts on local TV to recognise a traditional folk dance. The dancers were all dressed in white dishdash smocks adorned with ornate silver daggers tied around the waist. They went through their routine led by a lead vocalist until the climax, signified by an extra big unified hop from the whole group. Behind them he could see another troupe preparing to perform. Dressed in similar fashion to the first group, many also carried rifles slung over their shoulders.

Simon nudged him in the side. 'I've seen these dances on the tele, they take ages. Think I'll go buy a cola, want one?'

'Yeah, thanks, get me a Sprite if they have one, cola if not. I'll see if I can get to the front while you're gone.'

Simon ambled off, weaving his way through the spectators, now restless in the break between performances. Tomos turned his attention back to the show and slipped his way to the front, looking for a good vantage point. The sight of the rifle-carrying tribesmen made him edgy, he found it hard to take his eyes off them.

An inexplicable feeling of being watched persuaded him to scan round. There! Up ahead, his gaze was met by a pair of dark malevolent eyes set in a deeply-lined, swarthy face. The look of malicious intent only lasted a second before the crowd pressed forward in anticipation of the next act mercifully swallowing it from sight.

He moved back in shock. It wasn't the threat of latent cruelty that glowered blackly from those unblinking eyes that shook him, it was recognition. The face flashed through his mind. The day of the wadi flood - the dead body in the Land Cruiser - himself being pulled from the vehicle - a voice accusing him of letting a man die. The owner of that voice was the same owner of those hate-filled eyes. Or was it his imagination?

Seeing the dancers' rifles had reminded him of that day above the gorge. Had his mind tricked him? He inched forward. He had to be sure ... he needed a second look.

Why would the old man be here? Coincidence? That did not seem likely in a country the size of Britain. His blood froze at his next thought. Was this another set-up? Was this to be another assassination attempt? Was this Lihban all over again?

A hand landed heavily on his shoulder. Spinning round he instinctively grabbed a forearm and dragged his assailant out of the crowd.

'Whoa! What's up? Just say if you don't want your drink, OK?' Simon's surprised features emerged from the figures packed around him, clutching two bottles to his chest with his free arm.

'Sorry mate' Tomos offered. 'Listen, wait by here a minute while I go check something.'

'No chance, what's happening?'

'Not sure, maybe nothing,' Tomos added, moving off.

The new troupe started their routine accompanied by several drummers, the regular beat sounding like a dirge, making Tomos feel he was walking to his execution. Luckily, he only needed to fight his way past a few spectators before he spotted his man.

'There! It *is* him ... the old man from the wadi,' he breathed.

This time there was no doubt. What's more, he was armed both with a dagger at his side and a rifle held with both hands. Dressed in similar fashion to the dancers who were now in full flow, Tomos instinctively knew his adversary would not arouse suspicion. A second younger man, identically dressed and similarly armed, appeared at his side. Tomos briefly wondered if it was the same person who'd pulled him from the wrecked Land Cruiser.

'What's up mate? You do look sort o' nervous,'

'See those two dancers over by there ... the old feller and the young one next to him? I think they're after me.'

'No! Which two? Why? Anyway, two versus two; didn't think you'd run from odds like that.'

'Not normally, no, but look again ... they're armed and we're not. Problem is someone's already threatened to kill me, so let's not go looking for trouble.'

As they turned to leave, the old Omani looked Tomos full in the eye. He smiled a yellow-toothed grin and made a deliberate cut-throat gesture. His accomplice drew his own dagger and started walking purposefully towards them.

'Time to go', hissed Tomos.

Simon had seen the gesture too, and needed no second invitation. They jostled through the ranks of onlookers and emerged into the car-filled street beyond. The jeep lay ahead about twenty car lengths away, the intervening space haphazardly strewn with parked vehicles.

'C'mon, this way - it'll be quicker back along the beach,' Tomos shouted the words before leading the short adrenaline-powered sprint on soft dry sand which left them breathless. Hearts pounding, they reached the car. Simon jammed in the key and sprang the central locking. Simultaneously two doors were yanked open and both jumped in. Through the windscreen they could see the two Omanis walking unhurriedly towards them, rifles and daggers in hand. Simon threw the drinks into the back seat, checked his rear-view mirror, and swore.

'God no, we're stuck!'

Craning his neck, Tomos spied a grey pick-up parked immediately behind them. There was a saloon in front, another to their right, and the beach on the left, leaving them effectively boxed in.

'Shit, here they come! What the fuck are we supposed to do now?' Simon's voice was edged with panic as he turned the key in the ignition.

'I bet it's them that's boxed us in. Use 4-wheel drive and hit the beach.'

Simon did as he was told, brought the clutch up fast and wrenched the steering wheel hard left as far as he could. It wasn't the best way to start, and they very nearly stalled. With a lurch, the 4-wheel drive bit and the jeep turned sharply left onto the beach with an angry growl. As they bounced forward Tomos caught a quick glimpse of the younger Omani breaking into a run, his mouth forming an angry shout, his voice lost in the noise of the jeep's acceleration.

'We need to turn back the way we came!' Tomos shouted the words, jabbing his finger to emphasize his meaning. They'd left the windows open to allow some sea breeze to cool the jeep's interior and the inrushing air combined with the revving engine and his own heavy pulse created an almost surreal feeling, as if they had suddenly been plunged into a slow-motion nightmare.

Looking over his shoulder Tomos watched the younger man clamber swiftly into the grey pick-up that had blocked them in, before it too lurched onto the beach. He stuck his head out of the window to follow it and shouted as loud as he could at Simon.

'They're cutting us off! 'Head back along the beach the other way.'

Concerned only with gaining maximum speed, Simon had driven straight down the gentle gradient of the beach towards the sea - his only thought to put as much distance as soon as possible between them and the chasing vehicle. Their pursuers had chosen a diagonal, cutting off their escape route so that they were now driving between the jeep and the relative safety of the coast road back to Muscat.

'Keep going!,' ordered Tomos as Simon swung round to follow the coastline away from their pursuers. He eyed the beach ahead and the town to the right. They were roughly parallel to the tight knot of dancers and onlookers. He leant towards the steering wheel and punched the horn. If he could only alert the revellers they might see their plight. Help was desperately needed.

The echo of a fusillade of rifle shots rattled in through the open windows. Simon turned, ashen-faced to Tomos. 'What the fuck! They're all shooting at us! What the hell for?'

Despite the chaos and his pounding heart, Tomos felt mentally detached. His understanding of what was happening and their rapidly diminishing options were running through his mind at speed. 'It's OK. That's just the dancers firing their rifles into the sky. It's just part of their bloody act, nothing to do with us. Right, we should be able to outrun them in the jeep. Try turning in a big circle. Keep the speed up, OK?'

Simon nodded.

Bang!

Something slammed powerfully into the metal chasis at the back of the jeep. Both men instinctively looked back at the chasing vehicle, now about a hundred yards or so behind them. The old Omani was standing in the back of the pick-up, using the cabin roof to help steady his rifle. There was no doubting his intention. He fired again and the jeep bucked in response, its motion instantly changing to a rapid series of bumps, leaving Simon to fight for control.

A hit! One of the back tyres had burst. Was he shooting to cripple them, so he could finish them off at his leisure? The notion turned Tomos ice cold. The situation was desperate. With a flat, they couldn't possibly outrun their pursuers and once the punctured tyre shredded completely, they were done for.

He turned his attention back to the beach, looking for inspiration - anything to give hope. Having headed so far down towards the sea at least meant the sand was wet but firm. Ahead, a meandering thread stained the sand a darker shade as flowing water from the ebbing tide worked its way down towards the sea. They had already gone well beyond Quriyat, and with it the end of the blacktop road. There was no longer any hope of escape on the landward side; the beach stretched up to solid rock, the foot of the nearest hill an impenetrable barrier. Worse still, they were soon going to run out of beach altogether; that same rocky hill on his right curved seawards ahead of them to form a low rocky headland. Their options were running out.

Only seconds after the puncture, Simon took the only remaining option and started a slow turn back towards the sea. The change of direction came too late as they struck the meandering stain. The jeep howled and slowed to a shuddering stop, throwing driver and passenger hard forward. Looking down through his open window and with a sinking heart, Tomos saw why. They were stuck in very soft, saturated sand of a small stream; the watercourse having carved its own shallow channel in the beach. There was only going to be one chance of escape. It had to work first time.

'4-low! 4-low!' Tomos banged his palm on the dashboard. Simon, quick on the uptake, shoved the differential from 4-high to 4-low, instantly giving them maximum traction. His foot slammed onto the accelerator and the full power of the jeep came to their aid. With an almighty effort it lurched forward popping up and out of the mire. Tomos could almost feel the power running through the punctured tyre which with its loss of rigidity was the main wheel propelling them forward.

The jeep slewed violently as its driver fought for control. A spout of muddied wet sand belched up from the stream just below Tomos's window. Twisting violently round, he watched in amazement as the chasing pick-up ploughed into the same mire merely yards behind them, its greater speed taking it centre stream. He estimated it must have gone from 40 or 50 mph to zero in under a second. The sudden deceleration threw the old Omani straight over the cabin roof and onto the sand on the far side of the stream. He lay there feebly twitching, his rifle nowhere to be seen.

Tomos could just make out the face of the younger driver banging the steering wheel with his hand in frustration. Even as Simon drove the jeep out onto firmer ground, he could see the pickup digging itself deeper and deeper into the wet sand with every furious wheel-spin.

'We're gonna make it!' Tomos whooped. 'They look well and truly stuck, let's get back to dry land and change that wheel. If we're quick they won't catch us.'

They limped and bumped their way back to Quriyat, past all the celebrations; the dancers and audience oblivious to the events that had taken place no more than a kilometre from where they stood. Simon drove past the last of the parked vehicles before driving onto the welcome tarmac of the Muscat road. With no way of knowing if the two Omanis had accomplices nearby, they moved a little beyond the last parked vehicle before pulling over. Working like Trojans to replace the by now badly shredded tyre with the spare wheel, left them both dripping with sweat within minutes. Luckily there was still no sign of the pick-up.

'They're going to need a tow out, and if the old guy is badly hurt the driver will have to attend to him first,' Tomos asserted.

'Aye, and all the fisher folk are too wrapped up in the celebrations to notice they might need help. That should give us a bit more time'.

Wheel changed, Simon once again slid into the driver seat and this time they set off at high speed for the sanctuary of the city. As they thundered along, lost in their own thoughts, Tomos desperately tried to come to turns with what they'd just experienced. The one thought he could not avoid which rang clear as a bell, since it was of unquestionable logic, was that the stakes had been raised. Al-Hazbar must have been behind the attack, therefore, he, Tomos Morgan, was a target for murder. Not only that; his would-be killers were obviously prepared to hurt those around him if necessary. If this was going to continue he had no choice but to leave the country, for the safety of his friends if nothing else.

6

Tomos listened to the jeep's satisfying growl as they gunned away from Quriyat. 'Go as fast as you can - without crashing.'

'The idea had occurred to me. Mind telling me what the hell happened back there?'

'Let's just get home first, I'll explain everything then.'

It was a long anxious drive back to Muscat, one accompanied by frequent backward glances. As they neared the capital, Tomos relaxed a little, enough to give his friend the bare bones of his history with Al-Hazbar. Simon took in every word.

'Sounds like plain bad luck to me. Bad timing getting caught in that flood, bad luck getting blamed when you were trying to help, and very bad luck you've pissed off one rich, vengeful man.'

'Yeah, well, it's happened. Question is - what do I do about it?'

Simon didn't have an immediate answer, so Tomos resumed his rear-view checks. He'd noticed a small dot on the road behind them which was growing bigger by the second. Simon had seen it too, and both watched it with mounting concern. The dot was travelling way over the speed limit, a dangerous practice on that stretch of road. As it neared, it revealed itself to be a pick-up. It
closed in at breakneck speed, occasionally weaving across the road as it struggled for grip.

'Christ, it's them!' Simon jammed his foot down even harder.

The flash of a grey outline roared up alongside. They'd left it too late to do anything other than try to out-accelerate their foe. Tomos found himself gripping the side of his seat as he willed the jeep onwards. Looking across he observed the wide-mouthed laugh of an excited youth in the passenger seat. The driver, equally young, gave a loud blast on the horn as the pick-up started losing ground to the more powerful jeep.

'It's OK, just some kids,' Tomos gasped.

Simon slowed, and the erratic pick-up careered past them with another loud blast on the horn, its occupants jeering as they sped by.

'Can't take much more of this,' muttered Simon, 'I think we'll just about get back on this tank, last thing I want to do is stop for fuel.'

It wasn't until late afternoon that the dirty and dented jeep pulled into the forecourt of Tomos's apartment. Two cans of beer were plucked from the fridge and taken onto the roof.

Tomos looked out over the neighbouring rooftops. In the far distance, the Gulf of Oman was just visible, already dimmed to violet as dusk took control of the skies. He felt a spark of relief at the prospect of having someone to confide in. Simon wouldn't be able to help him, but the thought of sharing his problems was a welcome one. He cracked open his can; took a long drink; wiped his mouth with the back of his hand and retold his story in full.

This time Simon listened to the whole sorry tale, learning of Tomos's past events through the occasional sip of beer from both relater and listener. Tomos summed up the latest events.

'As we know, the old man was shooting to kill today. Well, to kill me at any rate. None of this has anything to do with you. I'm sorry you got involved. It's me they want; they won't be interested in you from now on.'

'Bloody hell, Tom, I would never have believed you if I hadn't been there. You can't carry on as normal with someone trying to kill you. Either go to the police or get someone - preferably another Omani - to go and reason with this man.'

'Like who? I've been thinking about this trip. It was Hassan my boss who suggested I went. I bet he was either asked, or told, to send me there. Thing is - did he know what was going to happen? If he did, then there's no point in asking him for help since he's obviously already chosen to side with Al-Hazbar. And I don't really know anyone else to ask. Abdul's only a kid. There's no way a big-shot businessman would listen to someone like him.'

'True, but Hassan may not have been fully aware of Al-Hazbar's plans. Either way, you'll have to confront him, if only to see where you both stand.'

'Don't worry about that, I'll be banging on his door first thing in the morning', that's for sure.'

'Good, you do that. I suggest you also go to the police. If anything happens to you and you've already pointed your finger at this guy, then he's an obvious suspect. At least that way the police might get their man.'

The recurring image of Al-Hazbar's face contorted with fury, flashed before Tomos. 'Yeah, it'll be a great comfort to see him caught as I look down from heaven.'

There was no obvious answer to that, and both men lapsed into silence. Tomos reconsidered Simon's words.

'You know, I seriously don't think going to the police will make any difference. He said he'd made a vow to get me, and he obviously means to see it through. In any case, this guy is all-powerful. I wouldn't be surprised if the police side with him, too.'

'I'll fetch another couple of beers, buddy, we need to lubricate the old brain cogs to find a way out of this.'

Alone on the rooftop, Tomos looked out again at the view. The housemaid from the villa next door appeared and started to unpeg a string of laundry. Sensing she was being watched, she turned and flashed him a friendly smile before returning to her chore.

He sighed and thought about what he and Simon had just discussed. To his mind there didn't seem to be an easy way out. Al-Hazbar knew where he worked. It would have been easy for him to identify his boss and approach him as he probably had with the wali. It was obvious Al-Hazbar meant everything he said, and he clearly had both the wealth and influence to carry out his threats. The logical conclusion he mused sadly, was that it was only a matter of time before he came up with a new scheme.

Simon reappeared with two more beers.

Tomos smiled appreciatively at his friend. 'Mate; you'd better make this the last one, you've still got to drive home.'

'After today, nothing worries me. Mind you, how am I going to explain all the damage to the jeep? Hope they don't take it out of my salary.' Simon sounded a little more cheerful, his eyes twinkling with returning good humour.

'I'll sort it all out tomorrow, one way or another. At least there's no blood to clean up.'

'Been thinking ... I heard you being called "the infidel" Has that got anything to do with this?'

‘Yeah, I’ve got the same guy to thank for that. It’s what he called me the day he came to the office, I didn’t realise anyone knew about that outside of Sohar.’

They supped their second beer and conversed in muted tones, ordinary topics of conversation too trivial to discuss with much enthusiasm. Fatigue was setting in with the waning of the adrenalin flush. Simon finished his drink, put down his can, and belched.

‘See what the boss says tomorrow before you jump to any more conclusions. I’m sure things will work out just fine.’

Alone again, Tomos’s thoughts moved to home and family, suddenly wishing he’d never left. He couldn’t believe this was happening to him. He wasn’t a *James Bond* type, able to fight off unseen enemies at every corner. God, he was just a boy from the valleys. What the hell was he supposed to do next?

Life in a Welsh valley was confined to the village itself and the surrounding hills, and for the most part could be considered safe. As a boy, the nearest he had come to any real danger was from wandering the open mountain above the village. He could still clearly remember the day when, aged ten, he had gone for a walk with a couple of school friends up the mountain and climbed the face of a disused quarry. Fooling around on the top, he’d ventured too close to the edge and found himself sliding down the slippery grass towards the lip and the drop to the rocks below. Shouting for help and with legs dangling over the edge, one of his friends had pulled him to safety just in time. That day had scared him, but it had been of his own doing. His upbringing had in no way prepared him for the sort of predicament in which he now found himself.

7

Hassan's black BMW was already filling its reserved spot in the ministerial car park when Tomos arrived the next morning. The purpose-built edifice that served as the Ministry of Water headquarters consisted of four floors. Ignoring the lift, Tomos bounded up the wide stairway to level three which housed his project. The open-plan office was already busy with early morning acknowledgements and catch-up gossip from the weekend's events. He worked his way through a dozen hurried greetings with a strained smile before reaching the far end of the room and the door to his manager's private room. He took a deep breath, rapped once and walked in.

Hassan bin Rashid was sitting at his desk. He was a tall handsome man, lithe in build and possessive of a wide white smile, always ready to charm. In his early thirties, his ambition and good looks made it easy for him to adopt a casual self-confident air. Normally his movements were languid and deliberate in nature, but not this morning. They shook hands and Tomos sat on the proffered seat facing his manager. Hassan appeared nervous, and when he spoke refrained from direct eye contact.

'I trust you had a pleasant weekend? I'm glad you're here, I need to speak to you about our work programme.' Hassan spoke in clipped tones that betrayed an English private school education.

'No, I did not have a pleasant weekend, quite the opposite in fact. Let me tell you about it. I went to Quriyat as *you* suggested, and someone there tried to kill me.' Tomos studied his manager's face for a reaction. He got one. Hassan visibly blanched under his gaze.

'*Really?* You look fine to me, I'm sure there's a sensible explanation, wouldn't you agree?'

'You tell me. Just to complete the story, I was chased along the beach while being fired on from someone with a rifle. Oh, and by the way, I recognised who it was.

'Oh yes? Sounds like quite a little adventure. So, who was this mysterious assassin?' Hassan stammered, affecting an air of sarcastic disbelief.

Tomos tried to control his rising anger; he knew it was probably a mistake to say too much, especially as it was mostly supposition on his part. It was particularly unwise to address his next words to his manager, but he just had to know where he stood.

'I saw him at a wadi crossing, up near Sohar. Someone died that day ... the son of a businessman ... perhaps you've heard of him ... Rashid Al-Hazbar?'

Hassan had been listening, head cocked slightly to one side, eyes fixed on the desk rather than Tomos's face. Tomos carefully scrutinised him as he spoke. There was a definite twitch at the mention of Al-Hazbar's name.

He continued. 'Well, the man shooting at me yesterday was also at the wadi, and I think he and Al-Hazbar are related in some way. Al-Hazbar is wrongly holding me responsible for the death of his son, and he's told me himself he wants revenge for that. Seems to me that he sent this assassin - as you call him - to murder me. Makes sense, as the guy would be able to recognise me.'

There was still no response from his manager who continued to examine his desk.

'And so I do wonder how your assassin managed to find me at the other end of the country. Quite a coincidence, don't you agree? However I remember it was your idea that I go there, and at a certain time too. It's all been a huge shock so I'm just curious to know what Al-Hazbar said to you.'

That did it. Hassan's dark eyes flashed in anger as he looked up. 'Now then Mr Morgan, you need to be careful what you're saying - very careful. I don't know this Al-Hazbar, and I'm not sure I believe your story. Many people in our country carry guns so I'm sure there's a rational explanation for your little misadventure. Now, if you've quite finished perhaps we can we discuss matters of work?'

Tomos studied his manager again before replying. He was sure he was lying. Why else did he appear so nervous? It certainly suggested he knew more than he was letting on. He wasn't getting anywhere like this, he needed to change tactic.

'I'm not blaming anyone here, you understand, but if you know this man perhaps you can help me. Go and tell him I'm very sorry for what happened to his son, but it had nothing to do with me...'

Hassan interrupted. 'I already said I don't know anyone by this name, so I can't help you. I suggest if you're not happy then you must resign and go home. Now then Mr Morgan that is the end of this nonsense, do I make myself clear?'

'Yes, very clear, and as I'm not happy I will reconsider my future here. I've got no particular desire to be murdered.'

'Fine, let's move on then,' Hassan shuffled some papers for no obvious reason. 'I've decided to swop you and James back to your original posts. You will return to Sohar to continue your good work. From there, you will be able to relocate easier to the new Khaburah office in a few weeks once it's ready. James will come back here to Muscat; this makes more sense as he knows this area better, so we can expect more effective work from him. I'm giving both you and James a week to get organised, so please expect to restart work in Sohar one week from today.'

Tomos stared in amazement at his boss. He felt sick. He should have realised this was coming. He wanted him out of Muscat so he couldn't make any more trouble, and at the same time deliver him back to Al-Hazbar's regional powerbase. This was not good.

'Very well, at least I now know where I stand.' Getting to his feet, he leaned across the desk, 'And I'll tell you what I decide before the end of the week.'

Without another word he turned and walked out, deliberately not offering to shake hands. It was an obvious insult; one he hoped showed his contempt. He was sure his boss was lying, closing ranks with the businessman, and he could only conclude he was an idiot for expecting anything else.

The tiny kitchen annexe partitioned off from the main office offered a temporary sanctuary. Luckily it was empty, and Tomos busied himself preparing an extra strong coffee, giving himself time to calm down before deciding on his next course of action. To his annoyance the door creaked open to reveal Suleiman; another newly employed graduate.

'Hello, I saw you come in. Abdul is on the phone from Sohar and wants to speak to you. He says it's important.'

Tomos sighed. 'OK thanks Suleiman.'

Reaching his desk, he picked up the receiver. 'Hi Abdul, it's Tomos. How are you?'

'I'm fine. Do you have a few minutes?'

'Yeah, I'm listening, go ahead.'

'I've been doing some research on Al-Hazbar. You know, if you want to find out about someone then it's not so difficult; in Muscat maybe, which is big, but up here in the north it's easy, everyone knows everyone.'

Tomos said nothing, just waited impatiently for his colleague to get to the point.

'Listen ... Al-Hazbar went to the police station last week when my uncle was on duty there. He was very angry and mentioned your name; spoke about you having made a fool of him again which cannot go unpunished.' Abdul paused for breath.

'You still listening, Mr Morgan?'

'Yes, I am, and I appreciate what you're telling me, please carry on.'

'Right, so Al-Hazbar wanted the police to issue a warrant for your arrest for not trying to help rescue his son in the wadi accident. My uncle knows of our connection and he pointed out that as you did not commit any provable or suspect offence there's no case to answer.' Abdul gave a low grunt of a laugh. 'Anyway, as the police refused to do as he asked, he really lost his temper. However what I really wanted to tell you was that, before he left, he said he knows people in high places and if necessary was going to wait for your return so he could take care of things himself. This is what I wanted to say

... The man is very dangerous. I think it's safer for you to stay in Muscat.'

'Thanks for the warning, Abdul. Believe it or not, I've just been told I'm being sent back to Sohar, but I'm not gonna play any more of these stupid games. No, it's time to end all this. I'm gonna resign. Congratulations, you're the first to know.'

'Sorry to hear that, but it makes sense. What else can you do?'

'Nothing - and your tip may just have saved me, so thanks again for your help.'

He replaced the receiver in deep thought. It was time to stop talking and time to start acting. He sat down, turned on his computer and typed out his resignation.

. . .

The letter was accepted without comment. As Simon later remarked, 'it was the only option you had, the only sure way no-one dies.'

On his last evening in Oman, Tomos went for one final run; his flight to Heathrow being scheduled to depart the next morning. As he ran, he recalled marching back into his manager's office to personally hand in his resignation; and the look of surprised indignation on Hassan's normally smug face.

"Pat pat pat." The soft but gentle rhythmic slap of his bare feet on the wave-kissed sands of Al Khuwair beach crept into the edges of his consciousness. He shrugged off the sounds of the outside world to focus on his private life. Was he right to quit, or should he have stayed to fight?

Whichever was the right answer no longer mattered. The die was cast, he'd made his choice. Tomorrow he would be leaving the Sultanate of Oman, moving on to pastures new. Hopefully all his worries would be left behind, and he would be able to start afresh; find himself a new job in a new country.

He took a moment to look around. On the horizon the beach terminated in a red-tinted low cliff on top of which sat the Inter-Continental Hotel. The foot of the cliff was still some two miles away and marked the end of his run. To his left he could hear the gentle hiss of the Gulf's small waves that rippled forward and gently retreated in their eternal lapping. The wavelets smoothed the sand in great arcs of overlapping oranges and reds, courtesy of the setting sun. They also methodically filled the shallow indentations created by his feet as he maintained his fast-paced rhythm. To his right, the dry white sands sloped up to a low sea wall which ran the length of the beach, beyond which the nearest dwellings were just able to peak their Moorish-looking rooftops into sight.

Swerving slightly left, he followed the line of compacted wet sand where he could maintain his speed. His breathing remained normal despite the exertion. His technique, honed by years of hard training and competitive racing was fluid and relaxed.

It was nearing low tide. Up ahead was a surprisingly deep creek that ran the full width of the beach, its waters flowing dark in the dipping sun. The creek was draining out to sea with the ebbing tide, the rapidly moving water presenting a natural obstacle to anyone on foot. It made him think of the chase along Quriyat beach; on that occasion the creek had been his saviour. His thoughts jumped to the incident that was changing his life. It had been dusk then too, the wadi flooded with water as he waded through it, only to be met by the stare of a man whose spirit continued to haunt him.

He came to a halt on the bank, tentatively stepped in and waded to waist depth, enjoying the sensation of the flowing water cooling his muscles. As he was wearing only shorts and vest, he easily swam the few metres to the far side.

Clambering up the other bank he jogged the final half mile to the end of the beach, deliberately running slowly to give his thin running attire time to dry. The glory of the day's end was all around him, an array of shimmering fingers reaching out in a final display from the fiery red ball of the sun as it touched the horizon far out to sea. The mood of the moment though was unusually lost on him. Preoccupied, he simply acknowledged the good timing of his eight-mile run; the end of it coinciding precisely with sundown. From the imposing hotel above, the occasional sounds of laughter drifted down upon him.

He walked to the top of the beach, vaulted over the sea wall and sought his Isuzu. He retrieved the key left hidden on top of the nearside rear wheel, opened the driver's door and jumped inside without bothering to change. Still barefoot, he drove the three miles through the wide streets to his flat in Al Khuwair. The sun dropped below the horizon, leaving ambient streetlights and starlight to reflect off the white-walled roadside residences in a strobe-like glow as he passed.

Inside his flat he headed straight for the shower. Refreshed, he grabbed a cold beer from the fridge - his last - and sat back on his bed. It still amazed him that non-Muslims were legally allowed to purchase alcohol courtesy of an alcohol passport which provided a monthly allowance.

In the corner of his room sat his suitcase, almost fully packed. On the bed, next to him, lay his passport. For no reason, he picked it up and flicked through it. His photo looked back at him, the face staring innocently with an expression full of hope and, it seemed now, complete naivety. On the page opposite was his visa for Oman with a stamped "valid from" date, of only nine months ago. With an angry grunt, he threw the little book back on the bed.

8

'Tea Mr Tomos?' Rodrigo's offer came courtesy of a smile exhibiting a full suite of yellow teeth. 'Come ... Lee will take over for a while.'

Tomos couldn't help grinning back, Rodrigo's wide ugly smile was irresistibly contagious. 'I'd love one. My mouth's as dry as a bone.'

He wiped the sweat from his forehead and followed the diminutive Filipino into the comparative cool of the air-conditioned porta cabin. The heat was to be expected in Libya at the end of August. Six weeks had passed since he had left Oman, six weeks of frenetic activity which had flashed by in the wink of an eye. An unsuccessful visit to the job centre back home in Wales had quickly prompted him to follow up the job adverts he'd seen two months earlier. Fortunately the Libyan post was still open, and after a telephone interview his application had been accepted. His immediate availability and his recent experience in Oman had weighed heavily in his favour.

So here he was, working on a project drilling water wells in Libya, and about to take tea with a Filipino in the middle of the Sahara Desert. Many of the project's drillers known as roughnecks were Filipino in origin. He knew a few by name, but found he got on especially well with Rodrigo.

Rodrigo busied himself washing out two mugs and filling a large Pyrex beaker with water.

'Tell me again, how long have you been working in Libya?' Tomos asked.

'Three years, my older brother also worked here for a year, but he went back home last month.' He worked as he talked, placing an electrical anode into the beaker to heat the water.

Tomos watched the tea-making with interest wondering how it was going to taste. The water he knew, had been pumped from hundreds of metres down, out of the recently-drilled borehole that lay beneath their feet. The well was one of many that formed a network drilled into the Nubian sandstone aquifer that underlay much of the Sahara in Western Libya. Tests on the water from this particular borehole had proven it to be of satisfactory quality for agriculture. Satisfactory for piping to the coast for irrigating fields - but not necessarily for making tea.

He doubted if Rodrigo knew or cared about the chemistry of the water, it was free and evidently palatable, and he guessed that was enough for his friend.

Rodrigo completed his dubious brew and poured out two mugs. They sat at the single small desk and pushed aside a pile of paperwork and dirty plates. Rodrigo was short, only five foot tall, chatty, and easy to talk to.

'Why'd your brother leave?' Tomos inquired.

'To be at the birth of his second child, a boy. Personally, I'm hoping the Libyans keep on expanding the well field by drilling more and more wells. I could do with another couple of years as the pay is so good!'

They finished the tea and chatted for a few more minutes before Rodrigo returned to his supervisory duties. Alone, Tomos carefully read and then copied the drillers log into his own notebook, along with the work plan for the next 24 hours. The log listed all on-site activities undertaken on the rig and would eventually be incorporated into a report he would have to write himself. Satisfied he'd gathered all the information needed, he set off for the main camp in an old and much dented Toyota Hilux that had been assigned to him.

The ground around the rig was deeply rutted. As Tomos navigated around the worst of the potholes, he passed the painted wooden sign identifying the site as "Well D16". This borehole was just one of over two hundred that stretched over an area about one hundred and fifty miles long by fifty miles wide. Well D16 was located about thirty miles west of the camp which lay roughly central to the well field and was home to several hundred workers.

The late morning sun beamed down from an un-blemished blue sky. The view through his windscreen revealed a mixed landscape that alternated between flat stony plains and giant sand dunes, many of them far bigger than those he had experienced in the deserts of Arabia. In every direction the vastness of the Sahara basked in all its majesty, one huge heat haze that fused in every direction with a perfect sky.

And the sky really was perfect, an entire hemisphere of burnished blue without imperfection from cloud or vandalism from aircraft condensation trails. In fact he hadn't seen a plane or their tell-tale traces since arriving in this largely ignored part of the globe.

The thirty miles back to camp took forty minutes, the hard-packed track being flat and almost devoid of traffic. He saw only one other vehicle, a flatbed carrying a rack of pipes. From their size he guessed they were destined for helping connect all the boreholes together, after which the precious water could be transported to the coast in one giant-sized pipeline. He wound up his window and switched on the windscreen wipers as the flatbed rumbled slowly past in the opposite direction, a mass of heavy machinery enveloped in a huge dust cloud which stayed airborne as an opaque plume, like the tail of a giant comet.

At base camp, he drove through the massive security gates and past the adjacent police block set just inside the perimeter fence, where he was waved through by armed security. He continued around the large pipe storage compound in the centre of the camp, and parked up in front of the British ex-pat quarters. The quarters consisted of a central corridor with eight rooms leading off, four each side, plus a social room at the far end.

After filing away his field notes he joined the other ex-pats in the nearby canteen block. The tiny dining room only had three tables, two of which were already occupied. At the far end of the room and already having their lunch, sat Vince and Ed, the senior drilling manager and drilling engineer. Matthew, another hydrogeologist sat alone at another table.

The Bangladeshi chef served him a basic curry and rice. Vince and Ed were deep in conversation and offered only a courteous nod in greeting as he took his place at Matthew's table. Like Tomos, Matthew had been engaged to supervise and analyse the results from various drilling tests used to assess the productivity of each well.

'OK Tom? Curry and rice today, just for a change,' even Matthew's chuckle seemed to have a Northern Irish accent.

'Alright Mat. Curry's my favourite. Had a good morning?'

'Not bad at all, been out at OBH1 with Drissa, but absolutely nothing of interest to report. Hope you've had more fun.'

OBH1, Observation Borehole Number One, was the nearest of all the observation boreholes. Every so often, the observation wells were visited to upload the automatically recorded water level data from the monitors installed inside them.

'Yeah, all good today ta. Been at D16. Had a good chat with Rodrigo, he seems to know a lot about how things work out here.'

'Yep,' Matthew gave a dismissive wave of his hand. 'All the Filipinos do; they don't keep secrets, unlike the Libyans. Take Drissa for example, he's always ready to have a moan about things, but you can't get him to talk much about Gaddafi, like he's scared of repercussions or something ... As if I'd say anything bad about him to anyone.'

Drissa was a Libyan engineer employed as a technical assistant and assigned to the British team where he also acted as a translator. Matthew chuckled again, 'I'd love to hear what really bugs him - if I could only get a few drinks inside him!'

Tomos spent the rest of the afternoon in the office writing up the latest pump test results. Vince and Matthew were also there, Ed had left to check up on one of the rigs. The time was productive and peaceful.

At 16:00, a radio message came in requesting a hydrogeologist attend site to supervise a drilling test. The estimated time was the early hours of next morning.

'Your turn, Tomos,' Matthew smirked. 'Better not drink too much before you go!'

After finishing in the office at 17:00, he went for a run. Apart from keeping him fit, it helped him reacclimatise to the desert heat, a much drier heat than he'd been used to in Oman. Exercise also allowed him to unwind. The work here was stressful. It was only after a month of working without a single day off, that he felt he was at last getting to grips with the demands of the job.

Even so, he reflected, everything still felt new and more than a little alien to him: the country; the work and routines; even the people. His daily run gave him privacy with his thoughts no matter where in the world he was, or how difficult life seemed. Even choosing his own route and deciding how fast to run furnished him with an all too rare feeling of being in control of at least one aspect of his life.

Rather than run around the camp, he took the Hilux to a region dominated by great rolling sand dunes that rose from the surrounding plain like huge ocean waves frozen in mid-motion. The blazing heat of the sun had abated, replaced by the warm blanket of early evening air. The day's heat lasted longer underfoot, radiating upward from the roasted sand.

A desert wind had started at noon, gradually strengthening during the afternoon. He parked in the dark pool of shadow that lay at the foot of the first great dune, conscious of the change in the air towards the far horizon. A perfect blue sky still smothered him but in the far distance it was collapsing into a sullen brown opaqueness that blended seamlessly into the great Sahara that stretched away to infinity. He had never seen a sky quite as threatening. Luckily it seemed a long way off, for the moment.

He felt free but lonely. The camp lay twenty miles behind him, the nearest rig another twelve miles ahead. There were no people closer than that. There was no sign of any life, no movement, the only sound was his own breathing and the whisper of a rising wind sweeping in from the desert to feel its way over and around the giant dunes.

Partly to minimise his laundry and partly to help stay cool, he ran barefoot and topless, wearing only a pair of shorts. Setting off, the heat of the sand burned the soles of his feet but was no longer hot enough to blister them. He jogged the low gentle slope of the nearest dune where it rose from the desert, then attacked the top half with vigour, fighting against the ever-steepening gradient and the soft sand underfoot.

Two steps forward one step back: the thought reflected his struggles as he forced his way to the summit. At the top, the dune curved away in each direction in an elegant arc. His efforts were rewarded with the sight of the maze of sand hills spreading away in a spectacular panorama beyond this first wall of sand.

He ran along the crest of the dune. The warm wind was strengthening quickly, whipping the grains upslope from his left and peppering his bare legs as he ran. Ahead, the whole length of the top of the dune began smoking with sandy plumes blowing up and over the ridge. In the lee of the dune the individual grains settled, the entire hill forever dynamic and changing. He ran awkwardly, each foot stumbling along either side of the razor-sharp crest. His legs stung, his feet were hot, and as he ran he tried to shield his mouth and eyes from the sand-laden blasts of wind.

This was crazy ... breathing in the grains would do more harm than good. Scanning ahead he spied two dunes to his right that curved back behind him. Following them would complete a short circuit. By the time he arrived back at his vehicle the sun was a finger's width above the horizon and the sand underfoot felt cold against his feet. The wind continued to pick up, sighing and moaning its way over the dune field.

The threat the air carried materialised when he was still ten minutes away from camp. The brown streak, once a distant smear, fell upon him like a demented demon. Sand grain bullets strafed the car, and despite his headlights, visibility shrank to nothing. He braked to a halt as the track ahead disappeared in the murk. He was going to have to sit it out.

The worst of the sandstorm passed in less than fifteen minutes and he was able to complete his journey. Safely back in his room, he showered, dressed, and just about made it back to the canteen in time for the evening meal. Everybody was in, and over plates of chicken curry, conversations were of the day's activities and the change in the weather. Vince, who had been in Libya the longest, enlightened his captive audience with tales of previous extreme sandstorms he'd witnessed.

The day entered its final hours like most others, with everyone gathering in the common room at the end of the corridor. The room had been decorated as a makeshift bar with an actual bar top across one end; a giant poster picturing racks of wine and beer bottles hung on the wall behind.

Vince and Ed brought along a bottle of ale for sampling. Both men were brewing their own beer in vats in their respective rooms. The water originated from the wells they were drilling, the sugar was bought locally, the hops and yeast posted to them to avoid being brought through customs. Vince had helped Tomos get started on his own brew, and he now boasted an oil drum of the stuff bubbling away nicely in his bathroom. Strictly speaking they faced the death penalty if caught in this alcohol-free state, but Vince had assured him the authorities conveniently turned a blind eye to such activities.

The relative merits of the two bottles were discussed; Vince's brew being given the nod in terms of quality over Ed's, much to Ed's disgust. Another two were brought along and tested to confirm the findings. At that point Tomos decided to leave, he needed to be ready if he got a call to work on the rig during the night.

'Gutted it's not my turn. You're sure to enjoy the excitement of it all; the getting out of a warm bed in the middle of the night with the added spice of a sand storm thrown in,' Matthew quipped.

'Yeah, can hardly wait to start,' Tomos retorted as he left. He didn't know why, but the deliberate sarcasm and Matthew's words resonated with his own intuition that a difficult time did indeed lie ahead.

9

The call to attend the rig came at 03:00. Tomos instantly awoke to a gentle knock at his door. It opened to reveal Fernando, one of the senior Filipino drillers on night duty in the radio room.

'Ah, Mr Morgan, radio call from H18; they expect to start the pump test about four-thirty.'

'OK thanks Fernando. Can you let them know I'm on my way?' He washed his face and dressed, making sure he wrapped his head in a black scarf given to him by Vince. Stepping outside, the cold desert air sliced through his clothing making him shiver. It was still breezy, though not as strong as before. There was a full moon and a myriad of tiny dots that etched out the band of the Milky Way in an incandescent swirl. Moon and stars bathed the desolate landscape in silvery white, battling for dominance with waves of blackened voids which came and went with the whining gusts that blew in small clouds of sand-laden air. Fumbling for the car key with one hand, he used the other to cover his mouth with the scarf; he'd already breathed in enough sand for one day. The chilled air surprised him a little, especially given the time of year. It had never really felt that cold in the deserts of Oman.

There wasn't much time to reach the rig before the testing was due to start. He silently cursed; his wake-up call should have been an hour earlier. Now he was faced with a drive of about sixty miles to cover in an hour, barely manageable even by day. After three miles, he swung off the main track and attempted a shortcut across the desert. It was a way he'd only driven once before, and then in daylight. He experienced a moment of nerves and self-doubt as he steeled himself for the trek ahead. It wouldn't look good if he arrived hours late, broke the vehicle on some unseen rock, or worse got completely lost.

He pushed on with only the reassuring drone of the engine for company. To navigate he followed the black rocky line which snaked ahead of him. The line marked the edge of a basalt outcrop, the surface remnant of ancient volcanic activity. Keeping the dark basalt to his right and the lighter-coloured sand to his left, he headed deeper into the desert. He kept an eye on the odometer; the shortcut reduced the drive from sixty to under fifty miles, providing he didn't get lost.

The terrain wasn't as flat or as smooth as he remembered. Several times he heard the exhaust scrape unseen rocks at the tops of imperceptible rises, only for him to be forced seconds later to accelerate through soft sand nestled in the trough the other side. The constant decelerations over the uneven terrain slowed him down, and he found himself throwing frequent anxious glances at both clock and odometer. Eventually he spotted what he had been praying for; at the top of yet another interminal rise he saw a bright steady light low in the southern sky almost directly ahead. It could only be one thing - the rig's spotlights used to allow work 24/7; a necessity where time was money. Thank God! At least he'd been going in the right direction.

Judging by the odometer there was still another fifteen minutes or so left to drive; plenty of time he congratulated himself. He headed straight towards the light and watched it brighten until it separated into four individual spotlights.

Concentrating on the lights instead of the ground proved a mistake as the nose of the pick-up dipped into a deep depression concealed in shadow. All four lights winked out in rapid succession quickly followed by the familiar heavy dragging sensation on the steering as his vehicle rolled into deep sand. The heavy pickup shuddered to a halt, the wheels spinning uselessly. He quickly put the vehicle into reverse which usually did the trick. Not this time however. The engine raced, the wheels spun, the clutch burned, and the pick-up rocked back and fore ploughing itself in deeper.

Damn ... just when he was so close, too.

Engaging low four-wheel drive would probably do the trick, but before trying it might be worth taking a quick look to see what he was up against. If he was unable to drive straight out of the sand trap, he could always dig himself free using the shovel stowed in the back.

Jumping down from the cab landed him into the sand heaped up around the front nearside tyre. Underfoot felt reasonably firm as he circled the vehicle inspecting each wheel, his small clouds of breath visible in the cold air. The only sound was the gentle creaking of the rapid cooling of the engine. A slight smell of burning clutch hung in the air indicating the wind had dropped to almost nothing. None of the tyres seemed too deeply embedded; he felt sure he could escape in low 4-wheel drive.

About to climb back into the cab he froze as the night calm was assaulted by the harsh metallic staccato retort of what sounded like machine gun fire.

What the hell was that? Gunfire? It sounded close by ... maybe a rack of drill pipes had been dropped at the rig.

Heart pumping, he jumped into the cab, slammed the lever into low 4-wheel drive and, keeping the revs high but steady, slowly took his foot off the clutch. He let out a huge sigh of relief as the pick-up shuddered forward. Within a few metres he was on top of the upslope and back onto firmer ground. Something was wrong however. Up ahead none of the rig lights had reappeared. There wasn't any reason for them to be off unless the generator had failed.

He flipped into 4-high and flashed his full beam. The reflection of the rig's sharp lines briefly dissected the canvas of dark sky, crazily resembling a streak of forked lightning. He pressed his foot on the accelerator and was astonished to see another pair of headlights sparking into existence. The vehicle they belonged to was only about fifty metres ahead and racing straight for him at breakneck speed. He caught his breath as the offending vehicle was momentarily picked out by his own lights before it veered off and blasted away towards the open desert. The vehicle registered in his mind as a dark, possibly black pick-up, very like his own Hilux. But what really made him gasp was the unmistakable shape of a large tripod-mounted machine gun in the rear, a figure wrapped all in black hunched behind it.

An armed pick-up at night choosing to avoid him must belong to bandits; no regular army vehicle would behave like that. Vince had told him there had been countless car-jackings in the area over the last couple of years, but the culprits only ever ambushed lone vehicles. He thought of the machine-gun. Had they just attacked the drilling rig? That was something he'd never heard of.

Keeping an eye on his mirrors and with headlights back on full beam, he drove slowly up to the rig and adjacent portacabin. All was quiet and still. No lights on anywhere. With the engine running, he sounded the horn hoping it would be interpreted as a friendly gesture. Nothing happened.

He killed the engine and wound down his window.

'Hey! Anyone around? Tomos Morgan here!' The portacabin door was pushed open from the inside and a torch was switched on, briefly bathing his windscreen.

'Hello? Mr Morgan ... Is that you?'

'Yes, it's me. Are you alright?'

More muffled voices from inside the cabin, then three figures emerged.

Tomos jumped down from his seat and strode over to join them. He recognised the torch holder as Paolo, an Italian geologist acting as site manager.

'You OK Paolo? What happened?'

'Bandits! When we heard your car we thought you might have been them returning. Lui ... can you fix the electrics?'

'It's done,' came a shouted reply. The background hum of a generator started, followed momentarily by the whole area lighting up as the spotlights switched on. 'They only pulled the cable.'

'I don't think they'll be back,' Tomos advised. 'I just saw them, looked like they were in a big hurry to get away.'

'You saw them leave? Good, come inside ... I could do with a drink. Lui, keep watch in case they return.'

They sat in the portacabin over two tepid mugs of very strong Italian coffee.

'We were still setting up for the pump test when three men appeared from nowhere,' Paolo explained. 'We saw no vehicles, so I think they must have arrived with no headlights ... maybe they parked far away ... too far away for us to hear, and then walked to the rig. With the earlier sandstorm, no-one was ever going to see them. They were dressed all in black, even wore black scarves covering their faces - and they all carried guns. Only the tallest one spoke, maybe he was the only one who knew English. Anyway, they made us all go outside and lie face down; we were shitting ourselves. For a moment I really did think they were going to shoot us.'

'It's OK, they've gone now. So, what happened next? What did they want? I thought I heard shooting.'

'Yes, when we were lying down one of them fired a machine gun into the sand right in front of our heads. Believe me, no-one dared move or look up after that. What did they want? Well, they ransacked the cabin but after a few minutes their vehicle drove up and they all got in. Once they'd gone we locked ourselves in the cabin until we heard you drive up. Because we were expecting you, I risked opening the door to make sure it really was you.'

'Did they take anything ... anything missing?'

Tomos looked around the small cabin. The only disturbance seemed to be the filing cabinet; all the drawers had been pulled open, their contents strewn haphazardly across the floor.

'They took the radio, so we weren't able to call for help; apart from that - nothing that I can see; they normally only hijack vehicles. Ah, that must be it... I guess they were looking for the car keys. I have my Nissan Patrol here; the keys are in my pocket ... see.'

Paolo laughed nervously and produced a set of keys from his trousers with a flourish. 'I wonder why they didn't search me, or even ask where they were?'

'I'm sure they would have, given time, but I bet the get-away driver saw the lights from my car and decided it was best to run. They couldn't be sure who was heading their way. I could've been military or armed police on patrol; wouldn't make any sense for them to hang around any longer than necessary.'

Lui appeared at the door. 'Another car coming. The headlights are on, so it can't be the bandits. It'll be here in a minute.'

Paolo and Tomos watched cautiously from the doorway as the newcomer pulled in. Tomos recognised the vehicle as one of the Libyan project vehicles. The driver's door opened, and Abbas stepped down. Abbas was a Libyan engineer appointed by the governing regime to ensure the project was being undertaken according to the terms of the contract. His job today was to ensure the drilling test was carried out correctly and on time.

One look around told him things weren't right. Paolo explained events again, and Abbas used the radio in his vehicle to report back to the main camp. 'The police are on their way,' he informed everyone.

'There's nothing more to do until they arrive, we'll probably try to set-up the pump test for the afternoon with the next shift,' Paolo declared. 'You can go back at least until we call in a new schedule.' He paused, 'or Abbas can, as we no longer have a radio.'

'Fine. Either me or Matthew will come back later.'

Tomos climbed into the Hilux's cabin and Paolo leant in through the window.

'You know it was maybe a good thing you missed the bandits for another reason.'

'Why's that?'

'When we were lying on the ground the leader poked me with his gun and asked me in English what my name was, and if I was British. When I told him I was Italian, he lost interest. I've no idea why he asked me that ... a bit strange I think.'

Tomos stared, his mind racing. 'Are you sure ... I mean that he asked if you were British?'

'I'm sure, but I don't know why.'

Tomos drove back to camp only stopping briefly to watch the spectacular desert sunrise, the orange red ball of nuclear fire lighting up its empire for another day. It was but a moment's relief from his preoccupation with the night's events. Despite the shock of hearing live gunfire and seeing armed bandits, his mind returned time and again to Paolo's final words and the reference to a British man.

The bandit could have asked the question for a million reasons. Since he spoke English it would make sense to seek an English-speaking Brit to question - or could it have been for another reason entirely?

The idea this was Oman all over again refused to go away. What if that bandit leader had been looking specifically for *him*? Did Al-Hazbar's influence stretch right across the Arab world?

The nagging thought stayed with him all the way back to camp. Aware of the time difference between Libya and Oman, he went to telephone Simon in the Muscat office as soon as he arrived at base camp. Usually, making a call meant travelling to Sabha, the nearest town, since the camp's own telephone was out of action more often than not, the line being frequently cut by bandits. These bandits were known to be local tribesmen who saw the exploitation of the groundwater under their land as theft by the Gaddafi regime. Cutting the telephone line to the camp was one way of fighting back, intended to disrupt and inconvenience.

Could they be the same bunch? Probably not, he decided. There were more than enough people with guns and grudges in Libya to account for all manner of things.

Given the telephone's history, it was a big relief to find it operating and to hear Simon's voice.

'Hi Tom. You OK?'

'Yeah, fine mate, you too?'

'Yeah, I'm alright. How's Libya? Take it that's where you're calling from?'

'Yep, it's OK, pays the rent I guess. Not so much fun as Oman though.'

'If you call being shot at *fun*, things can't be that great over there! Take it you haven't had any more problems.'

'No, so far so good. Have you heard any more from Al-Hazbar?'

'Not much. Abdul told me over the phone that he went to the Sohar and Khaburah offices asking after you, wanting to know where you'd gone. Abdul doesn't know where you are, and I certainly haven't told anyone. So, if no-one knows where you are, then I'd say you're perfectly safe for now.'

'Thanks, apart from my family I don't think anyone else knows.' Even as he spoke, his mind raced feverishly. One notion emerged like an unwelcome itch.

'Arrgh - damn! I forgot to remove Hassan's name as a referee from my CV when I applied for the job, the Libyans could've contacted the ministry in Oman without me knowing. If they did, then I suppose Hassan could know I'm here, which means Al-Hazbar might as well. I'm sure those two are in it together.'

'Oh ... not good. Easy mistake to make, though! Sure everything's OK over there?'

'Yeah, think so. Stay safe Simon and keep in touch. If there's anything new, can you phone my parents in Wales? You have the number.'

'Of course, no problem ... and don't leave it so long before calling next time, agreed?'

Tomos replaced the receiver before leaving the little wooden booth. He paid the extortionate fee to the Korean attendant who wrote the bill down for him, as he didn't speak English. Was he being paranoid? Was Al-Hazbar bitter enough to continue his vendetta even though he'd left the country?

The notion he'd been followed to Libya grew in his mind like a runaway train. With a sinking heart he realised it was a fear he was just going to have to live with.

10

Tomos found himself becoming wary of strangers. He was especially vigilant when outside the camp, often scanning the horizon for signs of trouble. Aware of his own paranoia, as he'd done in Oman, he concentrated on working hard at his day job. It took a while, weeks in fact, before he relaxed enough to be confident of portraying an everyday outward persona of calm normality.

He was able to relax a little more when the workload eased. A whole batch of borehole casing was condemned as being of inferior quality and this slowed the pace of the whole project. The casing was used to support the upper sides of the wells, to stop them collapsing. Without it, no more could be drilled. A new batch had been ordered but these would take weeks to arrive. The idle time afforded Tomos ample opportunity to explore his surroundings further and further afield.

Using Vince's knowledge, he tracked down many interesting new spots. One such place lay about eighty miles to the north-east of the camp in an area of low hills. A short walk up to a rocky ledge above a boulder-strewn slope revealed the remains of a World War Two machine gun nest. The immediate vicinity was still littered with bullets and empty discarded tins of corned beef, the stamped years of manufacture corresponding to the war - all still uncorroded in the arid climate.

He also became acquainted with more of the people working around him. In the middle of the security-fenced camp, a large rectangular open area of compacted ground acted as a pipe storage compound. The pipes were stacked around the perimeter leaving the central area open. Most evenings it was pressed into service as a makeshift football pitch.

One evening he stopped to watch a game between the South Koreans and a combined West African eleven. The Africans were a player short and he volunteered to fill in for them. After the game he stayed to chat to one of his new team-mates.

He already knew Isaac by sight as he was a camp fuel-pump attendant. Originally from Burkina Faso in West Africa, Isaac lived in a tiny wooden shack next to the petrol pump in a compound adjacent to the main camp. Isaac spoke French but was trying to learn English and asked Tomos if he would help teach him; something he readily agreed to. From then on, they met up for an hour twice a week after football, just to talk, and soon became good friends. Isaac practiced his English, and Tomos started speaking basic French again, something he hadn't done since school. They usually chatted in the stockyard sitting atop one of the large pipes. There was always a story to tell, and in halting English Isaac gradually explained how he came to be so far away from home.

'My village called Koutatenga, close to the capital city Ouagadougou, in Burkina Faso, West Africa. Life very hard there; my parents send me to school for some little time. I learned a little English. Problem was finding work after finishing school. I stayed in Ouaga ... as we call it ... with my aunt ... doing any work I find. Everything got very hard when the socialists took power. They forced people into the army. I did not want this. Me and two friends agreed we rather die trying to live better than suffer the army. We decide to try something while still young - that means one thing in Africa - try to go to Europe and make good money.'

'How did you get to Libya?'

'We pay to get lifts ... in any vehicle. From Burkina we cross the Niger border, then from Niamey we get a lift in lorry all the way to Libya. Very hard journey ... not enough food or water. When we get to some quiet place, the driver and his friend ... both had guns ... say they leave us in desert unless we give them all our money. I think we lucky to get here alive. After, we get to Tripoli, but have nowhere to live ... no money to pay the smugglers to cross the sea to Europe. Then there was a riot in Tripoli against the black Africans; many of us were killed. My two friends went to Tunisia to be safe, also good chance of work there. Me? I hear about this place. I know that where you find white people you find money. Also here must be safer than Tripoli, so I beg for lift here.'

'What's your plan now? Earn enough to pay for your passage to Europe?'

'I don't know. I miss home and wish I'd stayed there. My salary not enough to travel to Europe, smugglers want too much money - much more than I have. I think I try to save enough to go back home, even though the journey so terrible.'

Tomos was at a loss for words. He guessed Isaac's story was typical of hundreds if not thousands of others who'd made similar journeys. His life was easy compared to so many.

. . .

One favourite pastime of all the expats was to drive out into the stony plains of the Sahara. There, by scanning the landscape it was possible to pick out slightly darker patches of ground which on closer inspection sometimes turned out to be ancient fireplaces. By examining these Tomos was often able to pick up beautifully manufactured flint arrow and spear heads.

Rodrigo accompanied him the day he drove the Hilux far to the south west. Together they discovered an area where great pillars of sandstone rock protruded from the earth's surface like a monstrous version of Stonehenge. Over the centuries countless desert winds armed with abrasive grains of sand had carved the stone monoliths into fantastic shapes. The erosion was more pronounced nearer the ground resulting in many of the pillars resembling giant mushrooms. Walking through this wonderland they eventually found the purpose of their visit; ancient rock carvings of various animals etched by indigenous people long ago.

Tomos found a lion and a giraffe and various antelope while Rodrigo even found what resembled a crocodile.

Rodrigo was unusually quiet on the interminable drive home, and Tomos sensed he was mulling over something. Eventually, Rodrigo broke the silence.

'I had a friend back in the Philippines who was robbed one night in his own house. He recognised one of the thieves and so they beat him and told him if he went to the police they would return and kill him. Naturally my friend was so scared he never reported the robbery. Anyway he became a changed man after that - always nervous - and I don't think he ever trusted anyone again. You remind me a little of him. So, I was wondering if something bad has happened to you, too? Hope you don't mind me asking.'

Tomos winced before replying. Rodrigo had obviously seen through his mask of innocence but he wasn't keen to include anyone new in his personal nightmare. Still, sharing his burden might help, and in any case he liked and trusted Rodrigo.

'You're right. But it's all a bit strange and if I tell you, you may not believe me. If you do, you'll probably think I've gone a bit crazy, just like your friend.'

'Ha-ha, don't worry about that. If you tell me, then who knows ... perhaps I can help. What have you got to lose?'

Tomos gave in to Rodrigo's logic and related his story, including what was said by the bandit to Paolo, the fear he might have been traced to Libya.

'Us Filipinos are like one big family and there are a lot of us here doing all sorts of things, not just drilling. I'll ask around, see if anyone has heard anything.' Sensing Tomos was about to object, he quickly added, 'Don't worry, I'll be very discreet, I won't even mention you by name.'

'Thanks, I appreciate your offer, but don't think it's a good idea, just in case there *is* something going on.'

At base camp he dropped Rodrigo off outside his accommodation.

'Come on in Mr Tomos, take a coffee before you go,' Rodrigo invited.

Never having seen inside his room, Tomos covered his curiosity with a cheery "thank you". He was curious because his friend lived in a huge precast concrete pipe, some four metres in diameter and six metres long; one of thousands manufactured and destined to transport the water to Tripoli. Instead of being buried as part of a pipeline, Rodrigo's section had been turned into living quarters. He already knew one end had been fully blocked up while the other end was fitted with a door.

Rodrigo led him up a couple of steps and let him in. It took a moment for his eyes to adjust to the sudden change from bright sunlight to darkened interior. He tried hard not to show surprise at what he saw. A level floor had been installed; crammed along one side of which was a row of six beds, four were empty, the other two occupied by sleeping men.

So many bodies sharing made it very cramped, a little smelly and insufferably hot.

'They're on the night shift,' Rodrigo explained with a wave at the two sleeping forms.

His colleagues woke at the sound of their roommate's voice, and then sat up at seeing an unexpected visitor. Several lanterns were lit, and a bottle of highly illegal gin and a guitar appeared from underneath one of the beds. The Filipinos quickly lived up to their reputation for good hospitality. The bottle was drunk, jokes were swapped, and songs were sung.

It was well over two hours later when Tomos left the strange pipe house. It was good to have felt the stress lifted away for a while. As he walked a little unsteadily back to his own quarters, he clenched his fists in a physical effort to hold on to this feel-good sensation. Three months with no obvious threat from Al-Hazbar. Maybe it really was all over.

11

Despite a throbbing head Tomos was in work early the next day to prepare for a field trip with the Libyan engineer, Drissa. Gradually the other Brits made their way into the office. Everybody was engrossed in their own work when, an hour later than agreed, Drissa burst in.

'I must go home today; my father is very sick - maybe dying. I expect to be away for at least a week.' He gave his bad news to Tomos in a voice loud enough to ensure the rest of the room would hear.

'Really sorry to hear that, what's happened?' Tomos sympathised.

'Suspected stroke, no-one seems quite sure.'

'My sympathies, Drissa. Take as long you need - don't worry about work,' Vince added, walking over to join them.

'Thanks. I've arranged a police escort for Tom for today. It's better that way I think, with so many bandits about. Tom, you can pick him up from the guardhouse at the main gate when you're ready, he'll be watching out for you.'

Tomos and Drissa had been due to visit the furthest outlaying observation well. The planned task was to upload data from the automatic logger that tracked changes in water level. It was the most popular job as it meant a day away from the mundanity of the office or the more intense pressure of supervising the rigs.

Drissa left, and Vince looked at Tomos. 'You know the way?'

'Yes, I've been there once before ... not a problem.'

The policeman was ready and waiting outside the guardhouse when Tomos picked him up five minutes later.

'As Salaam al Aykum,' the greeting was snarled as he climbed into the passenger seat without even a glance at his driver; a small canvas bag held in one hand, a rifle in the other.

'Walaykum Salaam,' answered Tomos automatically, his eyes focusing on the gun, which he guessed was a Kalashnikov AK47 assault rifle. The policeman threw the bag into the back seat before carefully placing the rifle butt between his feet, the barrel held vertically between his knees. The overall shape of the AK47 was the only weapon Tomos vaguely knew, since it was so common worldwide, especially throughout Africa. In Libya, it told the story of Gaddafi's close links with the Russians. It didn't look well maintained; leading Tomos to briefly wonder if it would actually fire once the trigger was pulled.

'OK?' queried Tomos as they began their long journey west. His passenger slowly shook his head.

'No Inglaisee, no English.'

'Ah OK, no problem,' Tomos replied. He pressed the accelerator and settled back in his seat. A long uneasy journey lay ahead.

The uncomfortable drive was completed in necessary silence. For the most part, the policeman dozed, although Tomos noticed he never let go of the gun. He drove fast, forcing himself to concentrate to help pass the time. The track was a well-used one; it connected the camp to one of the very few tarmac roads that bisected the country north-south. After only twenty minutes he overtook one of the large pipe-carrying flatbeds; the vehicle and its driver semi-transparent behind a veil of choking dust.

Once they were ahead of the lorry, the full Sahara lay before them, an arid vastness unrivalled anywhere else on the planet. It wasn't until near the end of their journey that a line of hills gradually grew upwards from the horizon to break the endless plain; the uplifted bare rock a dark grey smudge against an otherwise uniform silver-blue sky.

After a little over two hours of quiet ennui and with 150 kilometres covered, the Hilux finally reached the tarmac road. Here, turning left would take them to the coast some five hundred miles northwards. Turning right, the road would eventually peter out, dispersing into a myriad minor tracks leading into the heart of Africa; to Algeria, Niger or Chad.

Tomos drove straight over the tarmac and pulled up thirty meters the other side, next to Well Number OBH9, the object of their trip. The location had partly been selected to make it easy to locate and partly to allow access of the heavy clumsy drilling rigs via the blacktop road.

He busied himself with his job. The first thing was to check the depth of the water level in the well. As he went to take the dipper-tape from the back of the Hilux, his escort jumped down from the cab and purposefully strode on past the back of the truck, rifle slung casually over one shoulder.

Dipper-tape in hand, Tomos walked over to the well, at the same time half-watching his silent companion gathering rocks into a small pile. He didn't know why, but he had an uneasy feeling ... Drissa dropping out of the trip and being replaced at the last minute by an unknown armed, so-called escort, who *couldn't* or *wouldn't* speak to him. What was wrong with him?

He was becoming an old woman; he needed to get a grip for God's sake.

He returned his attention back to the task in hand. The top of the borehole was covered by a padlocked steel lid that kept the sand out and prevented anything - or anyone - from falling in. Kneeling, he felt under the lip of the lid for the padlock.

Bang! Clang! The ear-splitting noise was followed by an almost instantaneous ringing echo.

Tomos jumped to his feet and spun round.

Bang! Clang!

He saw his companion kneeling as he took aim at the small pile of rocks.

Bang! The man loosed off one more shot, shattering the top rock into fragments - then looked at Tomos and smiled.

It was a surreal moment and Tomos felt a cold shiver run down his spine. OK, so the gun worked. He supposed his companion was bored and wanted some practice. Still, it was time to complete the job and get away.

He knelt back down and felt under the cover. His hand ran over the clasp and the empty slot where the padlock should be. It was missing. He stood up and looked at the well head; the protective cover did have a few unexpected dents in it. Without being locked down the lid lifted easily on its hinges to reveal the gaping mouth of the borehole. He peered in. At first only the unwinking black circle of the orifice met his gaze. Straining his eyes against the dark interior he managed to make out the smashed bracket bolted to the metallic lining at the top of the well. Clearly it had been broken into, and someone had removed the logger which automatically recorded the water level roughly 150 metres below his feet. The logger should have been connected to a cable which ran the depth of the well, at the other end of which was attached the pressure transducer. The transducer was sensitive to the depth of water and would send a signal up the cable to the logger every fifteen minutes. There was no sign of the logger or its cable.

He reached for the small pocket torch he always carried for site visits. It was a habit he had picked up in Oman; torchlight made it easy to check for snakes hiding in the cool damp recesses of the wells he had to inspect.

He projected the light downwards. The beam reached about twenty feet at which point a large angular boulder was lodged inside the borehole. Several smaller rocks on top ensured the blockage was complete, rendering the borehole useless. It had been sabotaged.

Heavy boots crunching on loose rock approached ... then stopped.

Tomos glanced up, then jumped to his feet. The policeman was standing ten feet in front of him, his assault rifle raised, the end of the barrel pointing straight at his chest. He could feel his heart race as the adrenalin poured through him. He was helpless. There was nowhere to run, and the policeman was too far away for him to rush. All he had to do was squeeze the trigger.

He watched helplessly as the man leered at him with a manic grin, enjoying the moment, enjoying his power.

He stared into the policeman's eyes trying to unnerve him. Incredibly it seemed to work. The ugly grin froze, the mocking eyes of his would-be executioner taking on a fixed unblinking gaze. Tomos hesitated. The man wasn't looking at him. Instead he seemed to be staring past his shoulder and into the distance.

Heart pounding, skin prickling with impossible tension, Tomos slowly turned round. Far away towards the southern horizon was a dust cloud. Not any normal dust cloud, this. It was a long sinewy snake, weaving along the ground. A vehicle was approaching; probably more than one, judging by the length of the trail.

A loud click prompted him to spin back. The policeman had lowered the butt of his rifle to the ground. The leer was gone and he licked his lips as if nervous. He glanced at Tomos, saw he had his attention and then pointed at the line of fast approaching dust - uttering one word in a trembling voice.

Gaddafi!'

The worm-like cloud was approaching rapidly, revealing itself as a convoy of vehicles. The agitated policeman laid down his weapon and stepped forward, raising his arms in the universal act of surrender. He looked over at Tomos, wide eyes betraying his fear. With a frantic signal, he urged him to do the same.

Tomos was aware many Libyans feared the hated dictator but was shocked at the strength of the policeman's reaction. Still, he cared more for his own immediate life than he did any possible threat from Gaddafi.

He moved fast. Eyes fixed on the policeman's face he deliberately walked over and picked up the rifle. His escort vigorously shook his head before pointing at the weapon and then up the road at the rapidly approaching convoy, the front of which had detached itself and was now racing towards them in a tight ball of dust.

'Gaddafi,' the policeman vehemently repeated, spitting out the word, before pointing at the rifle and making a cut-throat sign. The meaning was clear, if the rifle was spotted, they would be seen as a threat.

The whine of a racing engine grew louder as the lead vehicle gradually materialised from the dust ball, revealing itself as a camouflaged armoured car.

There was no time to lose. Tomos ran to his own vehicle and shoved the rifle into the back of the pick-up, concealing it beneath the heavy tarpaulin used to protect any cargo from being covered in sand.

His escort walked to the roadside, arms held high. Tomos sprinted to catch him up, also raising his hands. Just in time. The whine grew to a crescendo; then fell to a steady hum as the car drew up and stopped, engine ticking over. It was some sort of lightly-armoured Mercedes, its identity given away by the familiar badge, recognisable despite being sand-encrusted and partly-hidden behind thick bull bars covering the front grille.

A uniformed soldier brandishing a stubby machine gun as if it was a sword jumped down. He walked right around them before stopping to stand in front of the policeman. Gun pointing at the man's chest, he barked out some questions in Arabic. High-pitched squeaked replies betrayed the policeman's fear.

Tomos found himself sweating as he prayed their vehicle wouldn't be checked; even a cursory search would reveal the rifle.

More barked questions. Then without warning the soldier rammed the end of his gun into the policeman's midriff as hard as he could. Tomos's escort fell writhing to the ground clutching his belly and groaning loudly with every exhaled breath. He managed to stammer out the words '*Jabal Hasouna*' - the name of their camp - in between gasps from his curled-up position on the ground. The soldier peered past them at the pick-up, before giving a satisfied grunt and returning to the Mercedes.

Tomos knelt to help his companion to his feet as the armoured car sped away to continue its sweep ahead of the convoy. Once standing, and still panting in pain, the policeman raised his arms again and looked imploringly at Tomos to do the same.

Standing side by side with a man who moments earlier had appeared intent on killing him, Tomos watched the rest of the convoy pass by. Various light armoured vehicles were followed by tanks and troop-carrying trucks. Sandwiched right in the middle between two heavy personnel carriers bristling with weaponry, was a single black limo with tinted windows.

'*Gaddafi*,' the policeman wheezed once more, as if uttering the very name was punishable by death.

The convoy rumbled past and only when the final vehicle - smothered in a thick layer of sand from all its predecessors - had disappeared into the dusty horizon did the two men relax. The policeman looked at Tomos with a sheepish grin, before they walked back together to the Hilux.

He went to retrieve his weapon, but Tomos grabbed his arm and shook his head. After the smallest hesitation his escort shrugged and climbed unarmed into the passenger seat.

Tomos took his place at the wheel and turned the key. There was no more work to do at the borehole other than report its vandalised condition - something he was sure was another act of defiance against the government who the locals considered were stealing their water. He let out an inward sigh of relief; he didn't trust his passenger and just wanted to complete the long drive back to camp as quickly as possible.

Fortunately the policeman stayed quiet the whole way, allowing him plenty of time to think. Was Al-Hazbar still scheming against him? Or, was the policeman - his eyes slid to his silent companion - just having a bit of fun at his expense? The copper was a dead end; even if he could question him, he'd surely deny any intention of murder. His final question concerned Drissa. Drissa had set-up the trip, so the sphere of suspicion had to include him. It was a sobering concept; the idea that someone so close to him, someone he saw every day, might be conspiring to kill him.

He gripped the wheel hard. It was Oman all over again.

He dropped the policeman at the camp guardhouse, returned to his own quarters, showered, and lay on his bed. Fatigue swept over him and he fell into a fitful sleep. Assassins and dictators joined forces to chase him across an endless plain where he ran towards an empty horizon. As he ran, he sensed the mounting excitement of his hunters as they closed in for the kill.

12

The bad dreams continued. Worse, they joined forces with the daytime paranoia. The relentless pressure made Tomos consider once again if he should move on and leave Libya. He determined not to; his history would have to be faced up to one day; better here than home where loved ones might be put at risk. Meantime he did his best to struggle on. He worked harder, staying after hours to analyse data and reports, and spent any spare time on the rigs learning the intricacies of drilling.

His change in behaviour did not go unnoticed. Matthew even told him he looked stressed; that he ought to take a holiday. In fact the whole question of leave was becoming a major issue. He'd been in Libya six months and had so far refused to take any time off.

To make up for his lack of leave he phoned home regularly. Currently this meant the long drive to a post office in the central Saharan town of Sabha, the camp's own telephone line having once again been cut by bandits.

One late February morning he was in his quarters preparing for a trip with Ed to Sabha's post office, when there was a knock on his door and his name was called.

The door opened, and Vince's head appeared.

'Glad I caught you. Slight change of plan I'm afraid. I've just seen Matthew, and he's not feeling too well, so I hope you don't mind cancelling your away-day and covering for him instead?'

'Yeah, no problem ... nothing too serious I hope? He seemed fine last night.'

'Nothing life threatening, bit of an iffy tummy that's all; probably should have stayed away from Ed's brew - I did warn him. Ed still wants to go to Sabha by the way, but I'd like you to take a drive out to Well H22 and see what's going on with fishing out the end of the airline. The Libyans aren't happy about it, and we need to have a presence there to encourage the boys to hurry up.'

Well H22 was the latest borehole under construction by Paolo and his crew. Operations there had been suspended after the end section of the airline, a metal tube used to help clean the borehole, had accidentally become detached and was now lying at the bottom of the well. The Italians had designed a special "fishing tool" to hook it and bring it back to the surface after their initial attempt with an electro-magnet had failed.

'Paolo's rig, huh? Seems to attract trouble, that one.'

'Yeah. By the way Tom, any more thoughts on taking leave?'

Vince had been standing in the doorway. Now, he stepped inside and closed the door behind him. 'Got family troubles? Haven't we all? I'd just like to say that, as your manager, you need to go home for two reasons. Firstly, you won't solve anything by staying here; I don't know your problem but whatever it is you need to go and speak to people face to face no matter how difficult that is. It'll be worth it, you'll see. Secondly, we've all noticed a change in you, which I put down to stress. You need a break for your own good.'

His manager's advice was sincerely meant. Everyone was assuming he was having family problems, and so far he'd been content to let them do so; it was simpler than explaining the truth. Anyway, his life probably *was* under threat. What scared him was the idea of taking that threat home ... of risking those he loved. God forbid, he would never knowingly put his parents at risk.

'True enough. I've been waiting for everyone to calm down; they say time's a great healer.'

The lie came all too easily, the idea of blaming his behaviour on a family tiff having been silently rehearsed during many a sleepless night. Privately he hoped the concept of time being a great healer would also hold true for Al-Hazbar.

'Well, how about it? Will you go and book some of that overdue leave?'

'I'll think about it. I don't wanna go back too soon - but as I say, I'll think about it.'

'Well that's a start I suppose. OK, you best get going. Good luck at the rig, tell Paolo not to rush and botch things up.'

Tomos arrived just before the recovery operation was about to begin. The Libyan drilling supervisor was there, scowling at everyone and berating the drilling crew for slow work. In fact the crew were working flat out, or so it seemed to Tomos, as he watched the preparations for lowering the newly-fabricated fishing tool. Once it started its 500-metre descent beneath the desert, Paolo invited him into the shade of the portacabin to discuss other options in case the recovery operation failed.

The fishing went well, much to Paolo's relief. After witnessing the successful retrieval of the offending piece of pipe back to the surface, Tomos managed to return to camp by early afternoon. He settled down in the office to watch some CCTV footage taken from inside one of the newly completed boreholes. Having missed the canteen lunch, he'd resigned himself to munching his way through an old chocolate bar he'd been saving for just such an occasion. The office was very quiet, only Vince was in; presumably Matthew still wasn't feeling well enough to make an appearance.

He was halfway through what was arguably the world's most boring video, when the main door swung open and a desperate figure reeled in. It was Ed, almost unrecognisable from the Ed who'd set off alone that morning. This haggard version was breathing heavily, the eyes sunken in a glowing red face.

Vince leapt to his feet. 'Ed! What's up, mate? What's happened?'

Ed lurched over to the small fridge where they normally kept a few bottles of drinking water. He wrenched the door open, grabbed a bottle, and half-drained it in one long guzzle before turning to face his colleagues.

His face was burning red raw; his lips cracked from exposure to extreme heat, his voice a hoarse rasp. 'Got hijacked didn't I. Bandits came at me from nowhere, a black pick-up with a bloody great big machine gun in the back! No way was I going to argue with those buggars!'

'My God! Are you injured? They take your car?' Tomos asked.

'I'm OK. Yeah, they took the car alright. With a gun being waved in my face they were welcome to it. Made me stop, get out, and lie down. Some tall dude dressed all in black fired a machine gun into the ground inches in front of my head. If he wanted to scare the crap out of me, believe me, he succeeded.'

He emptied his water bottle and looked at Tomos. 'Before leaving with my car, he asked my name.' He took a deep breath.. '...Asked me if I was the infidel also known as Tomos. I don't think he believed me when I said my name was Ed. He took my wallet so must have checked my driving licence before he was satisfied.'

'What happened next?' Vince asked, handing Ed another bottle.

'Nothing ... they drove off in both vehicles, I reckon there must have been three or four of the buggars. Anyway, they just left me there. This was about fifty clicks from here. The only thing I could do was start walking back hoping to catch a lift. No water, though - and no hat. I thought I was going to boil away! I must have walked for hours before one of the flatbeds picked me up ... lucky really I even saw one.'

He finished drinking and belched loudly. The water seemed to be helping, every second his voice gaining in strength. 'They were obviously looking for a white guy called Tomos - and Tom here is the only one I know. If it's you Tom ... well, I don't know why these guys are so pissed off with you, but I wouldn't hang around in Libya for too long if I were you. Now, if you'll excuse me gents, I'm off for a cold shower and a kip.'

Tomos's heart had already dropped. All his old fears came welling up in a wave, sweeping through him and draining away all remnants of optimism. The hairs on the back of his neck had stood on end at hearing the phrase "Tomos the Infidel". There was no longer any doubt he'd been traced to

Libya; Al-Hazbar must have used his old nickname to describe him to his accomplices. He sank down into his chair shaking his head in disbelief.

With Ed gone, Vince turned to Tomos. 'It seems to me that if Ed heard right, it must be *you* they were looking for, which means you've got some explaining to do. You must know why these bandits asked for you by name?'

'I thought it was all over, at least I hoped it was. I'm really sorry for Ed. He probably wasn't ever in any real danger. It's me they want. Believe it or not, this all boils down to a simple case of mistaken identity.'

'Look, I'm not convinced Ed wasn't in danger. We've always had car-jacking's, it's part of life out here, but there's never been a hint of anything personal in it. You being asked for by *name,* adds a whole new dimension to things. As drilling manager I need to know about any new risks to personnel, so you'd better explain exactly what's going on.'

His secret was out, there was nothing for it but to admit to the whole sorry situation and try to find the best way forward. He gave Vince the bare bones of the story; witnessing the death of Al-Hazbar's son in the wadi flood and the subsequent threats made against him by the young man's father.

'I know Al-Hazbar asked my whereabouts, I just find it hard to believe one man's hatred can reach so far across the world.'

Vince exhaled deeply as Tomos finished his monotone account. 'You really should have told me all this when you started work, it would have made things a lot easier for everyone. I suppose this explains your reluctance to go home?

You don't want to take the problem back with you? Am I right?'

'Yep, that's about it. I can't go back in case Al-Hazbar follows me. Nothing's happened for so long now; I thought I was in the clear.' He slowly clenched and unclenched his fists. 'Obviously all I've done is bring my problems here.'

He looked over at Vince. 'Well, what next? Suppose it's for the best if I quit Libya, and try and sort things out elsewhere?'

'I'm afraid so,' Vince raised his hands in resignation. 'Life is dangerous enough here already. We certainly don't need any madman hell-bent on revenge to spice things up even more. Take my advice; book a flight home. I strongly suggest you also go to the police when you return; I can always back up your story about events here if necessary.'

'Dammit, this isn't how I wanted to finish! He looked hard at Vince. 'So be it; I resign, as from now.'

'I'm really sorry but maybe when you're back in Britain you'll feel more in control and be able to sort everything out. I'm going to check on Ed ... make sure he's OK.'

• • •

The talk in the canteen over lunch was all about Ed's trials and Tomos's history. Everyone was there, eager to learn anything new. Tomos was questioned relentlessly about what happened and what he thought might occur next. Ed was there too, despite his acute sunburn. He summed up most people's feelings by declaring that his assailants were probably just common car thieves who'd been asked by some outside influence to try and identify the location of a Brit called Tomos. The only logical conclusion was that Al-Hazbar knew

Tomos was in Libya but didn't know exactly *where*. Theirs wasn't the only camp, others were scattered along the length of the main pipeline route all the way back to Tripoli.

'So how did an Omani businessman manage to contact a bunch of rebels operating in the desert interior of a foreign country?' Matthew asked.

'My guess is that there's an Islamic connection here, perhaps Al-Hazbar has connections through Al Qaeda. A lot of the rebels living in the desert are thought to be associated with them,' Ed explained.

'Could be he had some shady business dealings with them, maybe buying and selling stolen vehicles or arms dealing,' Tomos ventured, aghast at the idea that Al Qaeda might be getting involved in a manhunt for him.

'Possibly he got a message out to the criminal network that you've wronged a fellow Moslem. Whatever his connections to Libya, I suspect he's offered a financial reward for your capture,' suggested Vince.

The idea was met with general agreement; a scenario that did little to ease Tomos's state of mind.

That evening all the British reconvened in the bar. The conversation initially centred on Tomos's problems but with nothing new to add it eventually moved onto other matters. When Vince and Ed began to talk about work issues, Matthew seized the opportunity to corner Tomos and pressed his friend as to why he hadn't confided in him.

'Sorry mate, I couldn't tell anyone, and if I did you'd have said I was crazy.'

'Well, let's just hope nothing else happens before you leave.'

'I see you're feeling better. Funny that ... now the day's work is done and the beers have appeared,' Tomos said, attempting to lighten the mood.

Matthew grinned, but before he could answer there was a loud rap on the door which was flung open. One of the Filipino drillers marched in. He scanned the men drinking along the bar, and his eyes flickered with recognition. Striding across the floor he offered his hand.

'Mr Morgan? Remember me? It's Carlos; I live with your friend Rodrigo.'

'Yes, I remember. What can I do for you Carlos?'

'Rodrigo is asking for you, he needs to talk to you urgently. Please come at once.'

From the British expat block to the pipe-house was a five-minute brisk walk. Outside they were greeted by a cold clear night, though only Sirius, the brightest star, managed to survive being drowned by the powerful lights of the camp.

'Is Rodrigo alright?' Tomos enquired, as they hurried along.

'The police came and arrested him early this morning ... said he'd been stealing from the stores during the night.'

'Rodrigo wouldn't do that - they've got the wrong man, or made it all up'.

'Oh, it's a false accusation, they never even said what was stolen. Anyway I know the police are lying,' concluded Carlos just before they entered the pipe. 'I'm part of his crew, we worked on the rig together right through the night.'

Rodrigo was lying on his bed, hands clasped behind his head. Seeing Tomos he broke into a welcoming smile and beckoned him over.

'Mister Tomos, very happy you have come to visit me.

Please forgive me for not coming to see you sooner.' Rodrigo called everyone mister. When Tomos had insisted he be called plain Tomos, Rodrigo had compromised and started calling him Mister Tomos. It had become something of a private joke between them. Not now ... the pun was lost as Tomos was wholly concerned with his friend's obvious distress.

'Carlos says you were arrested. What happened? Are you alright?'

Rodrigo winced before replying. 'I'm fine now, thank you. It's you I'm worried about. I'm very sorry, but I think I might have made things worse for you. You need to listen to what I have to say.'

'They beat his feet with a stick – look!' Carlos moved to his friend's side and helped him sit up with his legs stretched out. Tomos looked at the exposed soles of Rodrigo's feet and felt his stomach churn at the sight of the criss-crossing welts still oozing blood and swollen with dark bruising.

'Oh Rodrigo - why? Is there anything I can do to help?'

'Yes, please listen ... you may not have much time. The robbery was just a trick to arrest me. The police took me into a small room in their quarters and locked the door. They said it had been reported that I was asking questions about a businessman from Oman and they wanted to know why.'

Tomos felt his stomach turn over again.

'At first I refused to tell them anything and they got very angry ... told me I wouldn't be released until I told them where I'd heard about the Omani, and who had told me of him.' Rodrigo paused and took a sip from a mug of water that Carlos handed him, before continuing. 'There were three of them Mister Tomos. Two held me down; the other removed my boots and socks and used a cane on my feet. I'm ashamed to say that after five minutes I relented and told them what they wanted.'

Rodrigo hung his head and looked at the top of his feet as if they were to blame for his moment of weakness. 'I told them you knew the businessman from when you worked in Oman. Mister Tomos, listen ... this will get back to your enemy very quickly. If he didn't know you were here before, he will now. He must have the police on his side. I expect he's paying them for information, maybe even to capture you and hand you over. You must leave Libya immediately. It's your only chance.'

Tomos took a deep breath and stared at his friend. 'Rodrigo, I'm so sorry this happened to you. It's all my fault. Don't worry about talking to the police; anyone would have done the same in your position. Is there anything I can do to help you now – anything at all?'

'Don't worry about me, I will soon heal. Please ... if you want to help me, leave the country. You will save yourself, and I will not have to live with the shame that my betrayal led to your capture, or worse.'

There was a certain inherent truth in Rodrigo's words. Tomos was a hunted man.

He solemnly shook Rodrigo's hand. 'I'll never forget how you've suffered for me. There was no betrayal on your part. You did your best to help me; in my heart you'll always be my friend.'

The words came from deep within him, spoken without hesitation. Tomos hoped they didn't sound too pompous, but he thought he saw tears in Rodrigo's eyes as he departed.

13

Tomos returned to the common room deep in thought. He agreed with Rodrigo that Al-Hazbar would soon find him, doubting it would take long for the Filipino's information to find its way back to his old enemy. If he stayed where he was, then it was only a matter of time before he would be arrested on some false pretext, just the same as Rodrigo. His blood boiled at the thought of his friend lying injured on his bed; he would make Al-Hazbar pay for that one day.

The room went quiet as he walked up to the bar. Three heads turned as one to look at him. He took a deep swig of warm beer from his glass and waited for the questions.

'What's going on mate?' Matthew broke the awkward silence. 'Is your Filipino friend OK?'

'Listen guys, it sounds like things have taken a turn for the worse. My buddy's been roughed up by the local cops so they've just found out who I am. I'm assuming that means Al-Hazbar also knows I'm here too, or very soon will.'

'This is potentially very serious.' Vince groaned. 'After what you've just told us, you definitely have to leave as soon as possible. What's worrying me ... just how much influence does this Al-Hazbar have? Perhaps not so much in Tripoli as in the interior, but even so, you may not be safe there either.'

'We all know KLM is the only airline still coming to Libya and they only fly out on a Wednesday, that means the next flight isn't for five days,' Ed pointed out. 'That means five whole days of waiting either here or in Tripoli. Longer, if you can't get a late seat.'

Vince broke the short silence that followed. 'Right, first things first - everyone go and ditch all the booze in your rooms. Destroy or hide anything obvious you've been using to brew. If the police come here to search for Tomos, and find alcohol, then we're all in for the chop. Meet back here as soon as you're done and we'll decide what to do next.'

Thirty hectic minutes later everyone reconvened in the common room. The mood was sombre but ideas for action were more forthcoming.

Tomos spoke first. 'I'm not going home. You all know I haven't taken any leave yet. Well, the real reason was because I didn't wanna take my problem back and endanger anyone there. After what's happened to Rodrigo it's more important than ever I don't go to Britain. Somewhere else - yes, but not home.'

'If you do go somewhere else you might be able to get an earlier flight, the less time in Libya the better,' Matthew suggested.

'I still think the police are the main problem,' Vince remarked thoughtfully. 'We just don't know how they operate. If Al-Hazbar is throwing money around then it'll only take one phone call from the camp police to the cops in Tripoli, and they'll know they can wait for you there. Alternatively the police might well be on their way here as we speak, now that Filipino has told them Tom's here.'

Everyone looked at each other and then at Tomos, who felt not for the first time that the world was closing in on him.

'In fact, Tom,' Vince spoke slowly and carefully as he thought out loud. 'Go and pack a bag right now; I think you should leave straight away. Go to Tripoli and see if you can stay in a hotel, somewhere different to our normal place.'

'Whoa there, I've got it!' Ed shouted. 'You can fly from Sabha. There's a small airport there, it's much closer than Tripoli. If you can get a flight out of Sabha, you could be away in no time!'

'And you can avoid all the police checkpoints on the Tripoli road,' added Matthew.

'Not sure where you can fly to from there,' Vince sounded doubtful. 'But it's a good idea. How do you feel about it?'

'Guess what, I'm up for that. I don't care where I go. Anyway ... if I don't know where I'm going, neither will my enemy!'

Despite a few lame chuckles the tension remained; an almost tangible force in the air around them.

'OK. Tom, go and get your stuff together. I'll pop into the office and check on flights out of Sabha.'

Back in his room Tomos hurriedly packed his old rucksack. He also had a small sports bag into which, after hesitating, he threw his running shoes, shorts and singlet. Running might help keep him sane wherever he ended up.

He found his wallet, passport and small address book. Carrying all three, he clumsily dropped the book. Stooping to pick it up made him think of the names inside. There weren't many, mostly family and a few friends. An image of home thrust itself into his mind: his parents sitting peacefully in front of a log fire in their cosy cottage. He could not - would not - put them at risk.

Matthew knocked and walked straight in. 'Let me help you

mate,' he grunted, 'I can hardly believe this is really happening! I sure hope things work out for you buddy.'

They walked outside together, to the end of the block where they found Matthew's parked vehicle. He delved into his pocket and fished out his key. 'Here, take mine, it's much less likely to break down than yours. It does need filling up though.'

'Thanks mate,' Tomos half-turned to meet Vince who came sprinting around the corner from the direction of the office.

'No time for goodbyes! There's all sorts of lights on at the police quarters - never seen so many - so reckon they might be coming over any minute now. Just get going, for Christ's sake!'

'Thanks boys - for everything!' Tomos snatched the proffered key from Matthew, jumped into the driver's seat, fired the ignition and wound down his window. Matthew threw the bags into the back while Vince ran around to the driver's side.

'There's a flight to Niamey in Niger tomorrow morning, leaving at nine.'

'Nine o'clock ... Cheers!'

'Make sure you're on it!' Vince yelled through the open window as Tomos drove away.

Fighting to stay calm he headed for the camp exit. He had to pass right in front of the police block, unnaturally ablaze with light. As he warily eyed it, the main door opened and a figure emerged silhouetted by both the roof spotlights and the interior light that spilled out from the room behind. He turned his head away and looked fixedly ahead as he slowed so as not to draw attention to himself. Vehicles routinely passed in and out of the camp during the night, so the gates were never shut, and with so much traffic the vehicles themselves were rarely checked. He prayed tonight would be no different. Heart pounding, he raised one hand in acknowledgement to the duty sentry, the knuckles of his other white as he gripped the steering wheel.

No-one challenged him! Once through the gate he felt a little easier. Remembering what Matthew had said about fuel, he turned right. A few hundred yards along the track was the small fuel compound, manned twenty-four hours a day to keep all operations running. Time was money after all.

He swung in through the wide gateway and pulled up next to the two hand pumps in the middle of the compound. Next to the pumps was a small wooden shed which protected the two attendants who lived there; some shade by day and a little shelter from the cold wind by night. The duty attendant appeared and unhooked the nozzle. His body shape looked familiar, causing Tomos to look more closely and recognise the face.

'Hey Isaac, it's me Tomos. Can you fill 'er up as fast as you can?'

'Sure. Why the hurry?' Isaac sensed the urgency in his voice.

Tomos wasted no time in frivolous explanations; he trusted Isaac completely.

'Police are after me, need to get away quick.'

'Where are you going?'

'Niamey, Niger.' As soon as he spoke he regretted it. Isaac looked at him intensely. Something had occurred to him, and for a split second Tomos wondered if his friend would seriously consider selling him out.

'Can you take me with you? You know I want to go back, and Niamey is nearly home.' Isaac surprised him with the request even as he started filling the tank.

'Seriously? Are you sure? Could be dangerous ... what about money for a ticket? Also I need to go *now*. I'm sorry there's no time to even pack a bag.'

'I have everything here ... clothes, passport and a little money. Not enough for a ticket but listen ... if you help me get to Niger, I can help you lots when we arrive. I know many people ... maybe you can come home to Burkina with me. What do you think?'

Tomos didn't need to think. Travelling together could benefit them both, as long as they weren't caught.

'OK Isaac, you're crazy, but yes. Let me finish the petrol; if you're ready within two minutes we'll leave together.'

He held the fuel hose while Isaac ran into his little shack to reappear clutching a battered duffle bag. He was grinning, his teeth very white in the beam of the spotlight used to illuminate the fuel pump.

'All ready, let's go before these police arrive,' he exclaimed, jumping into the passenger seat. They swung out of the little compound and turned left, the road to Sabha taking them back past the main camp. A quick glance revealed the gate was shut, the first time Tomos had ever seen that ... a close escape indeed.

The first leg of the night drive to Sabha took four hours of intense concentration as Tomos divided his attention between keeping all four wheels on the unmarked track and scanning the desert for any sign of pursuit, either from the police or bandits. He was mindful of the fact that he was following the same path on which Ed had been ambushed only that morning.

Nervous though he was, Tomos was pleased that Isaac had not asked why he was fleeing the country. He took that as a bond of trust. Still, he considered he owed his friend an explanation, and so told him a little about Al-Hazbar and his present predicament.

Travelling mostly west it took nearly two and a half hours before they hit the tarmac of the Tripoli-Sabha highway, following it south for a further hour and a half. In all that way they saw not another single vehicle. Beyond the windows the desert appeared as subtle shades of an-almost black. Dunes and the ground's stony undulations shared the car's headlights and the heaven's starlight to create a teasing never-ending ocean of shadows that flowed away to invisible horizons.

Some ten miles shy of Sabha they pulled off the road and drove for about a kilometre until they found a depression just deep enough to conceal them from the road. Here they tried unsuccessfully to sleep until dawn, having agreed en-route there was no point in attracting unwelcome attention by driving through town in the middle of the night. Tired, dishevelled and hungry, they completed the final leg at sun-up. Even with the welcome companionship of Isaac, Tomos had never felt so alone and vulnerable in his entire life.

Sabha was bathed in weak morning sunlight when they passed through, the main street eerily quiet and empty. The international airport was situated on the other side of the town, the term "international" being a somewhat grandiose description in Tomos's opinion. Minor club aerodrome more like.

They left the pick-up in the small car park and walked to the terminal building. Tomos felt uneasy about leaving his vehicle where it could be so easily found should the police decide to check all the airports. However, there was little choice unless they were prepared to walk the two miles from town, which would have left them in an even more vulnerable position. Anyway, he consoled himself, Vince or Matthew would need to recover the vehicle, and they were sure to try the car park first.

The terminal was as dirty as it was small. There were only a handful of would-be travellers milling around, and a quick look at the manually operated departures and arrival board indicated theirs was the single flight due out that morning. The only other flight listed was an arrival due three hours later from Tripoli.

Isaac admitted it was the first time he had been to an airport. His growing curiosity about the whole procedure alerted Tomos that his friend was probably a little nervous about flying. They watched the tiny café open for business and sat down with two cups of cheap bitter coffee to wait for the ticket counter to open. Tomos carried little cash on him, since there was nowhere to spend it within hundreds of miles. With no other option, he purchased two one-way tickets to Niamey, using his credit card. He hoped Al-Hazbar didn't have the capability of tracing him through the transaction.

He agonised over the rights and wrongs of his actions, if he would manage to get away safely, and where exactly he was going. The wait for his flight to be called felt like the longest hour of his life. An official walked through the terminal to announce the departure, beckoning for all passengers to follow. Once through the departure gate, Isaac was waved straight through passport control by the Libyan in charge - his officious eyes already focusing on Tomos, who followed behind.

The officer held out an impatient hand for the passport and very slowly flicked through all the pages, one by one. Tomos's heart missed several beats.

Was he about to be arrested at the last hurdle? At least Isaac had got through safely.

He inadvertently swallowed, as he felt his face being studied and compared to his passport photo. The next few seconds might decide his fate. The officer in charge seemed to be enjoying his obvious discomfort. After an interminable age, he got the nod to pass. They boarded within minutes and he took his seat next to Isaac who looked more scared than he felt nervous. Only after they lifted into the bright North African sky did both men finally dare to breathe a sigh of relief.

Tomos couldn't help noticing Isaac still gripping the sides of his seat as the plane climbed steeply and banked at the same time. He didn't blame him. It must be his first ever flight, and this time yesterday he would never have dreamt he'd be flying home today. How would he be treated - as a returning hero - or as a failure who'd let everyone down? And what did his own future hold? Once again he was fleeing from an enemy he knew very little about. He had no idea where he was going or what he was going to do once he got there. His life was a mess, and he really didn't know what to do to put it back in order. Fate it seemed was still enjoying playing games with him.

He settled back in his seat and felt his head loll with fatigue. As he dozed, his thoughts sought comfort by imaging memories of home; Pontyafon village set in its South Wales valley. It was a landscape scoured out of the green hills by the hands of men, slaves to industries now long gone. Pontyafon's grey lines of tiny cottages created an unnatural intrusion into the majestic backdrop of hedged green grass fields that rose ever steeper before giving way to the open ferns and sheep grazed moors of the high mountain. The valley's river itself was invisible from where he lived, lying far below the level of the village, lost deep within the depths of the ribbon of black woodland that graced the waterway's gently curving banks.

He longed to be there and wished for it more than anything. To return a free man, without threats to himself or his family, that would be his aim. It was one he was determined to fight for, no matter what the cost.

14

It was only a matter of hours before the big Antonov 72 belonging to Libyan Air landed at Niamey international airport. The blitz of activity that followed allowed little time to dwell on past events or what might lie ahead. The plan, agreed on the flight, was that from Niger they would continue their journey on to Isaac's home in neighbouring Burkina Faso.

Isaac's help proved invaluable in obtaining two visas for Tomos, one for Niger on arrival and another for Burkina Faso, stamped at the Burkina Faso Consulate. At a branch of Banque d'Afrique Tomos endured the lengthy process of making a cash withdrawal. This entailed some considerable form filling in French, where he was once again grateful for Isaac's assistance.

A night in a grimy hotel provided a much-needed shower and a chance to catch up on some rest. Up at the crack of dawn, they checked out to prepare for the next leg of the journey. Breakfast was good. Sitting at a bench on the side of an already busy street, they hungrily devoured warm buttered baguettes with hot coffee served in tall glasses with generous lashings of sweetened condensed milk.

Isaac remarked how much easier the return trip to his homeland was, compared to the outward journey. A simple statement, but one that made Tomos reflect how others had suffered far more than himself. Isaac was proving to be a good friend indeed.

After breakfast they loaded their meagre baggage into a dilapidated Peugeot taxi. As they travelled Tomos tried not to look down at the road, clearly visible through several large holes in the floor.

'Most taxis sold cheap by French and Italian tourists,' Isaac explained. 'The Europeans drive them across the Sahara ... their big adventure ... then sell them here and fly home. People here don't have money for new cars; they just keep repairing the old ones. Believe me, I've seen much worse than this!'

Exhaust fumes billowed up through the floor in little choking bursts. The bone-jarring vibrations, courtesy of a long-deceased suspension combined with the loud rattle of the exhaust pipe, left the passengers feeling light-headed by the time they arrived at the sprawling central bus station. The driver only seemed to cope by poking his head out of his side window at every opportunity.

'Glad we made it, I'm not sure I would have survived another five minutes ... worst taxi I've ever been in,' Tomos grumbled good-naturedly to Isaac, after paying the fare.

'Don't worry; I will find good bus – but no guarantee!'

Looking around the terminal, Tomos felt grateful yet again for Isaac's friendship; finding out where to go was not going to be straightforward. Everywhere was a maelstrom of activity. He should have realised the station must serve the whole of Niger plus all the cross-border routes to neighbouring Nigeria, Benin, Mali, and Burkina Faso.

People, buses, taxis and bikes were everywhere, a continual swirling mass of impatience. It was a human kaleidoscope fabricated with the bright traditional garbs so beloved of sub-

Saharan Africans. Green, red, orange, yellow and white shirts and dresses danced and spun in the sun, a continuous stream of new patterns. The living canvas was painted with a background of red dust which hung in the air in little earth-bound clouds and stung the back of the throat, the gritty dryness palpable on the tongue. The ears struggled to disseminate an ever-changing cacophony of growling diesel engines, whining mopeds and honking horns.

People added their own rhythm as they talked or shouted; exchanging information, chit-chat, greetings or farewells. Acrid exhaust fumes from umpteen buses, taxis and mopeds mingled with the smell of humanity, open drains and rubbish strewn across the station. The whole experience was infused with occasional whiffs of freshly cooked exotic foods from vendors crying their wares. It was a great leap from the monotonous emptiness of the Libyan Desert; and Tomos found himself staring open-mouthed at every new sight and smell.

He successfully shrugged off the attention of a group of youths insisting on carrying his bag for an unknown charge, and followed Isaac through the bustle until they arrived at an ancient looking bus ringed by a small group of standing and squatting on-lookers. More questions and replies in French for Isaac, all too fast for Tomos to follow, until Isaac eventually turned to him to explain their options.

'This is bus we want, going to Ouagadougou ... but it has engine problem, driver is looking for a mechanic. Don't know what time it will leave ... maybe doesn't go today. We could take a bush taxi instead, but that is more dollars.'

Isaac pointed at a dirty but otherwise intact Peugeot estate, presumably the bush taxi. The driver was leaning on the bonnet watching them with interest, probably hoping to pick up some business courtesy of the bus's misfortune.

'We'll take the bush taxi,' Tomos replied without hesitation. Fascinating though the bus terminal was, he was desperate to rest and take stock of his situation so just wanted to get to wherever he was going as fast as possible.

They were joined by two other disappointed would-be bus passengers, the taxi driver anxious to maximise his profit. With the fares negotiated and paid, all baggage was piled high, seriously overloading the roof rack. The taxi crept forward, zig-zagging around numerous deep potholes, the driver honking to establish his right of way through the shifting maze of traffic and pedestrians.

Tomos found himself wedged in the back seat between a large lady and a thin older gentleman. The lady politely nudged him in the ribs with a fat elbow, and with a huge smile offered him a strip of dried meat from a pack that she was already chewing on.

Isaac laughed at him from the front passenger seat. 'Try it. It's called clichy ... very tasty.'

Outside the city limits the taxi increased speed, allowing a little cooling breeze to find its way through the half open windows. Tomos settled back into his seat to mentally prepare himself for what he rightly guessed would be a long and uncomfortable journey.

The drive to Burkina Faso normally took six hours, but on this occasion stretched to eight due to a lengthy unplanned delay at the cross-border customs and immigration control.

An official claimed Tomos did not resemble his passport photo, an accusation that proved fruitless to argue against. The same awkward officer then insisted that a requested sample signature also did not match the one in the passport. The upshot was that Isaac intervened on his behalf and quietly paid a small "admin" fee which immediately resolved all issues. Further delays at police and army road blocks necessitated further fees, leaving Tomos both out of pocket and distinctly unpopular with his fellow travellers.

The taxi did afford Tomos with his first glimpse of the West African savanna. His limited view left him with an impression of a flat, tree-studded landscape, a land of patchy roadside fields interspersed with swathes of tall wild grass.

Afternoon was nearly over when they arrived in the capital, Ouagadougou. A breeze had kicked up on their approach, surrendering the town to the grip of an eerie rose-tinted fog. Eager to see this West African city for the first time, Tomos was disappointed to find his vision limited to about twenty to thirty yards as the harmattan, the northerly wind, ushered in the red Saharan sands to smother the people and the city, filtering life through a translucent thin red veil.

They entered the city down one of the main arterial routes. The road was wide, the sides home to numerous stalls, and as they neared the city centre the road itself became busier and busier with increasing numbers of mopeds as people made their way home at the end of the working day. Behind the stalls most of the buildings were single storey with far fewer civic, commercial and industrial sites than in any European town.

At Isaac's request the taxi dropped them off at the barrage -

or dam and associated reservoir - which constituted the principal source of the city's water supply. Baggage unloaded, Isaac led Tomos on foot through a mile of busy streets to a small bar called Mon Amie on the south-eastern edge of town. The establishment belonged to an aunt he used to lodge with. From there, Isaac claimed he would organise a lift back to his village.

Both men arrived tired and thirsty. The aunt - a lady in her early fifties - enthusiastically greeted them, the warm welcome cemented with an ice-cold bottle of a locally brewed beer.

'Isaac! Hey! Ca va? Ca va?'

A young man, maybe nineteen or twenty years of age came running across the floor, gripped Isaac's hand and enthusiastically pumped it up and down.

'Tomos, meet my friend Non-non, my aunt's son,' Isaac laughed, a mischievous twinkle in his eye. Fending off streams of questions from both Non-non and his inquisitive aunt, Isaac explained in his own language that they wanted to get back to his village that evening. Non-non obligingly left, reappearing an hour later with a friend and two mopeds.

Isaac climbed aboard one to sit behind Non-non, and Tomos sat on the back of the other. No-one wore a helmet and with his rucksack slung behind him, Tomos clung precariously to the back of his seat for the slow ride to the village.

The mopeds followed the tarmac south for nearly two hours before turning onto the piste, or unpaved road. A further hour's ride ensued, this time much slower and bumpier over gullies that crisscrossed the track, the result of savage seasonal rains that eroded the exposed ground. Finally as dusk fell they reached their destination. Tomos soaked in the environment, discovering the village of Koutatenga to be an amorphous haphazard mixture of dwellings that included a small church and a mosque. He remembered Isaac saying that Islam and Christianity were deeply entwined in his homeland, insomuch that the normal extended families often encompassed both religions.

Halleluiah! The journey without an end had finally ended!'

Tomos felt like screaming his thanks. He might have done so, if he hadn't been so full of aches and wracked with fatigue that it took all his effort not to fall from the bike.

He looked on with relief and pleasure at the rapturous reception his friend received as the shout rang out that he'd returned. His family were so happy that he was back safe after being away for so long without contact, that no-one as far as Tomos could tell, questioned why he'd returned.

Several chickens were prepared for a communal feast which Tomos reckoned most of the village also attended. Being the exotic stranger, he attracted a lot of curiosity whilst being made to feel very welcome at the same time. A little dolo - the local millet beer - helped him relax, and despite his tiredness he even attempted to join in some impromptu dancing.

Aching with fatigue, he finally found his way to bed in Isaac's house, a large mud-brick cube. His room, a tiny alcove, provided minimal privacy. He leant over and blew out the light from a paraffin lantern, leaving him in comforting near-darkness. A square hole in the wall allowed the pinpricks of bright starlight that hung above the savanna to dimly illuminate a patch of the drawn curtain which partitioned off his section of the room.

The excitement of his new surroundings and the welcome he and Isaac had received had been so overwhelming, he wasn't sure he'd be able to sleep despite his exhaustion. The unglazed aperture - a poor excuse for a window - also allowed in the astonishingly loud harsh chirping of the bush crickets. He did his best to think of the noisy intrusion as a natural rhythm of nature, yet the insects and their brash calling remained stubbornly alien to his unaccustomed ear. It wasn't just the crickets. His whole situation, the uncontrollable train of events of the past few days all seemed to converge in his head to hammer home the message that once again he was alone and vulnerable, with a future he couldn't even begin to imagine.

Maybe he'd missed something, an opportunity somewhere or made a wrong decision; something he needed to reconsider.

He listened to the undecipherable hushed tones of his adopted family on the other side of the curtain until they fell silent. Only then did fatigue take control, finally leading him into a deep and peaceful sleep.

15

A thin needle of light poked tentatively through a gap in the rough timbered side of the pigsty. The ray of sunshine was the first of the new dawn, and its presence ignited a flicker of hope in the young woman locked inside. Grateful the night was over; she mumbled her thanks through prayer before straining her ears for any sound that might signal the end of her imprisonment.

She shivered. The cold from the earthen floor had long since seeped into her bones. Flung into the cramped space the previous afternoon, the little door had slammed shut behind her, the latch savagely bolted home, resonating the anger of her captor. Every eternal moment since had added to the weight of despair dragging at her soul.

The swine had been moved out to make way for her, but the nauseating stink lingered on, a saturating presence that permeated into her clothes, hair and body. Sitting up, she stretched her legs out in front of her; then brought them slowly up to rest her chin on her knees. She had to be careful. Every clumsy movement disturbed the muck on the floor releasing an over-powering stench, forcing her to retch anew.

Her name was Monique, and from the moment she had been conscripted into the army to serve her three years, trouble had dogged her. The army was tough, especially for new recruits like herself who had to live with the constant ache of hunger and the threat of physical abuse from superior officers. And it always seemed to be her who was singled out for the harshest treatment.

Not for the first time she cursed the misfortune in being born into the royal household of the Gourma people, a powerful tribe in that part of Africa. She was certain her royal connections were the root cause of all her suffering. A night in the pigsty was just the latest in a long line of punishments meted out by her commanding officer, Captain Jerome Zongo of the People's Army of Burkina Faso. Once Zongo had discovered her heritage, he'd gone out of his way to make her life hell. She often wondered whether his actions were borne from hatred of her perceived privileged upbringing or a desire to ingratiate himself with his socialist superiors.

Without room to stand, she hugged her knees ever tighter in a vain attempt to conserve body heat. Rocking slowly back and fore she tried to ignore the stinging in the back of her throat and the constant urge to swallow away the gagging odours.

This latest ordeal was punishment for stealing food. She and Sabine, her colleague and closest friend, had been so hungry they'd been left with little choice. Caught, they'd both been dragged to face the captain in the log cabin which served as the camp HQ. He'd made the punishment perfectly clear: a straight choice between a night with him or with the swine. Sabine had surrendered to the night in his quarters rather than face the trial of the sty. Having refused his crude threats Monique now felt a spark of satisfaction that she had survived thus far, her pride intact.

She shuddered, recalling his words after she'd refused his bed. "Think about it. You're a beautiful young woman, fine figure, only eighteen. Don't force me to make you old before your time; pain etches such ugly lines on a woman's face."

What did she care about lines? Romance and love seemed a thousand miles away, something that could only happen in a dream. Her left leg twitched, the unwanted warning of cramp. Unwilling to sleep with her head in the filth, she had chosen to sit up all night, praying out loud several times for deliverance from her suffering. Her eye refocused on the single ray of sunshine. What time was it? Surely she would be let out soon?

The sounds of the waking camp began with muffled shouted orders that were quickly joined by the faint call to prayers for the Muslim contingent of soldiers. A clang from the nearby kitchen preparing their meagre breakfasts was added to the background noise. The morning was well underway. Please don't forget me.

At last, the sound she'd been waiting for, the thud of approaching boots. The door was unbolted with a swift metallic rasp and wrenched open. The soft red square of the long-awaited dawn drew in a waft of sweet-smelling air. Blinking, and stiff with cold, she crawled out on muck caked hands and knees to face the beginning of yet another day of hell in the parched savanna.

Rising unsteadily to her feet she lurched away from a couple of amused onlookers. She was fully aware of the spectacle she posed; her uniform smeared with slurry, hair matted with filth. The odour emanating from her was such that even *she* found it repulsive. When this was over, she promised herself, she would do whatever it took to escape forever from these pigs of men.

16

Right from the start, the village of Koutatenga felt like a second home to Tomos and he quickly grew to love it. He couldn't say exactly why he felt that way, other than being grateful for the speed with which he was painlessly welcomed into the community. Although situated only fifty miles south of the capital city of Ouagadougou, the slow and simple lifestyles of the villagers hinted at generations of people living in harmony with the wilderness around them.

One of the first things he discovered was just how early the day began. Taking breakfast before first light allowed the women and older children to complete the heavier household chores before the sun rose high enough to dull the will to work. An early start also rewarded the men and boys, labour in the fields being far more productive before the day's heat strangled short any sustained physical effort.

On his first morning Tomos awoke to the sound of a cock crowing, a gentle reminder of the village life beyond the mud walls of his room. After dressing he found the bathroom ready furnished with a bucket of water which he later learned was drawn from the river a forty-minute walk away. The water wasn't too clean, earlier risers having already washed in it.

He splashed some water on his face before stepping into the main room. Sylvie, only twelve years old, was bent double sweeping dust out through the front door with a short-handled broom. She beamed a welcome, straightened, and walked over to join him holding out her right wrist - the hand itself being dirty from her work remaining politely unoffered.

Tomos laughed and shook the tiny wrist in greeting, mildly embarrassed at having risen so late.

'Good morning Tomo, did you sleep well?' she enquired in French, missing the 's' off the end of his name.

'Yes, very well Sylvie, thank you.'

'Are you hungry? I'll tell Mama you are up and want breakfast. Hope you don't mind eating alone, we've already finished ours.'

That morning proved typical of those that followed. The day always began with handshakes and greetings exchanged with each member of his host family, followed by breakfast usually made from the previous day's left-overs; or if the hens had laid, a freshly made omelette. It was a homely routine but one that Tomos grew to enjoy very much.

His unplanned arrival in Koutatenga created a new problem: how to explain to his family what he was doing in a remote African village. He ought to call home but first he needed to find something positive to relate. He was certain there would be a clamour for him to return, but that was the one thing he wasn't yet prepared to do.

For the moment he decided to better understand his new surroundings. Isaac helped, taking him to meet his neighbours, friends and relations. There was also a constant stream of curious visitors to Isaac's house, especially in the evenings when people had a little free time.

Isaac's family consisted of his parents, his older brother, Luc, and of course his younger sister, Sylvie. Another sibling, Benoit, the eldest brother, had already left home and Tomos now occupied his room. Even with Benoit gone it was a tight squeeze to fit everyone in.

For the next couple of mornings, Isaac proudly guided Tomos on hikes through the fields surrounding the village and into the wilderness beyond. Koutatenga lay on an arid plateau within the wide savanna belt south of the Sahara, a region dominated by a long hot dry season and a short wet one. The countless gullies that criss-crossed the thin red ferruginous soils bore witness to the short but savage rains that seasonally deluged the plains.

Tomos's first outing was a real eye-opener, especially the sight of the men toiling in the fields around the village, their bared backs shining with sweat, sinewy arms metronomically working up and down with hoe or machete. A thousand questions needed asking. Firstly, he felt compelled to ask why many of the labourers were wearing woolly hats when it was so unbearably hot.

'Oh, they pull the hat down to cover the face when the flies get too bad ... you'll see,' Isaac explained.

He was right. As they walked on and started to sweat they seemed to attract more and more flies, the unwanted attention made worse as the tiny "sweat bees" tried to crawl into eyes, ears and nose.

'Try not to kill any, it will only attract more,' Isaac warned.

While the men were away in the fields, children swept dust, sand or mud from the houses. Women followed their own morning ritual, starting with a trip to the river. Each returned carrying a heavy bucket of water perfectly balanced on top of their head.

Firewood was used for cooking. Seeing an opportunity to help, Tomos insisted on taking responsibility for chopping up the logs. He also paid his host family for his keep, his cash a great help to such a low-income household.

The landscape of the wild savanna fascinated him. It impressed itself into his mind as a living organism, a mostly flat skeleton muscled with knots of odd little hills, all held together by the slow-moving brown tendons of the many tributaries of the river Volta. The whole body of land was clothed in a hairy cloak of tall grass which grew way above his head, the long willowy stalks a rippling sea of yellow, the sun cruelly bleaching any enthusiastic shoot of green. Huge isolated baobab trees dominated entire patches of land, each great fat trunk supporting a canopy of short stubby finger-like branches. Elsewhere, small flat-topped trees dotted the landscape, coagulating into clumps near ponds and water holes and shaping the banks of streams where they grouped into woody thickets.

In those first days he spent hours exploring further and further afield, returning tired and hot but exhilarated at the sights, sounds and smells encountered. A month flashed by taking him into early April, a time of insufferable heat typifying the end of the long dry season. Any remaining green vegetation stressed into yellow during the desperate wait for the life-saving rains. Tall dense grassland trapped the hot air in stifling layers for anyone lured beneath; their shady promise nothing but a suffocating trap.

Once he'd learned his local geography, Tomos took to his lifelong habit of running - early evening being his preferred time. His favourite trail led him out of the village and along a narrow track to a small river, a tributary of the Red Volta. On the muddy banks he'd watch swathes of bright orange butterflies rippling; rising in excited huge bubbles that burst into a thousand individuals to gently float back to the water's edge as he passed. After a quick swim he would jog home as the sun went down. Dusk would bring out nocturnal animals and sometimes he would catch a glimpse of a warthog or a hare; one time in the fading daylight he spotted a genet, its cat-like body darting out almost beneath his feet.

The haunting call of the laughing dove reverberated through the village in the still savanna air during the hottest hours of the day. The mellow lullaby caressed the inhabitants to sleep, the soothing sound as much a part of the bush as the acacia and ancient baobabs that cocooned Koutatenga from the outside world. Tomos too, often dozed through the warmest hours, dreaming of lovely cold winter days back home. There was no electricity, no air conditioning, nothing cold or frozen to eat or drink. The only escape was to rest indoors or under the shade of a tree and wait for the air to cool off at the end of the day.

Tomos eased himself further into the family routine. Along with the wood chopping he also began tending the small family sty which sat unobtrusively next to the living quarters, home to a sow and six suckling piglets.

Visits from extended family and friends dominated the evenings. In his presence French was used rather than the tribal language, and the greetings and gossip helped improve his schoolboy French in leaps and bounds. The endless supply of jokes and storytelling backed up by buckets of laughter from narrator and audience, firmly consolidated his sense of belonging to the community.

After the evening meal, Isaac and Luc started to go out separately to visit their own circle of friends. Isaac became reticent when leaving without explanation and Tomos guessed he was seeing a girl somewhere. He himself stayed behind with Isaac's elderly parents and younger sister, Sylvie. Invariably they took chairs and sat outside, and by a combination of starlight and lamplight would shell groundnuts or do some other minor task. He recounted stories from home which were reverently listened to. In turn he was told tales about the village, tribal customs, and the way of life in his new home.

Under the bright star-studded skies often with a distant drumbeat emanating from out beyond the dark plains, he felt more relaxed than at any time in his life. If only he had the means, he felt he could live the rest of his days there.

17

Monique and Sabine parted company at the busy junction where the Avenue de la Cathédral met the Avenue Moro Naaba in the old town of Ouagadougou. Sabine shouldered her kit bag and ambled away towards her home nestled in a corner of one of the many grid-like streets in that part of the city.

Monique watched her friend leave, noting the weary tread and the tired shoulders so unlike the straight-backed stature of most African women. It wasn't surprising considering the long journey from the bush-camp. Six hours in the back of a noisy, fume-filled army truck over pot-holed roads through the heat of the day, was enough to sap anyone's strength.

Thank God she was nearly home. The thought sent her spirits soaring. The release for indefinite leave had come as a complete surprise, but now all she could think about was getting back to her own private space and the chance to pick up the threads of her pre-army life. She shivered in anticipation at seeing her family and old friends again.

The truck had dropped them not far from the municipal football stadium. She slung her own kit bag over one shoulder and set off towards home. Her route took her past the stadium, then through a large square at the far end of which was the entrance to the royal palace. She gave the palace a cursory glance before turning right and into the first of the avenue of houses marking the entry into her own residential quarter.

Her house lay about halfway along one of the streets leading off Rue Pange. With rising excitement, she pushed through the wrought iron gate set halfway along the crenelated wall and straight into the only home she'd ever known.

The first thing she saw was Pluto, her big mongrel russet-hued dog who came bounding up to greet her, long wet tongue hanging loose as he panted from heat and enthusiasm. Behind him lay the original mud-brick hut where she had lived her early years, now in a serious state of disrepair. Next to it stood the replacement, a one-storey breeze-block house consisting of three small bedrooms, living room and bathroom. Cooking was still practiced outside in the yard or occasionally under a small purpose-built shelter.

The sound of metal striking wood from somewhere behind the old house stopped as Pluto gave a welcoming bark. Monique's younger sister, Nadine, appeared from around the corner clutching a long metal stave used for splitting logs.

She gaped, dropped the stave and ran towards her. 'Monique!' She grabbed her sister's hand. 'I didn't know you were coming today! Great to see you!'

'It's so good to be back. How are you? Are Mama and Papa in?'

'Yes, they'll be so pleased to see you. Papa's sleeping, recovering from malaria. Mama's inside too.'

Together the sisters started towards the house. Monique's mother, Brigitte, met them at the door.

'I thought I heard voices! What a lovely surprise! Come on in and tell me how you are! Nadine - go and prepare some food for your sister. It's so good to see you; I've missed you so much!'

In celebration of Monique's homecoming, a chicken was bought, killed and prepared for the table. Later that evening the meat was served with rice as the three women dined and talked. It was everything Monique had looked forward to, especially during her darkest moments in the army.

The only negative was her father's illness. His recent poor health was contrary to the way she always thought of him; strong, intelligent and fearless. These were his traits she admired so much; the characteristics that had enabled Gaston to become a successful entrepreneur.

As a young man Gaston had been educated by Catholic priests but had quickly discovered that his talents lay not in religion but in business. On completing his studies he'd worked as a clerk for an American Aid programme, quickly rising to a managerial role. Paid a regular US-grade salary, he'd invested everything in building well-furnished villas. The risk paid off when he'd convinced a couple of foreign diplomats to rent them. From then on, his wealth had grown surprisingly quickly, right up until the day he'd lost it all; the day the new socialist government had brazenly confiscated all second homes from every citizen.

The conversation between the three women moved deeper into the affairs of Monique's father; and what she heard made her head spin. It was mad, insane, yet what she learned also explained a lot. If the news hadn't come straight from her own mother's mouth, she would never have believed it.

'There have been some big changes here. Things you need to know concerning your father ... concerning all of us in fact.' Brigitte's voice dropped to a whisper as if she feared someone might overhear. She sounded sad too, and clearly worried; the voice of a mother and a wife in troubled times.

'I know you weren't allowed to follow politics or the news while you were away, so I'll assume you know nothing.'

Monique waited for the story to unfold. Her mother was the eldest daughter of one of the five royal Advisors to the tribal king. The king was only a symbolic position; the president or head of the governing military junta ran the country. Nevertheless, the old traditions and customs still prevailed and so the king and his court continued to command great respect and influence at a grassroots level. Brigitte's father was the king's current Advisor for Farming and her marriage to the entrepreneur, Gaston, had been a very grand affair.

'The government is not popular with the people,' her mother began. 'As you know, our children have been coerced into the army and any successful private business has been taken over by the state. The military rulers no longer respect traditional customs and values. People are too scared to speak out; the government knows they're hated, so now they're taking steps to fight back.'

Brigitte looked sadly at Monique. 'Your father is a figurehead of the old democracy, a businessman who is respected in the local community. He represents the opposite of everything our new leaders stand for. Two months ago without any warning, armed soldiers came to the house and took him away.'

She fell silent and swallowed hard as she relived events. Monique was already aware the government had seized all her father's other properties, but she hadn't known he'd been taken.

'What happened next?' she asked softly.

Her mother composed herself before carrying on. 'Incredibly he was inaugurated into the cabinet, given the title "Deputy Minister for Finance", all against his will. I know they threatened him, but he hasn't told me exactly how. He had to make a radio broadcast in his new role and say how he had changed his views; how he now believed in the new government and urged everyone to support the state. I think they beat him, to force him to say such things. His health has deteriorated ever since, so he's really suffered with this bout of malaria.'

'Poor Papa, life is being so unfair to him,' murmured Monique. 'I'll see him now if he's awake.'

Gaston was still drowsy when she walked into her parents' bedroom. She raised the mosquito net and sat on the edge of his bed, gently taking her father's hand in her own.

The hand squeezed back as Gaston regarded her with hooded bloodshot eyes.

'Ah Monique, I thought I heard talking - and wondered if it was you. How are you?'

'I'm fine. More importantly, how are *you* feeling? Mama says you have malaria.'

'Huh, I'm almost over that now ... apart from always being very tired ... it's always the same. I seem to need to sleep all day.'

'And so you should. You can do whatever you want now Papa ... now that you're a big man in the government.'

'That? Huh ... Bed *is* the best place for me; anything rather than play those stupid political games.' Gaston looked fondly at his daughter before adding, 'Sometimes though, we are left with little choice.'

'Well, we're together now: you, me, mama and Nadine, Pluto, too.'

'Yes, my new post has some advantages. I managed to get you and Sabine posted back to Ouaga as I guessed things might be difficult. As I'm sick, I also arranged to secure you indefinite leave to help nurse me until I'm better.' Gaston gave a small chuckle. 'I even used the same excuse of compassionate leave for Sabine. A shame I couldn't get you completely out of the army, otherwise I would have done that, too. I hope I did the right thing?'

'So, it was *you* that arranged all this? I wondered what was going on; they never tell us anything. I'm so grateful - really happy.' She leant forward and impulsively kissed the top of her father's head.

'Well, I'm happy too. While we are on the subject of good news - there is one more thing I need to tell you.'

With a grunt, Gaston raised himself into a sitting position and turned to look at his daughter. His tone changed, the words now spoken with the authority of someone who was not to be argued with.

'I have been visiting the palace in secret these past few months and have had several meetings with the king. It's been a risk, as the government does not approve of royalty, but it's been worth it, believe me. The king has kindly enquired after your well-being; he's being very supportive in these difficult times. We both feel that the current regime cannot continue much longer, and with God's blessing we will see a return to the old ways. Monique ... I am so proud and happy to tell you that the king still wishes to take you as a wife. It's a huge opportunity for all of us, and one we should be celebrating. I hope that now you have seen the harsh reality of the world in the army you will agree this is wonderful news.'

His words hit like a rampaging elephant. All other emotions were swept away, leaving a nauseating emptiness in the pit of her stomach. She could feel her whole body tremble with shock, leaving her speechless. The image of the king, now in his early sixties, loomed large in her mind's eye as she tried to come to terms with what she'd heard. This was not the first time this arrangement had been proposed.

Through his father-in-law's position of Royal Advisor for Farming, Gaston often had cause to visit the palace, and it had not taken long before the king himself had noticed his beautiful elder daughter. To her parents' delight, an agreement had been made for Monique to be married to the king on her eighteenth birthday. No-one had asked her, and she had been devastated by the news. Despite his age, the king was a tall strong man and already had nine wives, most of whom had borne him children. It was the thought of becoming his tenth that filled her with revulsion. The timely intervention of the bloody *coup d'état* saw the socialists seize power and put a stop to proceedings. She thought it was over when all students under the age of twenty, including herself, had been conscripted into the army. She had been so sure that out of sight also meant out of mind - that some other girl would catch the king's eye and she would be conveniently forgotten.

With his daughter staying silent, Gaston spoke again.'You know you cannot refuse the king. It's all for the best, you must trust me on this. In any case, nothing can happen for the time being. The government will not approve the daughter of one of their ministers marrying the king; it's not a very socialist act. We will bide our time, wait if necessary for a change of government, but you must accept the inevitable. It's a great honour, after all.'

Monique drew a deep breath. Her father was unwell. She didn't want to upset him by arguing. The anguish she felt was slightly tempered knowing the marriage was not imminent. With a great effort, she forced herself to speak.

'You should rest, we can talk about this later. I need time to think about things.'

She helped to lay him back down, reset the mosquito net and went straight to the small bedroom she shared with her sister. After quietly locking the door and closing the shutter over the little square window above her bed, she flung herself face down on her old mattress. Quiet sobs of frustration and despair welled up, making her clench her fists as she wept.

Why should these old men decide every aspect of her life? What was the point of being able to think for herself, if she wasn't allowed to?

The sobs grew into a flood of tears as the full implication of her father's words struck home. The rest of her life would be lived without freedom, an endless hopeless desert with no prospect of passion or love.

18

A new problem presented itself to Tomos and gnawed at him like hunger, demanding a satisfactory answer. Many times over he'd seen women collecting water from the river, and seeing them weighed down with a heavy bucket of water made him ponder this arduous task. Koutatenga did possess a shallow hand-dug well but that had dried up; he was told it only contained water during the rainy season. The river flowed all year round, but the slow moving muddy waters of low summertime flows, teemed with bugs. In his own village in Wales, it would have been considered unsuitable for washing and cooking, let alone drinking.

It didn't take him long to decide to repay the village for its hospitality with something more substantial than just doing a few household chores. His professional expertise morally obliged him to help find a solution. What Koutatenga needed most was a proper borehole, one that would provide clean safe drinking water and potentially save hours of walking to the river. He broached the subject one morning to Isaac and his father.

'Really? You're willing to help fund a new well? Fantastic!' Isaac struggled to get the words out, his smile was so wide. 'That would indeed be a wonderful thing. If you're serious, we'll see the chief immediately.' The more measured response of Isaac's father failed to mask the gleam of interest in the old man's eyes.

Tomos was hurriedly escorted to the chief's house, a sight that set the neighbours tongues wagging.

They had already met; tradition had dictated the chief was the first person Isaac had taken him to meet outside his immediate family. Tomos estimated him to be around fifty years of age. Although of average height, he was heavily built with a corresponding large belly and boasted a white beard, putting Tomos in mind of an African Santa Claus.

They gathered within the low-walled compound surrounding the house, the largest in the village. Hearing it was important business, the chief ordered a chair to be specially brought outside and invited his three visitors to squash together on a wooden bench facing him. Being the most senior of the three, Isaac's father spoke, explaining how Tomos had offered to pay for a borehole. The chief clapped his hands together at the news and whistled loudly before speaking.

'This is the best news possible. I have been thinking about a borehole for a long time - years in fact. I know there's a government-owned drilling rig that can be hired, but the fees have always been too expensive for anyone in the village.'

'Can we get the latest price checked and see when it's available?' ventured Tomos.

'I am planning to travel to Ouaga to pay my respects to our tribal king. If you're willing, perhaps you can come too, and we can ask about the rig at the same time,' the chief suggested.

Although he genuinely wished to repay the village for their kindness, Tomos especially wanted to help Isaac. He sensed many were openly disappointed with his empty-handed return after getting so close to Europe; his reputation could only improve if he was seen as the man who brought the borehole-funder to the village.

The time had come to move on and make things happen. It would be a shame to leave Koutatenga, but it also felt good to have a purpose again.

19

Time flew by far too quickly for Monique's liking. Despite the demands of her new domestic routines, she couldn't stop thinking about her proposed marriage. That was until the day the nation turned on its head.

The sound of gunfire late one morning meant little at first; she assumed it to be a military exercise or some other pointless show of force. It was only her mother's cry from the living room an hour later that made her aware something was seriously wrong. Hearts racing, she and Nadine sprinted indoors from the lean-to where they had been cooking and chatting together over the open stove. They found their mother watching television - they possessed the sole TV in the street.

Brigitte was standing in the middle of the room, one hand clamped over her mouth, eyes open wide, staring at the screen.

'What's wrong ... what's happened!?' the sisters clamoured.

Brigitte shook her head and pointed at the TV. 'Watch ...'

Together they concentrated on the midday news bulletin. There was only one channel available, that being state-owned and broadcast twice a day; an hour at midday, then again for a couple of hours during the evening. The sombre newsreader was immaculately dressed in suit and tie. In perfect French he calmly announced to the world that a new government had taken control of the country.

In stunned silence the three women listened to the matter-of-fact account of how forces dedicated to the freedom and promotion of the nation of Burkina Faso had stormed the government buildings earlier that morning. All armed resistance from opposing forces had been successfully overcome with minimal loss of life. The new government regretted to say that unfortunately the incumbent president was one of the few casualties, along with an unstated number of bodyguards.

The newsreader explained how loyal troops had quickly liberated the national media centre to make this broadcast, to give the whole nation and the world the good news that the country had successfully shaken off the shackles of socialism enabling it to embark on a new path of order and prosperity for its people. The broadcaster ended the bulletin by asking all citizens to remain calm, and for all army and police factions throughout the country to pledge allegiance to the new government.

The screen began to repeat the whole broadcast from the beginning. Brigitte switched it off, before reaching out and taking one hand from each of her daughters into her own.

'I knew this would happen sooner or later. I so wanted things to change, but not like this. Oh, why today of all days was your father obliged to return to work at the Ministry? I was in the central market myself earlier and was sure I heard gunfire coming from the direction of the government sector. I'm old enough to know that can only mean trouble. I came home as quick as I could, to follow the news and be here in case I was needed.'

Monique knew she had to stay strong for her mother's sake. She looked at Nadine who remained silent, the worry plain on her face.

'I'm sure Papa will be fine. It may not be easy for him to come straight home though.'

'You're right, but we can do more than that,' her mother replied. 'We must pray together that your father will return safely to us.'

Obediently and in fervent hope, Monique and Nadine followed their mother's example; all three kneeling where they were. Brigitte led them in prayer, begging for the safe return of Gaston Tapsoba, husband and father to a loving family.

20

Tomos also heard the shots of the coup d'état during his first full day in Ouagadougou, having arrived the previous evening with the chief of Koutatenga. Bursts of sharp stocato gunfire coming from the government sector had reverberated throughout the city. It was not the kind of welcome he'd been expecting.

'Stay indoors until we know it's safe to go out', he was warned by everyone in Mon Amie, the bar owned and run by Isaac's aunt. Rather than pay for lodgings in Ouagadougou, Tomos and the chief had accepted the offer of free rooms in an annexe to the main building that housed the bar.

News of the coup d'état spread fast. The older citizens who'd witnessed such things before, discussed the changing politics behind closed doors; spies and informants could be lurking anywhere. However, the lure of the unexplored alien town proved too strong for Tomos, he ignored all advice and walked the city alone.

The prickly sensation of tension derived from potential danger permeated the city. It was carried in the air through the unnatural quiet and almost empty side streets and boulevards. He did feel edgy when outside; not least because of the heavy military and police presence, especially in the city centre. Armed men guarded government buildings and hung around major junctions perpetuating the air of nervousness among the locals. The general unease was fed by whispers of rebellion within the military where certain factions were rumoured to be loyal to the old regime. When no apparent resistance materialized, confidence in the new leaders swiftly grew. Less than a week after the coup, normal life returned to the capital as people gradually filtered back to work by day and to socialise by night.

For Tomos the turnaround was dramatically evident with the streets refilling initially with workers and shoppers, then students, and finally with laughter from cafés, bars and clubs. A full week of trudging the dusty roads helped him to familiarise himself with the everyday sights of a once-again living, vibrant city. The main highways teemed with streams of mopeds intermingled with cyclists, the thoroughfares bordered by throngs of pedestrians. Decrepit heavy goods lorries rumbled through the city, often leaning to one side on damaged suspension, colourfully festooned with opportunistic travellers clinging precariously to any handhold. Kerbs and junctions were ruled by rowdy hawkers. Youths pulled heavily laden carts of fruit, vegetables or firewood by hand, calf muscles straining as they sweated with their characteristic heavy determined gait. Young mothers rode helmetless on mopeds carrying their infants bound tightly on their backs, leaving only tiny heads, hands and feet, poking out from beneath brightly coloured wraps.

The streets themselves remained fundamentally alien, they were so different to the ones he knew back home. In Ouagadougou the main roads were typically wide straight avenues of compacted red dirt, potholed and without any of the street furniture and signs which infest European roads. As he walked the city, the sounds of laughter were never far away often emanating from homes where meals were being prepared over open fires. Music, a high tempo African beat, would spill out from the restaurants and bars which dotted the townscape; each venue a focal point of social humanity, pinpointed by rows of parked shiny mopeds.

. . .

The time spent together in Mon Amie, allowed Tomos and the Koutatenga chief to become better acquainted. The chief was called Wendbenindo, a tribal name meaning 'by God's grace', an appropriate title since God had gifted him with both a jovial manner and an infectious laugh. He was good company and conversing with him enabled Tomos to grow in confidence when speaking French. For the first time he was surprised to find that he could comfortably chat away without having to consciously translate every word.

Their appointment at a government office was a success. A contract was agreed, drawn up and signed, ordering the drilling of a well in Koutatenga in six months' time when it was expected the rig would become available. Tomos withdrew sufficient funds from his bank account - a transaction which halved his savings - and paid the fee for renting the rig and its crew.

He had one other important act to carry out in town; to telephone his parents. He placed his call from the central post office on his eighth day in Ouaga, the first day it reopened following the coup. After queueing for hours he was relieved when the phone was answered, especially at hearing his father's voice; dad was unlikely to ask the tricky questions his mother would inevitably put to him.

'Dad? It's Tomos ... how are you ... and mam?'

'Tomos ... about time we heard from you. We're fine ... where are you calling from? ... You still in Libya?'

'No ... things didn't really work out for me; I wasn't enjoying the work so decided to leave with a friend I met there. He's from Burkina Faso, that's where I am now. I plan to come home once I've helped drill a well in his village, but that probably won't be for some months yet. There really isn't much more to say than that.'

'I rather think there is son - but we'll leave that for another day. Why haven't you been in touch? Your mother's worried sick.'

'I know she must be. Look ... just tell her I'm really sorry for all this confusion and not calling earlier. I was travelling so haven't had a chance to ring before now. When I'm back I'll be able to explain everything much better than I can over the phone.'

'And when will that be?'

'Sorry dad, dunno. Could be weeks or months - I'll be in touch as soon as I know.'

'I suppose that's the best we're going to get out of you. Just stay out of trouble and call again as soon as you can.'

'Dad, I promise I will. Give my love to mam and tell her not to fret. Like I said ... I'm fine.'

Despite his guilt for making his parents worry, he couldn't supress a grin. Typical short man-talk with dad. Hopefully they'd be a little less concerned than before, although he'd bet dad was in for a telling-off for not digging for more information. He thought of Al-Hazbar and his threats - some things were best kept quiet.

At Mon Amie, he found Wendbenindo in fine spirits. Over a beer, he reminded Tomos that since he was in town it was obligatory for him, as a village chief, to pay homage to his tribal king,

'I've already been. In fact, I haven't long got back. I told the king about you, and he wants to meet you. Believe me, that's the same as a royal command - so you must go. I will accompany you to the palace myself. It's a big honour for Koutatenga; the king doesn't often request to see outsiders.'

'Well ... sounds good to me. Trouble is I don't know anything about him.'

'Then I'll tell you. Perhaps the greatest legacy of our once great empire is that we still boast a king. OK, so nowadays he's simply called the tribal king - the empire being long gone. You need to understand he's the direct descendant of the old emperors so holds great respect. He's still consulted on crucial decisions, especially those affecting the destiny of our tribe. In some areas his power rivals that of the president.'

'And now he wants to meet me. Are you sure?'

'I'm sure. Like I said, he told me himself. You can't refuse; it would be a huge dishonour for me and my village. Unthinkable.'

'Well I wouldn't want that ... so when do we go?'

'It's up to the king. He'll send for us when he's ready.'

The summons came early the next morning in the surprising form of a youth who delivered the request for them both to attend immediately. The messenger, barely into his teens, arrived on a heavy-framed pushbike that belonged to a decade long gone. He insisted on guiding his charges to the palace, ignoring the fact that Wendbenindo had visited the previous day.

Setting off, Tomos couldn't hold back a bemused shake of the head at his situation - being taken on a moped by a chief, to meet a king, guided by a boy on a bicycle. He had nothing of what he considered smart to wear but felt at ease in the traditional West African smock and trousers, both gifts from Isaac. The smock was made of light plain white cotton, open-sided and sleeveless, ideal for the climate. He enjoyed the sensation of the warm sunshine and the soft breeze against his skin as they cruised down the road at a stately five miles per hour.

At the palace grounds they followed a tall wire perimeter fence until they arrived at a gated entrance, outside of which were several gawping western tourists weighed down with cameras. Their guide stopped and without dismounting gave a nod to a middle-aged gentleman dressed in a long indigo robe standing alone inside the gate, before pedalling away, whistling as he went.

Indigo man waited until Wendbenindo parked his moped before walking over and introducing himself, much to the interest of the camera-clicking tourists.

Tomos watched as the two dignitaries went through a formal tribal greeting. Isaac had told him how the traditional salutation could go on for several minutes as each party enquired after the well-being of everyone in each other's household. On this occasion the greeting took a full two minutes before Wendbenindo introduced the stranger to Tomos as Mr Sanou - an Advisor to the king and the person who would also be their guide.

Sanou led the two visitors along a footpath inside the grounds - and via several vegetable plots - to the palace itself. In Tomos's eyes it wasn't a particularly impressive building, just a long single storey rectangular shape which rose to two stories at the far end. It was plain looking and appeared to be constructed mostly from traditional dried mud-brick, only the two-storey end being concrete.

Sanou led them through a door set in the nearest end of the building, and into a small unfurnished room. He gestured for them to wait before leaving via an inner door. Within a minute he returned and beckoned them to follow. Walking through, Tomos took a sharp intake of breath, instantly changing his opinion of the palace.

He found himself entering a large chamber. It was high-ceilinged, floored with plain white tiles, and had inner walls that gleamed in white-painted splendour. It was almost empty of both furniture and people, apart from a small cluster of men standing in the middle who gazed at the two newcomers with intense curiosity. However, it wasn't the size of the room or the people in it that made him stare in disbelief; it was the objects on the floor about ten feet in front of the waiting audience.

A throne consisting of a massive and ornately carved wooden chair was set halfway along the floor, a few feet in from the back wall. On either side sat a pair of equally massive wooden effigies of lions, each as big as a man. The total absence of anything else in the room only served to accentuate the dominating presence of the centrepiece.

'Most of the others are probably village chiefs visiting the city, just like me,' Wendbenindo whispered, as they joined the other expectant attendees.

They didn't have long to wait. Their escort left through a door set in the far side of the room and within five minutes it reopened - and in walked the king. Tall and powerful, His Highness strode purposefully across the floor with a flamboyant swirl of his traditional full-length, plain white robe, a multi-coloured pork-pie hat perched upon his majestic head. Scurrying behind him were two small bare-headed page boys, dressed in identical simple white cotton robes. Sanou was there too, shadowing a few discreet steps behind the little entourage.

The king took his seat upon the great throne whilst the page boys knelt either side of him, just in front of the lions. Sanou kept his distance, standing a little way behind and to the left of his ruler.

The formal meeting did not last long. One by one the Advisor beckoned the visitors forward, who knelt before their sovereign, heads bowed so low they touched the floor. Sanou introduced them, each man exchanging a few pleasantries with the king before the next dignitary was called. Following custom only the tribal language was spoken.

Wendbenindo and Tomos were left until last. Sanou introduced Wendbenindo who moved forward. Presumably since they had met the previous day, the king boomed a laugh and sent him back with a wave of his hand. And then Tomos heard his name called.

Uncomfortable at the thought of having to prostrate himself before another man, he edged himself to the front of the group and began to lower himself. The king laughed again - a loud raucous chuckle - and motioned him to stand back with the other guests. He then invited Wendbenindo to step forward again, who exchanged a few words on Tomos's behalf.

Concluding the session, the king addressed the group at large, which Tomos rightly guessed was a general 'thank you for coming to pay your respects' oration. Speech completed the king stood and left the room, drawing the meeting to a close.

Sanou guided everyone back through the palace to the outside gate, shaking hands with each guest as they departed.

Wendbenindo had already motioned Tomos to hang back, and as soon as everyone had gone, Sanou - speaking in French - asked them both to accompany him back to the ante-room in the palace.

Inside, Sanou smiled at the two guests. 'The king would like to speak with you both again. Please wait here while I go and see if he's ready to receive you, I should only be a moment.'

He returned within minutes. 'The king will see you now.'

A proud chief and an intrigued Tomos followed Sanou out of the building. They walked to the far end of the palace, scattering hens from their path as they went, and re-entered the palace through a door on the other side into a small hallway. Two chairs on one side of the room faced the king who was sitting opposite.

The king welcomed them in French, waving them towards the chairs. Tomos and Wendbenindo sat as directed, while Sanou took his customary place to the side of his sovereign. Close-up, Tomos noted the lined forehead and grey chin stubble betraying the king to be at least sixty, his age ably disguised at distance by the strength of his deep voice and imposing physique.

Staying in French, the king wasted no time in coming to the point, directing his words at Tomos. 'I'm pleased to meet you; I've heard how you're helping Koutatenga with a new well. This is very good. Tell me ... are you an expert on wells?'

'Ah, yes. Designing, building and testing them; it's what I do for a living,' Tomos replied, wondering if he should be adding 'your royal highness', at the end.

Nobody had advised him how to address the king, so he hoped he wasn't being disrespectful. Luckily the meeting was informal, and the king only seemed interested in him for his technical knowledge.

'That is good ... very good. I have my own farm. Unfortunately much of the soil has been washed away; infertile land and lack of water are the main problems. Do you think you can help? It would be good if you could give advice. I might be the king, but that doesn't mean I can afford to pay for experts to give their untrustworthy opinions. Outsiders, even the government, are fond of telling me I should do this or do that, without any consideration of our customs and traditions. What I really want is some proper technical advice from someone who cares and doesn't mind not getting paid. You seem to fit this role, so I'm happy to ask your help. What do you think? Will you at least take time to go and look?'

Tomos reeled. He hadn't been expecting this. It was clearly an honour, but he wasn't sure he would be able to assist much with a soil erosion problem, though maybe he could with the lack of water. Was he being asked in the hope that he would offer to pay for another well? That was something he couldn't afford, he needed to think of his ticket home.

The king was staring straight at him, head to one side, waiting for a reply. Tomos instantly felt guilty at thinking the worst of his host's quite reasonable request.

'Er, yes of course,' he stammered hastily. 'I'm very happy to help any way I can.'

The king beamed. 'Very well then, that's settled! I'm sure you'll find it all very interesting. My Advisor will make all arrangements. I give thanks to the village of Koutatenga for bringing me their guest.'

Business finished, the king stood and left without another word.

'Congratulations Mr Morgan, it seems you now have a royal appointment.' Sanou lightly applauded before pointing to the exit. 'Gentlemen, if you're ready, please follow me.'

Wendbenindo and Sanou chatted amiably on the way back to the palace gate, both sounding more relaxed now they were away from the king. Walking back through the vegetable plots towards the main gate they passed a couple walking the other way, a young woman holding onto the arm of a sickly-looking older man.

The woman was slim yet curvy, which immediately attracted Tomos's attention; he couldn't help stealing a glance at the woman's face as they passed. She must have sensed his gaze, for she briefly lifted her face towards his. For the fleetest of moments, they looked straight into each other's eyes. She was beautiful; easily the most attractive woman he'd seen on his travels. Without thinking, he turned to watch her walk away, his eyes fully appreciating her seductive figure.

The sound of Sanou sucking noisily through his teeth in the typical African manner of disapproval, returned him to the present. The Advisor was watching him, slowly shaking his head in annoyance.

'Mr Morgan, do not look at the young lady in that manner; she is of the highest rank and demands our deepest respect.'

Tomos mumbled an instant apology.

'No problem. I understand ... you're young and she's pretty ... but please don't do it again.'

At the main gate, Wendbenindo paused to explain his discussion with the Advisor. 'I suppose the first thing is - are you in fact happy to help the king? It's a rare honour to be asked personally, and it will reflect very well on our village.'

Tomos took a breath before answering. 'Yes, I said I would, so I will. Anyway, it probably won't be forever as I doubt I'll be able to help that much.'

'Good. I'm returning to Koutatenga, tomorrow in fact. The king is anxious that you visit the farm as soon as possible, and has asked Mr Sanou here to help in any way. I've been discussing possible arrangements with him and we think it best if you lodge with him rather than stay at Mon Amie. It's more appropriate and more convenient as he lives on the other side of town. From there it's not too far to the farm.'

Tomos immediately had misgivings. He felt comfortable at Mon Amie, he had friends there as well as his connections to Koutatenga, with which he felt an affinity. Moving in with a stranger was not a particularly attractive proposition. Wendbenindo must have seen the hesitation on his face.

'If you stay with Sanou it'll be easier for everyone.'

'No problem, it does make sense,' he replied without enthusiasm.

Sanou interrupted. 'You are of course very welcome to stay with me. I will personally collect you tomorrow morning.'

So that was that. Handshakes confirmed the arrangements and Tomos found himself being returned to Mon Amie by Wendbenindo. To the hum of the moped's little engine, he wondered what he was letting himself in for. He had a sudden worrying premonition about moving in with Sanou. Why did he feel that way? What could possibly go wrong?

He shifted uncomfortably on the Honda's plastic seat as he realised he didn't have an answer to either question.

21

As agreed, Tomos was collected by Sanou, who arrived at Mon Amie on a Yamaha 250cc motorbike. Approaching their destination, he noted the relative wealth of his new neighbourhood, his moving vantage point revealing a wide tree-lined avenue bordered by well to-do residences. Even the lack of hawkers and street children hinted at a degree of privacy and security lacking elsewhere in the city. As Sanou swung into his courtyard, a thousand rainbows sparkled from the protective shards of coloured broken glass cemented into the tops of long pristine walls that ran the length of the property.

Inside, the spacious garden included a lawn, flower beds, and a leafy grove of mango trees throwing cooling shadows over several motorcycles and a pickup. Sanou drew-up alongside the bikes and they dismounted. Looming above the treetops was a crenelated veranda, part of a sizable cream painted villa; the entire setting suggestive of someone used to comfortable living.

A child magically appeared running from under the trees chased by a tall handsome woman. Laughing, the child was scooped up by Sanou as she ran into his open arms to be fussed over.

Sanou smiled at Tomos. 'Please meet my daughter, Pogbi, and my wife Gabrielle.'

Tomos shook hands with both, the little girl shyly offering her hand, reaching out from the safety of her father's chest.

'Come inside, I'll show you around.'

The finery of the furnishings inside the villa did not extend to his room which boasted no more than a mattress on the floor and a hard-wooden chair and table. There was no air conditioning, relief from the stale indoor heat coming from a free-standing electric fan. He opened the one shuttered window, but was disappointed to find it did little to alleviate neither the gloom nor the sense that he felt more like a prisoner than a guest. He sat alone on the wooden chair that lunchtime and ate a meal of beans and rice served by Gabrielle, his new landlord having left on unknown business.

Things perked up in the afternoon when Sanou returned and invited him for a quick tour of the royal farm. They took the Yamaha and journeyed out beyond the northern fringes of the city. The gridded residential streets gave way to clusters of makeshift homes which in turn thinned out, then disappeared altogether as they entered the agricultural belt surrounding the city.

Sanou half turned to shout, 'Almost all these small plots you see belong to poor farmers without access to irrigation. The crops are entirely dependent on rainfall which is becoming increasingly unreliable.'

Having travelled for nearly an hour following ever-narrowing tracks, they pulled up in a field beside a tall thin black man dressed in long shorts and a faded red football t-shirt. He was carrying a machete.

The two Burkinabe greeted each other, and Tomos was introduced to the machete carrier, Adama, who Sanou described as the overseer.

Sanou swept his arm around. 'We are now standing on land owned by the king. We'll take a stroll, then you can see the extent of the farm and I can show you some of the problems we face.'

Tomos took in his surroundings with keen interest as they walked. He would never have guessed he had entered a farm as such. There was a lot he was going to have to learn.

'Why aren't there any boundaries like fences, separating each field or plot?' he asked innocently.

'Everyone with an involvement in the land knows who owns what, so there's no need. Besides, fencing is expensive. You will see that everything here is done as cheaply as possible.'

'I don't see any irrigation.'

'You won't, it's too costly. Like everyone else, our crops rely on natural rainfall. It's only the big commercial and government-owned farms that can afford irrigation systems. They grow cash crops like cotton for export but we mostly grow foods for eating, like maize and millet.'

Accompanied by Adama, they walked further into the farm where Sanou explained more. 'We do cultivate some other crops, but they only take up a small portion of the land.' He pointed out several small patches of bare earth, 'those areas are reserved for groundnuts and beans.'

'I see.'

They walked on and several stands of planted acacias drew Tomos's attention, other trees being few and far between. 'Are the trees part of the farm, too?'

'Yes, we plan to use them for firewood, some also for timber when they mature.'

One magnificent Baobab stood alone, its massively fat girth supporting its wide umbrella of short but thick branches, a thirsty and slumbering giant destined to sleep until the first rains.

'It's very old; acts as a meeting place for the labourers,' informed Sanou. 'The leaves make a very nutritious sauce.'

Between plots, tall yellow wild grass grew in thick swathes, very much as Tomos was used to seeing around Koutatenga; a landscape typical of the tree savanna of West Africa. Everywhere was tinder dry.

He tried to imagine what the landscape must look like during the rainy season; lush greens replacing the faded yellows of grasses and the deep reds of the bare sun-baked soil, the great baobab ruling over its domain dressed in its best leafy finery.

The guided tour continued and with it the enthusiastic commentary. 'One of the main problems we face is the briefness of the rainy season. Also, when it does rain, the downpours are so heavy they erode the soil.'

'And the soil erosion reduces soil fertility,' Tomos finished, beginning to understand the extent of the problem.

Evidence of the severity of the erosion was all around them in the form of numerous deep gullies carved into the earth. Sanou summed up the farm's difficulties.

'Productivity is low and there's not much money to invest. Most of the labour is undertaken in collaboration with locals who traditionally give time to work the king's farm. If you have any ideas that can help, Mr Morgan, they will be very welcome. Just to be clear, the king wants you to stay and work on the farm for one growing season, right through to the next harvest. That way, you will fully understand how everything works and be better able to help.'

'Fine with me, so long as I have enough money to survive that long,' Tomos agreed cautiously. It *would* be fine he consoled himself. After all, it was too early to go home and he needed to be doing something. At least this way he would be doing some good.

They completed a circuit, arriving back at the Yamaha where they parted company with Adama. Sanou and Tomos headed back towards Ouagadougou, this time taking a slightly different route, stopping at a tiny bar just inside the city limits. The bar consisted of a fridge run off a small generator, a great iron pot of home brew, and a couple of small tables with chairs. Awnings above the tables provided scanty shade for customers.

'I assume you drink beer?' Sanou asked without even glancing at Tomos, as he slid into one of the chairs.

A large rounded lady with brilliant white teeth set in a huge welcoming grin, waddled up from behind another awning at the roadside. She greeted the Advisor in her own language, the words lost on Tomos, but not the tone and body language. She and Sanou were obviously good friends.

'You like dolo?' Sanou waved towards a large earthenware vessel. 'It's our traditional beer, brewed from millet'

'Uh-huh - yes, I do actually,' Tomos replied, remembering the times he'd drunk the brew in Koutatenga.

The obese landlady took two wooden bowls and dipped them into the great pot, half filling each before handing them over. 'This is the best; I'm sure you'll love it,' she crooned encouragingly in French, her voice low and rich.

Tomos politely waited for his host to take a first sip, and was surprised to see him tip a little on the ground before taking a gulp.

Sanou must have seen the puzzlement on his face. 'It's a tradition to offer the first drop to the ancestors. We believe it honours them and keeps them happy, it shows they aren't forgotten.'

Tomos nodded and took a sip from his own bowl. The dolo was warm and syrupy, the pungent vapours tingling his nostrils as he raised the bowl to his lips. It was a difficult way to drink, and Sanou laughed as he wiped a dribble from his chin with the back of his hand.

'As you can see Mr Morgan, I'm very traditional. I believe in the old ways and I'm motivated to safeguard the customs of my tribe. As you will now be staying with me for a while, it is time you were told a little more about how things work around here.'

'I'd like that, thanks.'

'My full name is Arzuma Sanou. Now then, for your information, I am one of the royal Advisors to the king - a position inherited by my family through the generations.'

Tomos took another gulp of dolo before replying. 'I had no idea there were such things. How many royal Advisors are there? And what do you do?'

'There are five of us in all. They're very prestigious positions and we're all very loyal to king and tribe. Royal Advisors have historically been appointed to cover warfare, magic, justice, farming and administration of the royal court. I am the Advisor for Magic.'

Tomos almost dropped his bowl. African magic meant pins

being stuck into voodoo dolls, didn't it? He swallowed hard.

'And do you practice magic now, to defend the king?' he asked, hoping he didn't sound too sceptical.

Sanou smiled. 'Now that would be telling. Let's just assume such things belong in the past and leave it at that.'

'Why did you and not the Royal Advisor for Agriculture show me around today?'

'Actually, you saw his son-in-law yesterday at the palace, though I suspect you may only have noticed his granddaughter. The Advisor is an old man now, and rarely leaves his home. I expect the king wished you to stay with me as I'm also familiar with the workings of the farm, I used to labour on it in my youth. I also travelled to Europe in my younger days, and am therefore probably the most experienced in dealing with Europeans. Anyway, I serve the king; it's not my job to question his decisions.'

'Did you ever visit Britain?' Tomos asked curiously, latching on to the European aspect.

'No, I studied politics in France, the Sorbonne in Paris actually. After university, I returned to take up my new responsibility at court after the death of my predecessor.'

'I see. Thanks for letting me stay with you. I'll try to keep out of your affairs. I've no wish to be more of a burden to you than necessary.'

'Hmm, that is good of you, Mr Morgan. To tell you the truth I'm not very happy about the situation. Nothing personal ... but you do not represent our ways, and I stand against anything or anyone who threatens our culture. I admit the farm needs some modernising, but I believe we should also retain a sense of tradition in the way we achieve this.'

'What are the main traditions you want to keep?'

'I would say the types of crops we grow and using local labour which keeps a strong connection between the king and his people. It's a tricky problem, which is mainly why I freely admit it would be good to have fresh ideas. Anyway, what I also wanted to tell you was that while you are with us, if you respect me and my king, then we won't have any problems. Agreed?'

Tomos now understood the reason for the friendly beer and chat. He wasn't particularly welcome and would have to watch his step. They finished their dolo, and completed the rest of the ride home in silence.

It was the first time in Burkina Faso he had experienced any coldness towards him. He hadn't been invited by his host to stay in his home; Sanou was allowing him to stay out of a sense of duty. The Advisor's wife, although not unfriendly towards him, rarely spoke and served him his food with barely any acknowledgement.

Tomos found himself thinking more about his own home and realised how much he was missing his family. He particularly missed certain things; his favourite comfort foods, warm greasy chips or a packet of crisps. He also missed running on the mountain up through the village to the green fields and the woods beyond, before hitting the exposed moorland and feeling a cold refreshing wind on his face. Right now it was difficult to remember what cold wind or rain felt like.

That evening he strolled all the way into town to escape Sanou and his uncomfortable room. He enjoyed the walk; the main streets were still busy with traffic as people made their way home. The air was alive with strings of bright white headlights and red brake lights. In the city centre he drank in the atmosphere of the busy bar-lined thoroughfares. There was little remaining evidence of the coup, allowing him to relax in the jovial atmosphere, raising his spirits.

He toyed with the idea of phoning home just to hear a friendly voice. The notion grew and he headed for the Post Office and called his folks again. This time he spoke to both of them at length, enjoying the link with home, the familiarity of their voices. As before he gave nothing away, other than to say he was now helping the main tribal King with his farm. Using the pretext of no more change he ended the call before his mam could ask too many awkward questions. The conversation left him feeling uplifted. With luck the farm work would go well and his enemies would forget all about him. Returning home as a man freed from the death sentence imposed by his judge and would-be executioner was all he yearned for.

22

It was the quiet moments that Monique grew to fear the most. Those were the times she felt herself plunging deeper and deeper into a black abyss without means of escape. The coup d'état then her father's detention on top of her unwanted marriage; it was all too much. At the same time she watched helplessly as her mother and sister struggled to cope. Her mother prayed more and more often; her faith her pillar of strength. Nadine locked herself away in her room for hours at a time, taking little interest in anyone or anything. Monique worried for her younger sister but was at a loss to know how to help. The air of depression hung over them all, fuelled by the oppressive mid-April heat that incessantly beat down upon them day after day. By night the stifling air lingered indoors making sleep almost impossible. Minds and bodies were drained of energy; good news was desperately needed.

The mood in the Tapsoba household finally changed for the better when Gaston limped through the door one evening. Two weeks had passed since he had been taken into custody.

Monique saw a changed man to the one who had left for work the morning of the coup. He looked very frail and walked with the bent back and slow gait of a much older person. His every movement was slow and deliberate, as if he had to think how to move each limb in turn.

Over a family meal, their first together since his detention, Gaston explained how the new government had determined he wasn't a threat, and so released him. He had retained his cabinet position and even been granted a period of leave to recuperate, along with an apology for his incarceration by the new president. Despite repeated questions from wife and daughters he refused to divulge anything more. Eventually he lost patience.

'I have said everything that needs to be said, so let that be an end to it,' he declared angrily.

Days later, when Nadine was out of the house, Gaston admitted to his wife and Monique that he had been interrogated about his true political stance during his incarceration, but again refused to reveal details. Monique guessed he'd been beaten, possibly tortured, but did not pressurise her father to say more than he was willing to volunteer.

Gaston's traumas had come on top of his bout of malaria, leaving him very thin and weak. He barely ate, did not put on weight, and stayed housebound, often lying on his bed for much of the time in a state of extreme fatigue. Brigitte confessed to Monique she feared for her husband's physical well-being. Monique was also concerned for her father's mental state as he showed no interest in the wider world and little inclination to improve his health.

Gaston remained adamant about one thing; his eldest daughter would marry the king. It quickly became his mantra, his one overriding focus. Monique suspected that after all his setbacks her father saw the opportunity of her marriage as the best protection for the family against any future political upheavals. Such thinking did little to help her spirits; she began to despair of ever again being allowed to voice her own opinion should her father's plans come to fruition.

Gaston spent almost two whole weeks at home before venturing on the first of several outings beyond the end of the street. He never mentioned where he was going, but on returning from his third trip he shuffled through the gate and into the yard where Monique was busy scrubbing pans. Pluto ran up to greet his master, wagging his tail and alerting her to his presence.

'Hello Papa, you look happy. Looks like you're having a better day. Can I fetch you a glass of water?'

'Ah, yes. Then leave the cleaning and come and sit with me. I have something to say.'

A feeling of unease chilled through Monique. Dutifully she fetched a tumbler from the kitchen and filled it with bottled mineral water, not wanting to risk her father's health with anything else. She returned to sit beside him on a small bench set in the shade of the house.

Gaston sipped the offered water while absently fondling Pluto's soft ears before speaking. 'I've been seeing the king this morning, the third time this week. I have suffered so much Monique, but the king has stayed my guardian. I did not realise at first, but he used his contacts to intervene with the new government to plead for my release.'

'We're all indebted to him and very happy you're home safe and sound,' murmured Monique.

'We are indeed indebted to him, you're right ... I'm very glad you realise that. With this new government I'm confident of a return to more traditional ways when those close to the king will be in a very strong position. Recent politics has taught us we need all the protection we can get, and we now have an opportunity to cement our future as a safe and respected family.'

Gaston paused for another sip of water, but time seemed to stand still for Monique as she anticipated her father's next words.

'Monique, the king has been very patient, but the time has now come to repay our debt to him. I am very happy to tell you that today we have agreed that you will become his wife; the greatest honour possible for you and our family. The time has been set – six months from now, after the harvest - so there will be enough time to prepare for the wedding. You will then move out of course, to go and live in the palace.'

He leaned back against the wall behind him breathing heavily as if the effort of telling his daughter of her forthcoming nuptials had taken a great physical effort.

Monique felt numb, unable to speak. There was no point in arguing with her father once his mind was set. She must follow the customs of her people, even though the thought of being married to an old man made her feel nothing but revulsion. She forced herself to thank her father as expected; muttered her excuses and went to her room, all appetite for life drained from her by just a few words.

Lying on her mattress she tried to imagine her future giving unquestioning obedience to an old man - her husband, whenever demanded. It was too much to bear, and eventually the worry gave way to a fitful doze. She woke angry but refreshed, her mind determined and active.

Crying wouldn't solve anything and she wasn't married yet. There must be something she could do - something she could try. She ran through every alternative open to her. The trouble was there didn't seem to be any, apart from running away. Even fleeing wasn't really an option; that would only bring shame and worry to her family. She didn't even have a boyfriend to marry quickly, she thought despairingly. Her recent army days didn't seem so bad anymore; at least then there had always been hope for a romantic future.

She needed help, but who to ask?

There was only one person she could reliably turn to – Auntie Louise. Her aunt had always been there for her, always ready to give real advice or be her confidante.

She slipped out of her room, out of the house, and into the street. She wasn't ready to talk to immediate family yet, not even her own mother.

Outside, feelings of vulnerability and loneliness welled up making her blink away a tear. She couldn't carry on, couldn't do this alone. It was all too much, what if auntie couldn't help her either? She suddenly thought of Sabine. They shared so much history; as little girls they used to play in the street together. Sabine would understand what she was going through, her loyalty was guaranteed.

It was only a short walk to Sabine's house. The neighbourhood was similar - the same sized plot in a similar dusty street - one of the many laid out in a grid in that part of town. The gate was open so she walked straight in.

Here, the superficial similarity with her home immediately ended. Sabine's family were very poor; they still lived in a mud brick hut, a far cheaper option than concrete or imported breeze blocks. Even the yard looked run-down. A couple of scrawny hens pecked forlornly at the bare earth; the only vegetation being a sorry looking mango tree.

The front door was ajar and Monique could hear laughter inside. She clapped her hands loudly to announce her presence, and within seconds her old friend appeared.

'Monique! Can't believe my eyes! So good to see you! What's happening? Come on in and say hello to everyone.'

Sabine hugged her and Monique held her tight. 'Sabine please, I need your help urgently. I'll visit again soon I promise ... and stay awhile ... but come with me now, I can't do this alone.'

'Well, of course, Do what? Where are we going?'

'Other side of town ... sector twenty-three ... on the road to Bobo.'

Auntie Louise lived in an outer suburb, and as it was almost noon that meant a long hot walk. Monique looked over at the family moped. 'Is that free? Can we use it? We won't be gone for long, I promise. I need to see someone urgently. I can explain everything on the way.'

'Sure, I'll just change my shoes and get the key. I'll have to let Mama know I'm going out. Be with you in just a minute.'

Once both women were astride Sabine's little Honda, Monique explained her problem, shouting above the rushing wind and the montonous hum of the moped's 125cc engine, as she held onto Sabine's waist.

It seemed only minutes before they turned off the wide blacktopped boulevard which, had they followed it, would have taken them west, all the way to Bobo, the country's second largest town. Instead they slowly picked their way along a series of minor roads to the outskirts of the city, an ever-growing shantytown of makeshift shacks interconnected by a maze of dirt tracks.

Under Monique's instruction, Sabine stopped outside a neat concrete hut.

'You remember auntie from years ago? She's a very good fortune teller, the best. Some call her a witch, but she's always been very kind to me; if anyone can advise me what I should do, she can.'

Sabine smiled in acknowledgement. Witches and witchdoctors were part of everyday life. She recalled the time when as a girl she and her playmates recognised a well-known footballer who came to visit a neighbour. He played for a team representing a different part of town, and so they had diligently collected his dusty footprints from the street and taken it to their local witchdoctor who'd obligingly cursed the sand and therefore the feet that had made the imprint - thereby ensuring those same feet would never play well against their own team. As far as she could remember it had worked, becoming one more legend supporting common belief in the power of magic.

Auntie Louise didn't look like a witch. In her early fifties and well-rounded, she was all warm smiles and hugs as she welcomed her guests into her simple home. She produced two bottles of cola and invited her guests to join her inside, where it was cooler.

Monique got straight to the point and explained how her father had arranged her marriage, and how her own views had not even been considered.

'What are my options? Do I have any? And what sort of future can they offer me?'

Her aunt hadn't interrupted; just listened intently, tutting and shaking her head in empathy. Once she'd finished speaking, Monique rubbed her eyes before looking at her imploringly.

'Well,' her aunt offered brightly, 'why don't we see for ourselves what the future holds? Sabine, help yourself to another cola. We won't be long. Monique - follow me.'

Louise lit an oil lamp and led her niece into a tiny windowless lean-to at the rear of the house. Inside, she hung the lamp from a ceiling hook and closed the door. Pointing to a chair for Monique at one end of a small round table she took the seat opposite. With no ventilation it was suffocatingly hot. The shadows from the flickering lamp played tricks with eyes already struggling to adapt to the dark interior, adding a touch more mystique to the ritual.

Louise took two bags from under the table. The larger of the two contained fine sand which she poured onto the table before spreading it out evenly, completely covering the surface. From the smaller bag she retrieved a handful of cowrie shells which she passed to Monique. Without letting go of her niece's hand, she leaned across the table and stared intently into her eyes.

'You know what to do. When I say so - think positively - then cast the shells onto the sand. Right, whenever you're ready.'

Monique threw the cowrie shells seven times. After each cast Louise the witch surveyed how they had fallen, and the imprints they left. After the final throw she leaned back and closed her eyes for a moment before speaking.

'This is all very unusual. The future is uncertain ... so many people involved ... let me see.' She stared worriedly at her niece. 'I see death ... that one thing is sure ... I don't necessarily mean yours,' she added hastily. 'It could be anyone. I also see a white man. How he can be involved in your affairs I do not understand. Once betrothed to the king, a woman's life is set. There is also another man, one of evil intent who is watching you. You need to be very careful in all that you do. As for the marriage itself ... the magic isn't showing me anything ... that doesn't mean it will be good or bad ... I just don't know at this moment.'

'Thank you, auntie.' Monique tried not to sound disappointed. She had secretly hoped to be told what she could actively do to avoid the wedding and find happiness.

'Don't worry dear, there'll be plenty happening in your life; much of it has the potential to be very good. You just need to be careful, that's all. Things - men especially - may not be all they seem at first sight. If you stay patient but wary, it may yet work out for you.'

Monique grabbed this kernel of hope. If things could still work out, she would do everything in her power to help herself.

She thanked her aunt again as they exited the lean-to. The bright sunshine further reinvigorated her spirits, and she smiled when she found her best friend finishing off her second cola.

'C'mon Sabine, drink-up, let's go. I've kept you away long enough, and I've got a life to live!'

Back at Sabine's house they shared a bottle of beer while Monique explained what her aunt had said. Her aunt's words were hopelessly lost on Sabine who was still gushingly excited about her best friend marrying the king.

'You're mad. I would give anything to marry him. Just stop and think - it's a life of security; there's not even much work to do because my mother told me the housework is divided up among all the wives. What an opportunity for an easy life! A chance in a million! I'm sure you'll be allowed occasional visitors, so we can still see each other. Any woman - not just me - would be more than happy with that.'

Monique drank a full draft before answering. 'You know what I'm like. I don't see why I should have to bend to the will of a lot of old men. God has given me a brain, so I also have an opinion. The fact is I don't wanna marry an old man, especially one who's already got lots of wives. There's no love or passion there, I'll just be a faceless number.'

'You're much too stubborn for your own good. Come on, finish the beer and I'll take you home. Just remember to recommend me to the king next time you see him - I'll marry him like a shot!'

Seated behind her friend on the small Honda again, Monique couldn't help wishing it were true; that it was Sabine and not her who was due to wed the king. One good thing was that her aunt had given her the determination to live life to the full until the wedding day. Six months to do what she wanted for the first and perhaps only time in her life.

. . .

Sabine prepared her family's meal alone that evening. A late return meant she was still cooking over the open charcoal fire in the yard well after nightfall. As the eldest daughter of three, most of the household responsibilities fell to her. After serving the staple dish of tao - a dough made from millet flour with a sauce created from okra - to the rest of the family, she returned to the fire and served herself.

She was close to Monique, seeing her as a real sister. But their differing army experiences, courtesy of the brutality of Captain Jerome Zongo, had driven a wedge between them. Today was the first time she'd seen Monique since their return from the bush camp all those weeks ago. She'd been genuinely delighted to see her friend but meeting her had also resurrected painful flashbacks of army life, especially those involving the captain. Now they came flooding back in an unstoppable wave.

She stared at the burning charcoal in the remains of the fireplace. Dull red eyes glared back at her. They dimmed even as she watched the last of their heat evaporating into the cold night air; their defiant spirits ebbing away.

The memory of her night with the captain rudely thrust itself upon her. Disgust with herself and hatred for him flared inside her. She had been sadistically raped that night, and she burned for revenge. But how to achieve it?

Monique was the key. Her family had influence. With this new government, the boot ought to be on the other foot. A proclaimed socialist like Captain Zongo ought to be running scared. If only someone could inform the new powers in charge of his crimes, then surely he would have to pay the price for his evil deeds. Monique's father could tell someone in authority. If *he* didn't, then her mother could do so through her connections with the royal family.

Sabine's path seemed to light up before her, just as the last embers of the fire turned black. She inwardly smiled at her idea. She had made her decision. She would visit Gaston, Monique's father, and explain how the captain had mistreated them both. A proud man, she was certain he would take steps to avenge them and free her of her shame. She only hoped Zongo would realise it was she who was behind the troubles that were about to come his way.

23

Monique also had an idea, one that came to her several weeks later as she lay tossing and turning, unable to sleep. She had been running through all the various threads of her life, trying in vain to find one that ended in anything other than marriage to a man she didn't love. One unravelled out of the confusing knotty mess, the result of a visit she had made that morning with her mother to her grandfather's house. It was something he'd said that she now latched onto, giving her the wispiest strand of hope.

Her maternal grandfather, despite his advanced years and reduced mobility, retained the official title of the Royal Advisor for Farming. He had decades of experience as the man in charge and as such demanded respect from those around him. He had been angry ever since learning the king had asked an outsider - a white man no less - to help with the royal farm without consulting him first. Worse, the king had asked one of the other Advisors to show the stranger around and even ordered the man to lodge with him. He had made sure Brigitte and Monique understood his feelings.

'It's intolerable that I wasn't included in any of this. I am the Advisor for Farming, so *I* should have been asked, not that upstart Sanou. I might as well not exist anymore. I know I'm not as active as I used to be - and I may even have suggested the same arrangement - but not to be consulted at all! Well ... it's unheard of! Totally unacceptable and humiliating.'

It was only now, with time to herself, that she was able to knit together all the different connections. Her grandfather's voice came to mind, specifically the reference to a white man. As a frequent visitor to the palace, she knew all the main players and there were definitely no Europeans or Americans among them. Yet she *had* seen a white stranger at the palace only the other day. *And* he'd been in the company of Sanou. He must be the one the king had requested help from.

The last thread fell into place. As Monique didn't know any Europeans, he *had* to be the one - the one her aunt had predicted she would meet. A thrill ran through her, and she couldn't think of anything else. They had noticed each other that day at the palace, the strings of fate drawing them together, making the connection at a most fundamental level. That could not be ignored.

She didn't have much time; nearly a month had already passed since she'd learned the date of her betrothal. No more than five months remained until the wedding; the ticking clock hung over her, haunting and taunting her with her impotence. She fully intended to grasp this opportunity; any action was better than meekly accepting a lifetime's sentence. Tomorrow she would go to the farm, where, God-willing, she would meet with a stranger in the hope he would become her saviour. The prospect of such a meeting was exciting, and she lay awake for much of the night as she imagined endless possibilities.

. . .

After preparing breakfast for the entire household and sweeping out, Monique washed and changed into her best dress: a patterned batik of bright yellow flowers on a blue background. Her mother raised an eye but said nothing as she wheeled the family moped out through the gate and into the street. She breathed a small sigh of relief. Her father hadn't spotted her; he may well have asked where she was going, possibly even have stopped her going out altogether.

She arrived at Sabine's house too late to catch her friend. They'd spent a lot more time together since visiting Auntie Louise, so were familiar with each-other's daily routines. Sabine had even admitted telling her father about Zongo. Monique couldn't hold that against her; she'd suffered so much more at his hands.

'She's already left for the central market,' Sabine's younger brother, Pascal told her. 'She won't be back for at least a couple of hours.'

Pascal was an academic, very bright, and at sixteen years of age was aiming to get into the university of Ouagadougou. He was a big hope for a better future with a real chance to land a well-paid job and earn money to help support his extended family. Today he was also the real reason for Monique's visit.

'Pascal, you're the only man that can help me, that's why I'm here. No questions though, it's for the good of the king.'

The last part was a lie, but she was in no mood to risk not getting her way. For single women it was imprudent to travel so far out of town alone. With a male escort, even a youth, she would be perfectly safe.

Pascal was no match for her in a debate. Climbing aboard the moped, Monique supressed a grin. As if she'd ask a boy to go with her to do urgent business for the king! Whatever was Pascal going to think of her once they got there?

The constant whine of the moped's 125cc engine gradually faded from consciousness as she considered her next move. If she could only find her man, there might be a chance of something life-changing happening. Then there were the optimistic words of Auntie Louise, who was always right. Besides, a strong inner voice was reassuring her that some bigger part was about to play out.

She directed Pascal to the farm. The route was difficult to remember; she'd only been there herself on a few occasions, and then as a passenger. In fact, with no signs or boundaries they only realised they'd arrived after catching up with a small group of machete-armed men jogging along in single file.

Pascal pulled up alongside the leader.

'Hey, what's the problem?' he shouted.

The man barely glanced at the youth before answering, '*bushfire - straight ahead!*'

Monique craned her neck to peer around Pascal. Not too far in front of them, great spirals of brown and black smoke were rising vertically in the hot, still air, eventually dispersing in wispy curls high up in the deep blue of the African sky. She'd spotted them earlier but thought nothing of them, the sight being common enough at that time of year all over the savanna.

The leader must have detected doubt as the couple next to him stared into the distance. 'We're all going to help; it's a lot worse than it looks. All this land belongs to the king. We have to move fast, if the fire isn't stopped it could spread to neighbouring farms!'

'Ride on! Let's see if we can help too!' Monique yelled in Pascal's ear.

They skirted an area of open grassland. The land was parched and the grasses would light in an instant if the fire approached; a thousand million matchsticks waiting to be struck. They rode on for a few more minutes until a straggly line of working men emerged through the swirling brown mists drifting down from the raging bushfire that lay beyond.

As they neared the inferno, the smell of burning vegetation hit them, followed by a quiet rustling which grew to a roaring crackle as the fire itself came into view. Monique gaped as the extent of the blaze became apparent.

The gang leader was right; left to right the fire was at least a hundred meters wide, how far back it went she had no idea.

Pascal slowed, allowing Monique to watch transfixed at the nearest flames. Vivid red and yellow tongues licked voraciously upward devouring the tall grass. The frond-like heads burned most fiercely, whipping around in crazy circles in the fierce updrafts like demented demons.

'Close enough - stop here,' she yelled, feeling the fire's heat beginning to fan her face. Together they dismounted and ran to join the end of the line of firefighters.

She understood what the men were doing. There was no water to quench the flames, so they were using the only other method of fighting back: containment. Each man was armed with a machete, that invaluable tool to agricultural labourers throughout Africa. Stripped to the waist, a ragged line of black torsos shone with sweat as they laboured in a race to clear a swathe of land ahead of the advancing line of fire. The heat from the raging inferno was incredible, the nearest flames no more than twenty yards away.

Pascal hesitated before approaching the man who seemed to be in charge, a tall thin figure dressed in long shorts and a faded red football shirt. He signalled his intent to help, and was immediately handed a machete. Monique watched him take his place in the line of sweating men, his skinny arms working in long diagonal swipes as he hacked at the roots of the grass. Pascal was unused to physical work so would surely suffer the next day.

She scanned the line of men again, and her eyes froze about halfway along. She hadn't seen him at first. The white man was dressed like all the others, bare-chested and wearing a pair of ragged trousers. It was no wonder she hadn't noticed him; the exposed skin on the back of his arms and neck - already deeply tanned - was blackened from the smoke which drifted over the labourers in little clouds of ash.

Her saviour was going to have to wait. No doubt it was inappropriate for a girl to undertake firefighting, but she wasn't about to let etiquette get in the way of doing her bit. The already cut grass needed to be moved away from the fire so there was no chance of loose sparks igniting it and ruining all the hard work. Starting behind the nearest man she quickly gathered together a bundle of the loose stalks and carried them away before returning for another.

She moved her way along the line of sweating labourers, carrying bundle after bundle to safety. Her efforts did not go unnoticed, and it wasn't long before the shadow of the man in the football shirt loomed over her, demanding to know who she was and what she thought she was doing.

On hearing her name, he peered more closely before bowing himself away, thanking her for her valuable efforts.

The men worked fast, grim-faced in their efforts to stay ahead of the fire, its leading edge marked by a black cloud of thousands of flying insects fleeing the advancing line of death.

Monique worked behind each man in turn, eventually gathering an armful of cut grass from behind the white man. He turned around as her shadow fell on him, and they locked eyes for a second time.

. . .

Tomos instantly recognised the young woman gathering the grass he'd been scything moments before. He wrenched his attention away from the fire, struggling to recall the circumstances where he'd seen her. Of course, she was the lady from the palace.

The woman flashed him a smile as she stood up, and he felt himself grinning back. Circumstances precluded idle chat, which was just as well as he was momentarily tongue tied. Their mutual gaze lingered for a whole two seconds before the woman turned away, her bare arms hidden under a heap of cut grass.

He returned to his labours with renewed vigour, working harder as he fought to catch up and keep pace with the men around him. He was only wearing cotton trousers and an old pair of trainers, and could feel the heat singeing the hairs on his arms and chest as he doggedly ignored the smoke and ash that fell onto his skin. His lungs burned with every intake of breath.

The firefighters kept up their hard work for another hour until the overseer called time, more reinforcements from neighbouring villages having arrived. Calabasas of water were handed out to the thirsty workers.

Tomos stopped work, stood up straight and stretched his aching back. He could see the fire was well on the way to burning itself out. A vast blackened area of scorched earth highlighted the extent of the blaze. Where the red of the flames still licked upwards, the heads of the grasses continued to whip around in their furious dance of death. There was more black than red now. The ring of cleared ground had done its job; the remaining fires could probably be left to burn out harmlessly.

A hand touched his arm. He turned to find the same woman from earlier standing beside him. Her other hand offered a tin mug of water which he accepted automatically, his eyes transfixed by her perfect features. He tore his eyes away and drained the mug in a single gulp.

'Come,' she laughed, eyes sparkling, 'follow me, there's plenty more over there.'

He followed her to a small stand of acacia under which where a few plastic bottles of water. He neither knew nor cared where they had come from, his thoughts being entirely centred on the woman. Two labourers chatting under the trees fell silent and ghosted away with curious stares, leaving them alone in the acacia's dappled shadow.

'I picked this up earlier; I was told it belongs to you.'

Tomos gratefully retrieved the shirt which she held out, and donned it before speaking. 'Thanks. I'm Tomos, by the way. What's your name?'

'Monique ... Monique Tapsoba.'

'I recognise you from the palace. What brings you here today?'

'I could say the same about you. Why is an outsider working so hard on our land?'

'Oh, I agreed to help out on the king's farm. Mind you, fighting bushfires was never part of the plan.'

'Ahah, they're very common this time of year. Some people even start them deliberately; maybe this one was, too.'

'But look at you ... you worked so hard as well ... and now you've spoiled your dress.'

Tomos immediately bit his lip in annoyance at his clumsy choice of words.

Monique turned away. 'I'm so dirty - in such a mess. I must look horrible.'

'No, no, not at all - I think you look beautiful.'

She *was* beautiful. For the first time he was able to look at her properly and drank in the classic high cheek bones and the large child-like almond-eyes. Also for the first time he saw the intriguing tribal scar cut deep into the top of her left cheek. It spoiled the otherwise perfect symmetry of her face, but for him it simply added to her mystery.

'I'm sorry - I didn't mean to be rude.'

'It's alright, I *am* in a mess, can't deny it.'

'Hey Monique, can we go yet?'

Tomos looked up at the unwanted interruption and saw a skinny youth nervously approaching.

'Pascal, yes, I've kept you away too long already,' Monique responded.

'Monique, listen,' Tomos spoke hurriedly. 'I would love to see you again - how d'ya feel about meeting up sometime, maybe go for a drink?'

'Yes, I'd like that.'

'How can I find you?'

'Where do you live? Perhaps I will find *you*.'

'I'm staying in Ouaga at the house of Arzuma Sanou. You know him?'

'Oh *him*. Yes, I know. Let me think ...'

In the pause that followed, Tomos noticed the youth, Pascal, giving Monique an exasperated look before walking away.

'I think I'd better leave now,' Monique breathed, also watching the retreating figure. 'There's a bar called La Forêt a couple of streets away from where you're staying. I can't promise, but I may be there tomorrow around sunset.'

'OK, hope to see you there.' He watched her leave until she was fully out of sight. Only then did he re-join his co-workers, whistling a meaningless happy tune as he went in search of Adama the overseer, the bushfire already half forgotten.

24

Tomos went shopping the next day for a new outfit in the sprawling central market. It was not an activity he normally enjoyed but today was different. He set off with real purpose despite his aching back and blistered palms, courtesy of wielding a heavy machete for hours.

Women hadn't been on his mind for a long while, and meeting Monique had made him realise just how much he missed female company. His own clothes were little more than rags; a new shirt and pair of trousers would make him more presentable.

It was still well before dusk when he arrived at La Forêt. He already knew the place, having escaped there once to get away from the loneliness of Sanou's house. Sizeable yet secluded, it boasted a couple of indoor tables, though most were set outside in a courtyard enclosed by a low wall, the top of which was currently occupied by an attentive vulture.

Somewhere, a Bob Marley tape was playing, the gentle melody hanging in the air, the bar an oasis of tranquillity. Within the yard the only clients were a couple enjoying a meal, fully engrossed in their food. They were oblivious to him, and to the vulture hungrily waiting for a chance to seize any scraps.

Tomos selected an outside table away from the diners and sat facing the street. The barmaid approached, and he ordered a bottle of his favourite beer. There was no sign of Monique, so he stretched himself out and prepared to wait. He still felt as if he were a puppet acting out his life. At least this evening there was something real and desirable to look forward to.

His beer arrived. The barmaid gave him an engaging smile as she opened the bottle, scrawled the bill on a scrap of paper and placed it under his glass.

There was a change in the air; a cooler hazy sky having replaced the usual stifling warmth. The difference felt good, like the rising but excitable tension before a major rugby game. He straightened his aching back again and took a sip of the cool beer; he was determined to enjoy the evening no matter what.

He didn't have long to wait. Two women entered, arm in arm. It wasn't until they walked up to him that he recognised Monique. She looked stunning, instantly putting him at a loss for words. Her hair had been neatly plaited with long extensions since yesterday. A smart yellow and green figure-hugging batik dress highlighted her curves.

She laughed; a chuckle that politely covered his hesitancy. 'Why Tomo – did I say it right? Fancy meeting you here,' she exclaimed, shaking him by the hand. 'This is my best friend, Sabine.'

'Hello Sabine, pleased to meet you. It's Tomos actually but Tomo is fine by me. Are you both happy to sit outside?'

Monique laughed again. 'Definitely; it's the first cool breeze we've had for ages.'

'Great, err... what would you both like to drink?' Tomos enquired, signalling to the barmaid.

Two more beers were ordered, a slightly disapproving look on the barmaid's face as she glanced at the newcomers.

'So, tell me more about yourself Monique. I'm dying to know all about you.'

'OK, but you go first. To start with, where are you from, with your funny accent? And what are you doing in Burkina Faso?'

'Well, my accent is British ... Welsh actually. I travelled here with a Burkinabe friend that I met in Libya where we were working. He invited me to come and see his country and I stayed with him in Koutatenga until recently. Anyway, to cut a long story short, I was asked to help out on the royal farm. It was suggested I stay with Sanou ... been there for nearly a month now; the rest you know.'

'So, you're British. You're the first one I've met. I knew you were different as soon as I saw you. The king generally doesn't like outsiders in court, especially the French, given their colonial history in our country.'

The mention of colonialism was always an awkward moment. Since his arrival in West Africa, Tomos often found it mentioned early in conversation; he always assumed it was to judge his reactions.

'I'm not surprised,' he retorted, 'but it's your turn now. I wanna know more about you.'

Monique shrugged. 'There's not much to say. Like I already said, my maternal grandfather is one of the royal Advisors, that's why I often visit the palace.'

'Oh, which one is he?'

'Advisor for Agriculture. Tomo, you need to know my grandfather and Sanou don't particularly get on. It might be a good idea if you don't tell Sanou we've met; if grandfather gets to hear, it'll only upset him.'

'Sure - no problem. And what about you, Sabine? Anything I ought to know about you?' Tomos asked light heartedly.

Before she could reply, a roll of thunder rumbled across the heavens, the first time it had been heard in the capital since the end of the rainy season, nine long months ago. He watched the unfeigned delight show itself on both Monique's and Sabine's features. The thunder was the sign all the country had been waiting for, the start of the rainy season. A second roll of thunder followed, this time accompanied by a sudden gust of cool wind which blew a dust ball into the courtyard from the street.

Sabine was the first to react. 'Hey, you two, I think we'd better move inside sharpish. Tomo ... the most important thing you need to know about me is that I hate getting wet!'

Bottles, glasses and unpaid bills were snatched just in time, the heavens emptying as everyone dashed indoors.

Inside they sat and listened to the passing storm as the rain fell in a great thumping staccato upon the bar's corrugated iron roof.

'At last ... the farmers will all go crazy now planting the crops,' Monique half-whispered. 'I guess you'll be busy too?' she added, giving him a sideways glance.

'Only during the day, my evenings tend to be free,' he replied.

Another round of drinks was ordered. The ambiance was relaxed and friendly, as was the conversation. Tomos was now comfortably able to follow the French language, although he was painfully aware of his own shortcomings when speaking it.

The rain continued to pour down for the next thirty minutes, a steady drumming that drowned out the soft music and hushed conversations from the other customers. Tomos found the rainfall vaguely comforting, like an old friend who had joined them unexpectedly. It was only when it stopped as suddenly as it had started - making him look up, that he realised the night had silently crept in, unnoticed by all.

Sabine touched Monique's arm, and spoke in their native tongue. Monique nodded.

'Tomo, I've enjoyed meeting you, and thanks for buying the drinks. Wish I could stay longer but we both have to get back.'

'Sure, can I walk you home? It's dark outside.'

Monique laughed. 'No; but thanks for the offer. I'll be in touch again; drinks are on me next time!'

Tomos reluctantly stood and shook hands with both women. Again, the merest lingering of fingers with Monique before she and Sabine were gone into the night.

Alone, he ordered one last beer. The evening had been so different compared to anything he'd experienced for far too long. He'd really enjoyed himself in a way he'd almost forgotten. His drink arrived, and he reclined in his seat wondering what the next days and weeks might bring.

The alcohol had relaxed him. His guard was down and the nagging thoughts of his past took advantage. He found he didn't care. The fleeting notion of a possible future in which he might not be alone, could maybe even be happy, was what mattered most. He had to accept the past and move on.

25

Monique proved right, with regards to the onset of the rain meaning busier times. Sowing of crops was the order of the day, and all available farm labourers set to work to make the most of every drop of moisture. Although not expected of him, Tomos insisted on spending long hours over the next few days doing his share of physical labour. He also started to put forward his ideas for improving the existing farming system. Contour ploughing to reduce soil erosion was one such idea; the planting of more tree crops for cash was another; the two concepts happily accepted by both Sanou and the overseer.

Shortage of wood for cooking fuel and construction was a pressing problem for the rapidly growing capital city, so he also pushed for a significant part of the farmland to be given over to establishing tree saplings for this purpose. The trees would provide much needed income when felled in seven or eight years' time. They would also provide shade; thereby allowing ground crops such as groundnuts to be cultivated beneath their canopy; maximising the productivity of the land.

Understanding the importance of giving everyone a vested interest, Tomos also suggested that if the villagers could plant their own crops around the trees and be allowed to harvest a certain amount of firewood for themselves, then they could tend both their crops and the trees, benefitting everyone. The farm would gain its main profit from the selling of the trees when they reached maturity. Once all the ideas were discussed and accepted, Sanou agreed to investigate the practicalities of implementing them.

Agricultural work tended to finish well before nightfall, allowing people to use the last hour of daylight to travel home and prepare for the evening. Tomos had adopted the early start of his co-workers and was often to be found at the farm shortly after dawn, Sanou having lent him one of his older mopeds.

Day after day, during and after work, he waited in vain for news of Monique. None came, and the lack of news weighed heavily upon him.

26

Monique eavesdropped with increasing nervousness as her best friend chatted excitedly to guest after guest in the dusty forecourt masquerading as a garden. It was 7 o'clock in the morning, and everyone in Sabine's extended family had already arrived at her house; the gathering being a wedding party organised in honour of one of her cousins, Phillipe from Ouagadougou. The bride-to-be lived in a village eighty kilometres away. Monique had managed to beg an invitation for herself and Tomos.

Her eyes were anxiously drawn to the gate again and again. She and Tomos hadn't met since La Forêt, two weeks ago, and she'd only just sent the invite so wasn't sure if he would come. The wedding party was due to leave soon; it would be terrible if he was late and missed the bus.

She forced a smile to greet the few guests she was acquainted with. With every day that passed she wished she were someone else. For any other local young woman, marrying the king would be a dream come true. But she wanted so much more. The whole world was changing - evolving - and she wanted to be part of it.

Being promised to the king was the highest honour possible, and one which demanded a certain standard of decorum from the bride-in-waiting. If she was going to cultivate a relationship with Tomos to avoid getting married, then early discretion was vital. So much for that! She'd already made a mess of things. One little drink with him - that was all she'd had - and some nosey troublemaker had reported her to papa. The disconsolate thought was triggered by the memory of a conversation she'd had only two days ago. Her father had walked into her room and berated her.

"I've just heard what you've been up to ... out meeting a boy ... a foreigner indeed! I despair of you, I really do. You are a fool and a disgrace. You dishonour me and the king; you even dishonour our ancestors and traditions. Don't you realise what you're doing? If the king finds out he's likely to call off the wedding, and that is more shame than I can take. What's wrong with you girl? Do you never think?"

Monique had remained silent, had fought the temptation to scream at him: *What is the point of thinking if I'm not allowed an opinion?*

The sullen look she gave her father must have infuriated him further.

"Nothing to say for yourself girl - only a stupid look? You can thank your mother for not getting a beating. You can also thank Sabine. Don't look at me as if I'm mad! You must know Sabine has told me all about your army captain."

Her father had trembled as he spoke. "Well, he soon won't be troubling anyone again. I've used my new influence to issue a warrant for his arrest, though it seems he's already gone into hiding. Just as well, if you ask me. It's more of a punishment if he's a hunted man. You see, I do care for you and fight to protect your best interests. So let this be the last I hear of you and this white boy - any boy for that matter - you understand? Do not let me down again. It's only five months to the wedding; surely you can behave yourself for five months!"

Five months! Her father's words echoed inside her head, a taunting reminder of her impunity that snapped her back to the present. She had every intention of seeing Tomos again; God willing she prayed he would turn up today. She had to admit he was very likeable ... handsome too. Could she persuade him to help her? Being a European he could be her ticket out of Africa; maybe even help her stay safe in his own country.

Her only plan was to continue seeing him in the hope something helpful might develop. With father watching every move, today was her first opportunity to see Tomos again. She clung to the encouraging lifeline Auntie Louise had thrown her. The white man she'd seen in her vision *had* to be Tomos - and surely his influence on her life *had* to be good - so he *must* be worth pursuing.

Tomos was the last guest to arrive, guided in by the ever-reliable Pascal. Monique raised a hand to beckon him over as he walked in through the gate, prompting him to wave back. The unfeigned delight that lit up his face sent Monique's spirits soaring.

'Hi, so glad you could make it.' She thought he couldn't possibly know just how glad.

'Great to see you again, thanks for asking me along. What exactly is going on here?'

Monique stifled a giggle as she watched him gawp at the happy gathering. The mood was light-hearted, the yard echoing with laughter. Sabine's house was the most central of her extended family and therefore the most suitable as a meeting place before departure.

A bus coughed up alongside the front gate and belched out a cloud of diesel fumes from a rattling exhaust.

'C'mon everyone, we don't want to be late.' Sabine's mother bustled among the guests.

The wedding party eventually organised themselves enough to file on board and with a double blast of horn and black smoke, the bus shuddered off.

Monique felt she must be the only person aboard so fraught with inner worry. She imagined the king and her father on one side, Tomos on the other. Which would decide her fate?

'Are you alright? You seem very quiet,' Tomos asked from the seat next to her. As he spoke, he reached out to hold her hand.

Monique smiled back, giving his hand an encouraging squeeze. 'I'm fine,' she murmured. 'I'm not feeling my best today. I think it's the bus ... I've never liked them.'

'If what Pascal told me is right about the distance, it won't take long to get there. I'm sure you'll feel better once you get into the fresh air.'

The journey passed without difficulty, a big relief for Monique as it meant less time to ponder the unknown. Even the roadblocks did not delay them long; some good-natured banter with the duty officers saw the old bus and its happy passengers waved through with barely a pause.

The constant chatting and laughing continued most of the way. Monique half listened to the gossip, feeding the juiciest bits to Tomos. His reactions to every story indicated that he at least was enjoying the whole experience.

The sixty kilometres to the village of Nazougou took an hour and a half, long enough for the sun to have risen high in the sky by the time they arrived. The bus lacked any air conditioning, the only relief coming from little breezy puffs of air that squeezed in through tiny gaps around the edges of ill-fitting windows. It was noisy too, and the passengers gradually grew hot and uncomfortable. The last few kilometres along an excessively potholed track that took them to the centre of Nazougou finally took its toll, waning conversations to silence.

Monique gratefully climbed down from the bus with the others. There wasn't much to look at: a large area of red dirt surrounded by a few circular mud huts with conical thatched roofs. Through some scrubby bush, the welcoming bridal party approached them, several elderly gentlemen to the fore, shadowed by a train of curious children.

The two groups met and greeted. After some discussion Monique informed Tomos that the wedding was to take place immediately before the day became unbearably warm.

The ceremony was conducted beneath a mighty baobab, the tallest and fattest one Monique had ever seen. It was a truly magical setting. The wedding was a Christian one and the priest, a local man, orchestrated the rituals in the local language. Monique whispered a translation of the key words. Goodwill prayers were made, hymns were sung, and lengthy congratulations concluded the marriage for the happy couple.

Watching them enjoying their wonderful ceremony was hard for Monique. This was how a marriage should be ... two people in love choosing to be together.

After the nuptials the bride and groom retired from view. Most of the adult Nazougou inhabitants drifted back to their daily routines leaving the children to stare at the visitors, especially Tomos, much to Monique's amusement. Sabine's family stayed in the shade of the baobab and began complaining about the lack of hospitality from the host village.

'This is all part of the traditional way of doing things,' Monique explained. 'The host village is obliged to feed the guests, but they will tease them by making them wait until they're really hungry!'

'You seem much better now,' Tomos remarked. 'Can we go for a walk while we're waiting?'

They headed off along the nearest trail through the bush. After a few hundred yards, their way was interrupted by a scrawny blackened acacia adorned with trinkets, its thin branches reaching out and over the path.

'Stop,' Monique touched Tomos's arm. 'We can't go past - see the fetishes.'

Tomos looked at the branches and saw numerous hanging wooden ornaments and what looked like bits of cloth tied to the ends of the outermost twigs.

Monique tugged insistently at his arm. 'Come ... we can't stay, it will only upset the locals if we're seen here.'

'But what does it mean?' Tomos asked, as they turned around and headed back towards the big baobab.

'Oh, I don't know. Probably in this case someone has decreed it a sacred area, it looks like the tree was hit by lightning which is a bad sign from the ancestors. Sorry, I don't believe in such things, but out here in the villages most everyone does; whether Christian or Moslem makes no difference. Traditions die hard.'

It was mid afternoon before the locals returned to the baobab meeting area. In single file willowy women brought food with them in various pots and bowls carried expertly upon erect heads. The rest of the village followed in dribs and drabs. The serving of the overdue meal helped lighten the mood and it wasn't long before both groups were intermingling and trading friendly jibes.

'The insults are another tradition,' Monique happily informed Tomos between mouthfuls of beans and rice. 'Best watch out; another is the local girls being allowed to throw cups of water over the visiting young men!'

The sun had completed most of its daily arc by the time the revellers climbed aboard the bus for the long ride back to the city. A combination of fatigue and full bellies making for a much quieter mood than on the outward leg.

Half an hour into the journey, Monique sensed Tomos's form relax to the gentle vibration of the bus's motion.

'Wow, look at that sky,' he breathed softly.

Together they watched the passing landscape. The savanna stretched out around them in all directions - the African plains rolling away to infinity. Above the horizon, thick dark clouds were gathering, a first glow from far off lightning in their midst hinting at an approaching storm.

Monique sensed the mood was right to take a chance; the moment had arrived to speak about bigger matters. She laid her head on Tomos's shoulder.

'Everything alright' he asked softly.

She smiled up at him. 'I haven't said thank you for coming today. It's been so nice to spend time together. I wanted to see you again, but it's not easy for me to find time to go out.'

'Wish we *could* see more of each other.'

Monique thought of her aunt's words. She had never actually explained how the white man would influence her life *for better or for worse.* It was time to find out.

'It's Sunday tomorrow, you won't be needed on the farm. I thought maybe we could spend another day together ... just the two of us.'

'Hmm, sounds good. 'Have you got somewhere in mind?'

'Yes, actually I do. We can stay at my uncle's house tonight; he lives not far from this road, just as it enters Ouaga. There's just the two of them - him and his wife. They only got married last year, no children yet. We can spend the evening together, and all of tomorrow - just the two of us. What do you think?'

Tomos looked down at her, surprise clear in his expression. 'Yes, sure; I'm happy to do that, but won't your family wonder where you are?'

'That's great. Don't worry about my family, I'll ask Uncle Bertrand to let them know where I am.'

The bus passed through the city limits and dropped them off at the first proper suburban road. Monique watched their diesel-belching ride until it disappeared out of sight around the corner at the end of the street before she took Tomos's arm.

'Come ... it's this way. I'm sure you're going to love Bertrand and Marie.'

'Tell me about them,' Tomos asked as they walked.

'Uncle Bertrand is on my mother's side. He's about ten years older than me, and when we were growing up he always looked out for me. We're still very close. He's a vet, and his wife Marie - she's lovely - works as a receptionist in one of the large hotels in the city. By local standards they're quite well off.'

As Bertrand's house came into view, which from the outside resembled a flat-roofed bungalow, Monique reflected how she had arranged the visit in advance. She wanted the right setting to tell Tomos about her planned marriage, only then would she know where she stood. The right setting meant being somewhere they could both be at ease without fear of being disturbed. Uncle Bertrand's place seemed ideal. So far, so good; he had agreed to stay over. All she needed to do now was wait for the right moment to tell him everything.

Every time she considered the risk she was about to take, she could feel her stomach knot. Would he support her - or would he run?

27

Bertrand and his wife Marie served up a genuinely friendly and enthusiastic welcome; pumped handshakes and a gush of warm words relaxing their guests in an instant.

'We're going to have sundowners on the roof, why don't you join us?' Bertrand asked.

'Thanks uncle - that alright with you, Tomo?'

'Love to, it must be great to be able to sit out and enjoy the view.'

The roof overlooked the nearest shacks, the backdrop of the savanna beyond an inspiring vista to accompany the conversation and beer drinking. Before them, the race between the approaching thunderstorm and the encroaching night unfolded.

Bertrand and Marie were easy company to keep; both were chatty and neither dominated the other. They conversed for half an hour until the setting sun lost its race against the black clouds. When the now familiar first gust of cold wind announced the rain was about to start, everyone scuttled inside carrying their chairs with them.

The rain lasted for twenty minutes, just long enough to churn the street outside into a sea of mud. As soon as the downpour finished, Marie offered both her guests the chance to freshen up. Bertrand provided Tomos with a set of traditional lightweight cotton trousers and smock.

'Hope they're comfortable ... make yourself at home. 'I'm sure you and Monique are both hungry so I'm off to get some food - a take-away, African-style.'

Tomos was left sitting alone in the main living room while the two women disappeared together into the kitchen.

Marie spoke to Monique in her own language. 'Well, your man seems very nice, but does he know about your engagement? Bertrand will do anything for you, but you must understand if this gets out it won't do any of us any favours.'

'I understand. I just want a little time with him before I tell him everything. We'll be gone in the morning I promise, no-one need ever know we were here.'

'You really like him, don't you? He likes you too; I saw the way he looks at you.'

Monique took a deep breath. 'Yes, I do like him ... a lot. I'll be a married woman in four months' time. That's the end of my freedom ... my life. I thought maybe if Tomo and I got to know each other, he might be willing to help me somehow.'

She felt her shoulders sag. 'But the more I think about it, the more I think time's too short - and why should he help me anyway?'

Marie smiled sympathetically. 'I understand. Take my advice; live for the moment. If you like him so much - go to him; don't have any regrets for the rest of your life. Bertrand need not know anything; it'll stay our little secret.'

. . .

Monique filled a bucket with warm water, threw in a sponge and picked up a towel. Marie was right ... this was her moment.

Carrying the bucket and towel, she walked past Tomos, beckoning him to follow her out through the main door.

Mystified, he followed her to a small round mud brick hut at the far end of the yard.

'It's the original house, used when the main house was being built,' she whispered.

Once inside she placed the bucket on the broken concrete floor. The roof was fully open to the night sky, the original thatch long gone, the small indoor arena bathed in the radiance of a full moon already visible after the passing squall.

She closed the wooden door behind them and turned to smile at him, the contours of her face highlighted by the soft light from above.

'Let me do this for you ... you're a very special man to me ... in more ways than you know.'

She walked slowly across to Tomos who didn't move or speak. Putting her arms around his neck, she looked into his eyes and kissed him gently, hearing his breath catch in his throat as his body tensed.

She slowly undressed him until he stood naked in the middle of the floor. At the first touch of the wet sponge he flinched, then looked up at the night sky savouring the moment as she took her time in bathing him, his youthful body now gold from months of African sun. He drew deep shuddering breaths as he returned her caresses, unfastening her dress and letting it drop to the floor. No words were spoken; the intimacy developing into mutual desire and need.

Time passed in a sensual blur ... nothing else mattered but the here and now. Passions ruled as they became completely immersed in their pleasure of each-other. It was the most special of times - something Monique knew she would cherish forever.

She left first, her mind and heart still racing with the echoes of physical love. In the lounge she winked at Marie who was alone watching television. When Tomos entered a few moments later, she saw him blush as Marie looked him up and down.

'The clothes fit you well, Tomo'. I hope you're hungry. Knowing my husband, he'll bring back far too much to eat.'

'Oh, I'm hungry Marie - very much so.' He nodded at the television, 'Who's playing? I didn't know you liked football.'

Marie laughed, 'I'm a strange woman; I love my football ... It's France versus Germany tonight. Sit down and watch. One of the French players was born right here in Ouagadougou, so I'm hoping he can score.'

Bertrand returned with a takeaway of rice and meat. They ate, plates on laps, watching the football. It had been a long stressful day and Monique began to feel more and more tired, the conversation faltering as the evening wore on. She was sitting next to Tomos, and eventually her head rolled onto his shoulder as she dozed.

Bertrand noticed, and stood up. 'I think it's time we all went to bed ... too much food and drink. I know I'll sleep well tonight.'

Monique brushed her teeth in the bathroom. It had been a wonderful day and she hadn't wanted to spoil it by spilling her bad news. She caught sight of her reflection in the mirror. Her image looked older and wiser than she felt.

The day had gone so well. If the next was half as good, maybe she *did* have a future after all.

28

Saif parked his silver Audi against the kerb near the end of Byron Street in Pontyafon. He glanced up and down the rows of houses each side of the road before his gaze came to rest on number five. He looked contemptuously through the rain-lashed windscreen at the front of the grubby little terrace house; one grey hovel in a line of grey hovels, all strung along like shabby clothing hung to dry under a washed-out sky.

The locals must be crazy to choose to live in such a place. He liked that; the concept nicely complemented his preconcieved sense of superiority.

Outside of the car's warm interior the wind gusted and swirled, peppering the windscreen and side windows, the tiny droplets of water sparkling in the feeble sunshine. The watery sunlight marked the passing of the latest in a series of early summer showers. The Welsh climate was more than living up to its reputation for rain, being unusually cool and wet for the time of year, even for Wales.

Saif often wished himself back in the heat of the Gulf of Oman. He inwardly smirked at the realisation that he soon might be, once he'd successfully carried out this latest assignment.

He quickly ran through the proposed routine in his mind, simple - but sufficient to fool a couple of old folk. A shiver of resentment ran through him; he didn't mind lying, he could do that all day long if it suited him. It was being ordered to do the bidding of Al-Hazbar that rankled. He didn't care to admit it, but like so many others he was just too scared to refuse his bidding.

With a grunt he zipped up his expensive sheepskin fleece, stepped down from the car and a moment later rang the doorbell.

A smell of homely cooking wafted through the front door, which was opened by a short stocky man boasting a thick mane of grey hair and great bushy eyebrows.

Saif by contrast was tall and olive skinned, with a mop of black hair and dark eyes that radiated friendly warmth. He drew himself up to his full six-foot height and gave a wide cheery smile before speaking.

'Please excuse me, but am I addressing Mister Gwyn Morgan, the father of Tomos Morgan?'

'You are indeed. And who might you be?'

'Please forgive me for not warning you of my impending visit, but I only had your address, not your telephone number. My name is Saif. I represent the Ministry of Water in Oman, Tomos's old employer.'

He was confident his words, spoken in perfect English, radiated sincerity.

'Really? You'd better come in out of the rain.'

Gwyn called for assistance as he showed Saif into the dry warmth of the living room.

'Beth! We have a visitor here ... about Tomos.'

Saif eyed the middle-aged lady that walked in carrying two plates laden with joints of meat. She carefully placed the food on a wooden dining table already laid out with cutlery, before approaching.

Gwyn introduced them. 'This is my wife, Beth. Beth - this is Saif, from Oman.'

'A pleasure to meet you, Beth.' Saif flashed his best whitest smile as he offered his hand to the slim bespectacled woman who stepped forward, her eyes bright with interest.

He looked around the small room and waved despairingly at the laden table. 'Ah, I hadn't realised you were about to eat. How very inconvenient! Would you like me to come back another time?' He was certain he sounded genuinely concerned at the timing of his visit.

'No, no - not a problem at all; please take a seat. Would you like a cup of tea?' Beth replied hurriedly, waving towards a comfortable looking leather armchair.

'Have you heard from Tomos? Is he alright?' Gwyn interceded.

'Oh ... he's not here? No tea, thank you, Mrs Morgan. How very unfortunate, I was so hoping to meet him. You see I bring good news. As I said, I represent his old employer, the Ministry of Water.'

As he took his place in the armchair, Saif noted the brief exchange of glances between husband and wife. Good, he had their full attention. 'You see, I'm not sure why Tomos left his post, or how much he's told you, but we would like him back. Our work at the Ministry has continued in his absence but is not yet complete. The message has come down from the minister himself that we'd like him to return to finish off the great work he was doing there.'

It was Gwyn who replied. 'Well, he left because he wanted a change. Perhaps if he'd been told at the time he was doing a good job, he might've stayed.'

Beth glanced reproachfully at her husband. 'Oh Gwyn, leave it. Let's hear what the gentleman has to say.'

Saif threw her a grateful smile. 'It's all very simple. I have been asked to contact him to see if he would like his old job back. We are even prepared to increase his salary, naturally all expenses paid as well. If he's not here, all I need are his contact details.'

Beth took up the initiative.

'Tomos is in Africa ... but from what he's told us, it's not working out too well for him over there so he'd definitely be interested in hearing about his old job. In fact, thinking about it ... yes, I'm sure he would really want to know what you have to say.'

'Splendid, do you have any contact details for him? An address or telephone number perhaps?'

'We don't have a proper address. He's staying with someone in Ouagadougou in Burkina Faso. Unfortunately we don't have a telephone number either – he calls us when he can from a public phone,' Gwyn admitted glumly.

'He's helping the king with his farm,' Beth exclaimed proudly. 'That's the big king who lives in a palace in the capital city. Tomos was always willing to help others,' she added impulsively.

'Well now, who would have guessed that? Your son is clearly a talented and resourceful man. Ideally the Ministry would like him back as soon as possible. I'll recheck to see just how long they are prepared to wait; today was only to ask about his availability. I think it best if I get back in touch with you when I have a few more details to pass on to Tomos.' He paused, before adding, 'Hmm, thinking about it, it's probably not even worth mentioning my visit to him until I can confirm what the minister would like to do next.'

'Did you know our boy, in Oman?' Gwyn asked curiously.

'Regrettably no, I'm merely an employee of our government; in this case acting on behalf of the Ministry. Well …' He stood up before any more awkward questions could come his way. 'I won't keep you good people from your delicious lunch any longer. If you will please excuse me, I have to get back to London immediately.'

He tried not to laugh out loud as he walked back to the Audi. He waved a last goodbye to the ignorant old folk standing respectfully in their doorway, before driving out of the village. Two miles down the road he pulled over and retrieved a large mobile phone from the glove compartment. They were the latest gadget, all the rage back home. He wanted to laugh again at the thought that Tomos's parents probably didn't even know such devices existed. He thumbed through the short list of contacts until he found the name of Rashid Al-Hazbar. With luck, the information he'd just learned would be sufficient to allow the infidel to be found. Over there life was cheap, it would be relatively easy to deal with him.

As he dialled he smirked again, this time at the image of the little terrace, home to the vulnerable parents. There was more than one way to inflict vengeance and suffering; and his employer had no mercy whatsoever.

29

Jerome Zongo scowled as he paid the young woman whose services he'd just used. Life had been one long struggle since he'd been hounded out of the army. Back then he'd commanded respect. When that wasn't enough his position always allowed him to get his way, naturally that included any woman in his charge.

With the prostitute dismissed, he showered, dressed, and discreetly left the gloomy hotel stepping into an equally gloomy street. It was early evening, emphasised by the fact that even the combined power of the cheap lighting fronting the seedy bars in this poorer part of town struggled to outshine the moon and stars.

At the end of the street he turned into one of the quieter joints, Le bar de Paris. Inside there was no sign of any of his small circle of friends. Choosing to sit alone in a corner, he ordered a beer, sat back, and surveyed the rest of the clientele with contempt.

What did any of these wasters know of real life? The army was hard. He was hard - he had to be. Sure, he'd had privileges, but he'd earned them through hard work and discipline. The silver spoon brigade was the worst - they'd never known hardship. These idiots would never even have survived his childhood. *Hateful, worthless, think they're noble pricks.*

Anger and bitterness welled up inside as he recalled his ejection from the army by those he was utterly opposed to. The right wing had won again; everything he and his comrades had fought for had been swept aside as if they'd never existed. With the new government had come the witch-hunt for known socialists like himself. Hateful retribution for actual and perceived wrongs was particularly swift and savage against those from the armed forces.

Zongo shuddered. His drink arrived and was quickly poured, experience having taught the barmaid this particular customer was not to be kept waiting. He drank deeply, his fist tightening around the emptying glass as he fought the anger. Luckily he'd been warned to go AWOL just in time. Apparently, the new Deputy Minister for Finance was personally after his head.

Why the hell had a so-called socialist cabinet put a known capitalist into such a powerful position? It belied belief, and it meant he had to pay the price for carrying out his orders. OK, he accepted he'd done some bad things, but only to teach the protected the harsh realities of life. They should thank him for having educated them.

He'd recently discovered that the deputy minister who was after him, Gaston Tapsoba, had had a daughter in his section. He remembered her clearly, the only woman who'd ever dared refuse him. It must have been that same bitch who'd informed on him, kick-starting the formal inquiry which could yet lead to his court martial and imprisonment - if he was caught. This Gaston and his wretched daughter might cost him everything he'd worked so hard for over the years.

Zongo knew the charges against him: rape and cruelty to two women. He barely remembered the rape victim - she was just one of many. He easily recalled the other; it was Gaston's own privileged bitch of a daughter who'd repeatedly spurned his advances. He hadn't even touched her, and now she must have used her father's influence to force him out of the army - to have him hunted down like an animal; the inexcusable indignity. He'd been reliably informed that it was Gaston's signature on the arrest warrant. Getting caught meant a life sentence. Unthinkable! Now the same uptight snob was betrothed to the king, no doubt chasing further privilege and power. It was all so unfair.

The grudge he held against the woman, Monique - he remembered her name - was nothing compared to the burning hatred he held for her father. Gaston Tapsoba was the source of his downfall. He had been keeping tabs on him; he already knew where he lived and something of his activities. If an opportunity for revenge should ever present itself, he would be ready. He had sworn that.

Zongo finished his drink and was about to leave when Koné entered the bar.

Yousef Koné, an ex-army colleague, was a man feared and detested almost as much as Zongo. Like himself, Koné's support for socialism was no secret and he'd also left the army in a hurry.

Zongo signalled his presence and Koné joined him in the corner.

'I've been looking for you ... got some news,' Koné grunted.

'Tell me.'

'I've just come from the Hotel Independence. Someone's turned up you might be interested in.'

Zongo waited impatiently. Koné often hung out in the bigger hotels hoping to meet some rich tourist he could take advantage of. Like many Africans, he was multi-lingual.

Unlike Zongo he was also capable of being charming when there was something to be gained. He was good at fleecing tourists, offering them anything from girls to guided tours.

"Be friendly - chat to them - find out what they want; then charge them whatever they can afford. It's simple really," he once divulged.

'There's a couple of Arabs just come over from the Gulf somewhere. You know Arabs - easy rich pickings. Naturally we got talking and they were only too eager to tell me what they were after.'

'Well, get on with it.'

'Some white guy ... I thought nothing of it, until they mentioned the guy's British and is working the king's land.'

Zongo sat bolt upright.

'Thought that might get your attention ... The only Britisher I know of, is the one rumoured to be seeing that bitch from your old camp. You know, the one you caught stealing - she was royalty, wasn't she? The Arabs were sure about his connection to the king, so reckon that nails him. Anyway I told them I thought I knew him, and would confirm by tomorrow. I've got his name ... Tomos Morgan. Mean anything to you?'

Zongo carefully voiced his thoughts. 'The name ...? No, it doesn't.' He frowned. 'But you're right ... I've heard of the Brit on the king's farm too ... but no idea what he's called. Yes, it must be him, can't be anyone else. Did they say what business they had with him?'

'No, but I got the feeling they don't like him. Listen – they've got money, lots of it. If we play our cards right, I'm sure there's something in it for us.'

'Hmm, you've done well. I'll go and meet these Arabs. With luck, it sounds like we might be able to help each other.'

'Right ... I'm telling you this because I thought you might already have a connection. They were *my* contact first, so make sure you don't forget my usual cut if you make a deal.'

Zongo's mind went into overdrive: Koné was right - if the Britisher *was* the same one he'd heard about, who knew where it could lead. A good payment for information ought to be the very least to be milked from a few gullible Arabs.

. . .

Taking Koné's place, Jerome Zongo met Rashid Al-Hazbar the following evening. From the hotel lobby, he was shown to an expensive suite by an older Arab who introduced himself as Malik. Inside the plush apartment Zongo critically studied his host, a tall goateed man who strode purposefully over to welcome him.

Al-Hazbar was dressed immaculately in what looked like an expensive tailored suit, the epitome of a successful businessman.

'Welcome ... thank you Malik, I can look after our guest from now on.' Malik was politely waved out of the room by his superior.

'Mr Zongo? I'm Rashid Al-Hazbar. You're very welcome - please make yourself comfortable. Your colleague Yousef said he might send someone else to help me. I'm afraid I don't speak French, are we OK to talk in English?'

'Yes, I speak English. I worked in Ghana in my youth before my army days.'

'Ex-army, eh? Excellent, exactly what I need. Can I offer you a drink? Take your pick: whiskey, beer or non-alcoholic if you prefer?' Al-Hazbar pointed at the suite's mini-bar.

'Maybe later, if there's something to celebrate. Let's not waste time. Just what is it you want?'

Al-Hazbar's features hardened. 'Right then, I have some unfinished business with a certain Tomos Morgan. I pay very well for what I want... tell me ... just how far are you willing to go?'

. . .

Zongo had quickly realised Al-Hazbar was not as gullible as he first hoped. To agree terms for him to kill Tomos, he'd been forced to admit much of his past army experience, something he was uncomfortable with. On the flip side, his lie about being personally acquainted with certain people working alongside Tomos had helped his cause; a handsome fee for his services having been agreed. In fact the deal was better than anything he could have dreamed of. With the huge payment promised for the execution of the outsider, he would be able to afford to emigrate; start a new life, a life without having to continually look over his shoulder. He was surprised to find the notion of committing murder did not horrify him at all - quite the reverse, he could feel the adrenalin pumping at the mere thought of it.

After sealing the deal, he got busy. Al-Hazbar had stipulated the job had to be finished within two weeks. Zongo guessed he must be planning to leave the country after that.

Al-Hazbar seemed confident Tomos was working on the Royal Farm. Zongo immediately confirmed this by going there himself and speaking to some of the labourers. He also made certain he understood all the unmarked boundaries as well as the paths preferred by Tomos on his rounds.

Next, he took a day to drive to a remote spot in the bush. There he dug out a cache of arms he'd buried before quitting the army. Many others had done the same. In times of political uncertainty it was sensible planning to have recourse to weaponry, should it be needed. He retrieved his Russian AK47 sniper rifle and a belt of ammunition before reburying the other items. All that remained now was to pick the place and time, something which needed great care. That apart, he was ready.

30

By mid August the rains had turned the savanna into myriad shades of green. All life thrived, but it was the insects that truly ruled both land and air. Flies were everywhere and no-one - human or beast - was able to escape for more than seconds from their insistence of continually crawling over body and face. For every poor farm labourer working the land each and every day, flies were the crowning misery of their hardship.

Tomos suffered along with his co-workers. The prospect of another day enduring the sticky heat and orifice-loving flies awaited him as he rode to the king's farm on Sanou's moped. Only two months remained to the harvest - then he'd be off home.

The implications of that were clear. Leaving Africa meant leaving Monique unless she came with him. They had started meeting in secret at Sabine's house a couple of times a week. The secrecy was at Monique's request. When pushed for a reason, she had admitted her social status implied a marriage to an equal from her tribe. She had pleaded with him to help her escape such a marriage before it could be arranged, the secrecy of their own relationship she deemed necessary for family honour and to maintain her value as a bride.

'I hate it, but if I do get married some day, then my monetary worth is very important,' she had confided.

The idea of Monique having a financial value made Tomos feel sick. Her situation seemed so unfair and she'd been so distressed he'd agreed to do whatever she asked. On top of which, he had to admit he was beginning to fall in love. He shouldn't get involved any further, he knew that. Not now, not with all his other problems; but love was mighty persuasive, a force powerful enough to choose its own destiny. If he could just obtain a visa for her, she could leave the country and be free to make her own choices in life.

He shut his mind to the possibility of being part of Monique's future; his immediate duty still lay with his promise to help the king.

Arriving at the farm, he parked behind a rough wicker shelter. The thin shade provided would be just enough to prevent the plastic seat of the moped becoming too hot to sit on for the return journey.

All around him the millet was nearing full maturity, the feathery stalked spikes - already as tall as a man - nodded gently in the weak breezes that ruffled across the savanna. He intended walking around the various plots to inspect the crops, but was distracted by a smartly dressed elderly man who was being directed towards him by Adama.

Tomos held out his hand in welcome as the man approached. He wasn't that old close-up, he realised; it was the thin torso and shuffling gait that aged him prematurely.

They shook hands, but the newcomer wasn't smiling. 'Mr Morgan?' he enquired in slow English with a strong African accent.

'Yes, that's me. It's OK, we can speak in French if you prefer,' Tomos replied in a friendly voice.

'Very well, thank you,' the switch to French was effortless. 'I am Mr Tapsoba, Monique's father. I believe you may have heard of me?'

Tomos drew a careful breath. This was something he hadn't been expecting. Monique had told him a little about her father. He knew he was called Gaston and was highly unlikely to approve of his daughter seeing anyone, especially if they weren't of high social status from his own tribe.

'I'm very pleased to meet you sir, I was hoping we could meet soon.' He doubted the lie sounded convincing.

'Is that so? Well we meet now, and we have some talking to do. Walk with me, I have lots to say.'

With a sinking feeling Tomos fell into the slower step of the older man. On either side of them the millet stalks continued to bob their bearded heads as if acknowledging their passing. Ahead of them, and beyond the last field, a straggly copse of stunted acacia marked the boundary on that side of the farm.

Gaston Tapsoba wasted no time. 'I have heard rumours of you and Monique being together, so please do not insult me by denying it. You do not deny it, do you?'

'No, Mr Tapsoba I do not. In fact I ...'

The old man waved him silent. 'Later ... you need to listen to me first.'

The two men walked on in silence while Mr Tapsoba gathered his thoughts. 'Now you seem like a good man to me, Mr Morgan, so let me begin by saying that what has happened cannot be undone, and I am prepared to draw a line under it. I know my daughter better than anyone, especially how impetuous and stubborn she can be. I'm sure she is at least as much to blame as you.'

'Mr Tapsoba, please ...' Tomos began, only to be waved aside for a second time.

'Before you speak there is one thing I have to ask.'

The old man stopped, turning his head to look him squarely in the eye. 'Are you aware that Monique is due to be married to the king? Has she told you about this? The wedding is due to take place immediately after the harvest.'

Tomos stared in disbelief as a wave of nausea swept through him. He imagined he might have been asked to leave the country, or even to marry Monique to avoid scandal or some other such thing - but not this. Was he making it up to scare him off? Surely it couldn't be true; if it was, why hadn't Monique told him?

The two men continued to stare at each other in silence, one waiting for an answer, the other too stunned to speak.

Without warning, Gaston suddenly and inexplicably collapsed backwards - an invisible shove from an invisible hand pitching him forcefully to the ground. The sound of a gunshot rang out a split second later.

Tomos stared at the crimson fingers spreading across the front of Gaston's white cotton shirt, his body lying motionless in the dirt. He'd been shot!

The realisation triggered his muscles in a flash, instinct spurring him to a sprint for cover into the nearest field of millet, his body a lithe blur. The unmistakeable retort of a second gunshot assaulted his ears just as he reached cover. The bullet whizzed past him at head height, whistling harmlessly into the midst of the leafy screen. Monique's father had been shot! It was no accident – whoever it was had meant it. Now he intended to shoot him, too!

Anger coursed through him. Unarmed or not, he'd catch the cowardly bastard if he could. He was sure the shots had come from the direction of the acacia trees, directly ahead of where he and Gaston had been standing. He stumbled as he turned to fight his way through the thick stalks, trying to head in the general direction of the acacias.

'C'mon man - run!' he snarled to himself. He frantically beat away the scratchy leaves obstructing his path. The millet might be shielding him, but the stalks felt more like prison cell bars preventing him reaching his target. The plants thinned and disappeared, replaced by a stretch of open ground beyond which stood the thicket.

Too late!

A car thickly covered in dust was parked the other side of the trees. Even as he sprinted across the intervening patch of ground, it growled into life and sped away.

Tomos watched it go, seething with anger. 'What the hell was *that* all about?'

. . .

Zongo was ecstatic as he accelerated away from the scene of his crime, despite missing with his second shot. Like a good soldier he'd laid his plans well, picked the ideal spot for the ambush and fired off a perfect first round. When he'd recognised Gaston walking towards him, it was as if the old man was being delivered to him as a gift. He immediately realised this was likely to be his best chance to exact revenge on his persecutor and remove the source of charges against him, both at the same time. The opportunity had been too tempting, so he'd switched his primary target from Tomos to Gaston.

It was a shame the Britisher had got away. Still, once Malik had reported what he was capable of, Al-Hazbar would be forced to accept that he was still the best man for the job. He would arrange another opportunity to get his quarry. He did not intend to give up on the rest of the money.

He ignored the surly unspeaking Arab next to him, and grimaced. The royal farm was a surprisingly busy place; every second in its vicinity increased the risk of being caught. It was the reason why he'd preferred to take a solitary shot rather than use rapid machine-gun fire - a single shot was much less likely to draw attention. Unfortunately Malik had panicked, and in his haste to get away the fool had grabbed him just as he'd pulled the trigger on his second shot, causing him to miss.

For the drive back to Ouagadougou, Zongo followed a long circuitous route that would see them re-enter the city from a completely different direction. His application and prudence were already paying off, he was getting away with murder.

Gaston was dead. He was certain of it. That was the most important thing. He felt a great weight had been lifted from his soul. Redemption was sweet indeed.

31

Gaston Tapsoba was declared dead by the investigating military police. The official statement was made immediately after they'd examined and covered the body, concealing it from the fascinated eyes of the loitering labourers. Gaston had been a popular figure; the whole situation was now highly inflammatory. Being a government minister the first assumption by police and public alike was that he must have been murdered in a politically motivated act.

Once the police learned Gaston had come to speak to Tomos, he was interrogated relentlessly, held in custody at the farm until sundown that afternoon. His statement to the police had been a simple one. He explained how he'd escaped by stumbling through the millet, emerging just in time to see a car speed away. His account, he knew, would be backed up by the several farm workers who'd simultaneously arrived on the scene. He just hoped they didn't conclude from his dishevelled, wild-eyed state that he was the culprit, running from the crime. His bare arms bleeding with scratches from his rampage through the sea of sharp leaves would not help his case.

Together, he and the workers had confirmed the awful truth of Gaston's death, a bullet hole clearly visible in the centre of his chest. The sight was one he would never forget; the sandy earth turned black-red from the blood oozing from the inert body.

The police made him repeatedly run through his movements up to the time of the shooting, even re-enact Gaston's final walk through his beloved fields. It proved particularly awkward when he was questioned as to why Gaston had come to the farm that day seeking to speak to him. Revealing his relationship with Monique would have meant incriminating himself with a possible motive for murder. After all, with Gaston gone he would have a better chance of marrying his daughter. Instead, he stated that Gaston had been shot before having a chance to say *why* he'd come to see him.

He also refrained from mentioning the second shot which had been aimed at him, afraid that it would have complicated matters and detained him even longer. He was convinced it was only because he told the police he was working at the king's invitation and was staying as a guest of the influential Arzuma Sanou that they finally agreed to release him.

Freed, but still confused over motives and worried for Monique, he stopped at the first bar he came across on his way back to town. He unconsciously scratched at the mosquito bites covering his arms while he waited for his drink. He'd been made to sit under a tree during his interrogation where his already red raw arms made an irresistable target for the blood sucking insects. He needed a moment alone to think and decide what to do next. Monique would have been told by now, and he could only imagine what she and her family were going through. Would they blame him for Gaston's death? Should he stay away, or go and offer his support?

He understood that Gaston was involved in politics, and guessed that might be cause enough to be hated by those with opposing views. But what about that second shot? It had been fired after Gaston went down, so *he* must have been the target. Who would want him dead? Al-Hazbar of course! Who else?

But why shoot Gaston? Maybe Gaston was the main target and the assassin had tried to kill him as a possible witness. Then again, maybe he had been the target and Gaston was shot by accident.

He slowly shook his head. None of it made any sense. His beer arrived and he downed it in one, unusually oblivious to its taste. He determined to see Monique as soon as possible. Whether she would blame him or not, he felt obliged to tell her what he knew. After that, things would be out of his hands.

And with all that had gone on, there hadn't been time to get his head around the bombshell of Monique marrying the king. He simply had to find out the truth about that.

32

At Sabine's, Tomos pleaded with Pascal to go and tell Monique he wanted to see her. Sabine as always made him feel welcome while he waited; her eyes almost popping out at hearing his news.

He stayed in the yard slowly resigning himself to not seeing Monique that evening. The street outside had fallen quiet and his watch read 10:45 when at last he recognised the drone of her moped. Sprinting over, he opened the gate, and watched her apprehensively as she rode in and dismounted. They hugged without speaking, taking comfort from the closeness before stepping back, both unsure where to start.

Sabine briefly appeared, also hugged Monique, the soft words between them conveying the shocked sympathy of a close friend. She glanced back at Tomos. 'I expect you two want to be alone for a minute, I'll go fetch something to eat,'

They sat together on the concrete step outside the front door and whispered in low, hushed tones.

'No-one can believe the news, we've had so many visitors to the house, everyone from kilometres around coming to say sorry or find out what's happened. Lots of public wailing - especially by mama, that's how it is in Africa – there was no way I could've got away any sooner.'

'I know, but you're here now, that's what matters.'

Monoique sniffed and rubbed her eyes. 'I'm so tired, but had to come and see you. It's good we meet here, mama is so upset I don't think she can take any more. I'm afraid she might blame you in some way, and where would that leave us?'

'I'm so sorry for you and your family. I can't believe what's happened. I want you to know I'm here for you; I'll do whatever I can to help.'

'I'm scared. Mama can barely speak, and Nadine has locked herself away in her bedroom. I have to go back to them ... can't stay long.'

'Yes, of course, you must do that ...'

'It's all my fault he's gone. If it hadn't been for me, Papa would never have gone to see you. My fault he's laying cold and dead,' Monique's whisper was hoarse.

'No, it's not your fault. You're not to blame. Whoever did this had their reasons.'

'Tell me what happened - all of it. I need to know.'

Tomos did as he was asked. Monique recoiled at hearing he'd also been targeted.

'Oh no - I'm so sorry. Are you OK?'

'I'm fine. I know it's not the time ... but I have to ask you something. Your father told me you're engaged to the king. I thought I was hearing wrong - is it true? Why didn't you tell me?'

'How could I? You would never have even looked at me. No man would. I'd already decided you were the one for me - I couldn't jeopardise everything by telling you too early.'

'I wouldn't have let you down; you must realise how I feel about you.' He took a deep breath. 'Well, there's also something I haven't told you about me.' He was interrupted by Sabine calling them inside to eat. Neither had an appetite, but it seemed churlish to refuse her kindness.

Over the simplest meal of millet and tao sauce, he revealed his history in Oman: how a businessman called Al-Hazbar had sworn revenge on him. Monique and Sabine listened in numbed silence. Monique looked in despair at him, as if her world was in danger of complete collapse.

'I was hounded by an officer when I did my National Service,' she offered sympathetically, 'so I have an idea what it's like.'

'I don't know if the shooting was aimed at me - or your father. I'm tempted to think he was the target, and I was just a witness they didn't want hanging around.'

'If Papa *was* the target we'll probably never know who killed him or why,' Monique concluded bitterly.

Tomos shook his head. 'How will you and Nadine manage without him?'

Monique gave a stiff shrug of her shoulders. 'Probably my maternal grandfather will take care of us. Times will be tough for sure, especially for mother.'

They talked for a few moments longer, then a last hug at the gate before they parted: Monique to her grieving family and Tomos to his lodgings.

He felt little relief at being spared a similar ending to Gaston; his overriding emotion was still one of anger. He had only one thought in mind - to find out who was responsible and bring them to justice.

33

Midnight had passed by the time Tomos arrived at his lodgings. Arzuma Sanou was waiting for him and insisted they sit in the living room. No-one else was about, so he supposed his landlord had told his wife and daughter not to disturb them.

The Royal Advisor for Magic clearly wanted to talk. He got straight to the point.

'I've been at the palace most of the afternoon. The king demanded to know every detail about a murder on his own farm - a murder of one of his closest friends. I had to admit ignorance of the matter - you cannot imagine how humiliating that was.'

'Sorry to hear that,' Tomos replied disconsolately.

'The king has ordered me to use every means to find the culprit. You were there. Tell me everything that happened ... leave nothing out.'

'Sure, but I've already told it all to the police, several times.'

'The police won't find the murderer ... I will. You're already in trouble by the way ... we've all heard the gossip of you and Gaston's daughter. Don't you know she's intended as a royal bride? The king himself invited you into the royal circle; your actions threaten his credibility.'

'I swear until today I didn't know she was in an arranged marriage. In fact, that's why Gaston was at the farm ... that's what he came to tell me .. now you know something the police don't'.

'Carry on, I'm listening.'

'We were walking together when he asked me if I knew about Monique and the king, which I didn't by the way. Next thing, he was dead. That's it. As soon as he finished talking he was shot. I chased after the murderer but he got away. I did see a car driving off ... so dirty I couldn't even tell what colour it was, let alone read a licence number. I'm sorry, that's all I have to say.'

'You never saw who shot Gaston?'

'No, not even a glimpse.'

'You know, Tomo; I have a network of contacts throughout our tribal lands as well as the city. When you first met the king, I made enquiries in Koutatenga about how you came to be in our country. It seems you had a few problems elsewhere ... someone's been trying to kill you ... am I right? It seems to me they might have followed you here to finish the job.'

'I have considered the possibility,' Tomos conceded.

'Good ... tell me more about it. I need to follow up all leads.'

Since Sanou was already aware of his problem there was little point in trying to hide his past. Relenting, Tomos gave the barest bones of his history with Al-Hazbar and his oath of revenge.

'I don't see how he could've tracked me across Africa to Burkina Faso.'

'I'll soon find out if he's involved,' asserted Sanou. 'It's inconceivable that such a desecrating act as murder on the king's land go unpunished; the whole ethos, mystique and respect of the royal dynasty could be tarnished.'

'I have an idea ... we can work together. Let's use your contacts to find out if Al-Hazbar is in the country. I can identify him of course. If he's here we can confront him and discover the truth.'

'We can rule him out if he's not here, I suppose. I'm not interested in your past - only in finding out what's happening here and now. No-one gets away with murdering a royal Advisor; I'll use all my powers to find the guilty man.'

'Go on.'

Sanou smiled. 'Tonight I shall appeal to my ancestors for help; rest assured they will tell me what to do.'

'I'd like to know what you decide.'

'You will. Now, what about Monique Tapsoba? The king isn't pleased you've been seeing her. It doesn't reflect well on me either, so I will ask you one more time for your own good, and hers, let the relationship go no further. If you carry on, it will end in tears for both of you.'

Tomos stayed silent. His dreams of a future with Monique looked doomed, and what the future held for her, he couldn't even bring himself to ponder.

34

Tomos saw neither Monique or Sanou for the next two days. Frustrated with the lack of action, his hopes of tracking down the murderer through Sanou's contacts also faded until late one afternoon when he wheeled the moped into the Royal Advisor's sumptuous garden. His host was idly swinging in a hammock slung next to the bike stand.

'Ah Tomo, have some papaya.' Sanou climbed down and handed out a piece of fruit. 'Good news at last.'

'Thanks, what's up?'

'News on your Arab, of course: what else?'

'Your ancestors helped, then?'

'Indeed they did. What I really want is proof of identity of the killer to take to the king. That would be the first and most important step in restoring everyone's faith in the monarchy. We may be about to find out if your businessman is involved.'

'So, he's here? He must've been behind all this. Why else would he be in the country? If he's to blame it means Gaston must've been shot by accident ... can't see why else he'd be attacked.'

'You realise you're not helping yourself by saying that. If true, it means you brought this problem here.'

'I know, I was hoping it wasn't the case. So, what's your plan?'

'Well, understand this. I have contacts everywhere - all from my tribe, and all of them loyal to me. The government is stupid enough to believe their spy network is the biggest and best - rubbish! It's mine! Now then, my contacts tell me that

Rashid Al-Hazbar and a colleague called Malik, checked out of their hotel yesterday. However my people at the airport confirm only Al-Hazbar left the country on an Egypt Air flight bound for Cairo; the obvious route for anyone heading to the Gulf. That means his assistant is still around somewhere. Finding him was tricky. Still, a Gulf Arab's not a local, and I now know exactly where he is.'

'Right. Arzuma listen ... I'm impressed, but I've got business with him. I need to see him first. Where exactly is he staying?'

'Not so fast. I too, have business with him. We shall go and visit him together. With luck you will see how the ancestors - or magic if you prefer - will help us both achieve our aims.'

'What d'ya mean?'

'Ha, I've used the old ways in my role of Advisor for Magic, something I rarely do. Officially I have ultimate tribal rights over not just magic - which for my tribe is an ancient form of voodoo - but also traditional knowledge. I'm talking about ancestral knowledge gained and handed down through the ages from father to son. Anyway, the time is right; I was waiting for you. We need to leave immediately.'

Unusually it hadn't rained that day, and the earlier heat prevailed making the climate particularly hot and sticky. Even the breeze from the twenty minutes' ride to their destination offered no relief. By the time Tomos dismounted, he was coated in red dust from his shoes to the knees of his jeans. A ring of sweat had pooled around his cotton shirt above his trouser belt. Ignoring his discomfort, he took in his new surroundings.

They were in a part of town unfamiliar to him; the national football stadium they'd passed, now half a mile behind them, had been the last landmark he'd recognised. A sign reading Hotel Oasis in large welcoming letters arched above a wide entrance to the nearest building.

A youth in long, baggy shorts and grimy t-shirt was squatting outside the hotel's entrance. He strolled over to join them, bowing to Sanou. The lad's heavy pushbike seemed familiar. Looking more closely Tomos recognised the messenger who had previously guided him and the Koutatenga village chief to the royal palace.

The youth mumbled something to Sanou, who nodded and beckoned Tomos to join him. 'I am reliably informed that Al-Hazbar's colleague, Malik is staying here. He hasn't left his room all afternoon.'

Tomos's heart raced. 'About time ... let's go get some answers. One thing, though; if he's who I think he is, we should arm ourselves. I haven't forgotten he's already tried to kill me at least once.'

'I think he'll behave himself. You just watch ... it will be an interesting experience for you.'

'I'm *sure* it will,' Tomos muttered under his breath.

Inside the lobby they were met by a giant of a man, presumably the hotel owner. Solidly built as well as tall, his muscles bulged from beneath the vest adorning his torso. He respectfully greeted Sanou by name.

'This way please.' Keeping to the ground floor, he led them to a room at the end of a corridor leading from the lobby.

Tomos raised an eyebrow. Nailed to the top of the door frame was a crudely-carved wooden effigy dressed in an all-white Arab robe, the holding nail hammered right through the doll's midriff.

The burly hotel-owner unlocked the door and they pushed their way in.

Malik was lying on his bed. Far from immediately jumping up and attacking them, he simply rolled onto his side and squinted at them.

As Tomos suspected, Malik was the same man who'd pulled him from the wreckage in the wadi flood and then tried to kill him during the car chase along the beach in Oman. His face was only just recognisable. Puffed up cheeks, once swarthy, were now mottled with ugly grey blotches. Only the eyes were the same; a little more sunken into that deeply lined face but still filled with brooding malice. He was wheezing non-stop and dripping in sweat despite the air conditioning. The room stank of vomit - a trace of urine; maybe something stronger.

Sanou didn't wait for the old man to protest their forced entry.

'Hello Malik ... that is your name isn't it? Let me introduce myself ... Sanou. Some people call me a witchdoctor.'

Malik nodded weakly. His eyes, bloodshot under blackened hooded lids, shifted from Sanou to stare at Tomos. He showed no surprise his identity was known.

Too sick to care, Tomos surmised.

'You are unwell ... in pain? I expect you need help. Am I right?' Sanou prompted.

Malik slowly turned his attention back to the speaker. He was clutching his stomach, his pallid face running with beads of sweat. He spat out his words in short gasps. 'I've been poisoned - I know it. Have you come here to taunt me with your Englishman - or have you come to help?'

'You've been attacked by magic. It is my privilege to know such things; the proof is on your door. You know what I mean.'

Malik's replied with a loud groan. He leaned over the side of his bed and retched. Panting, he lay back; globules of dribble glistening as they rolled down his chin.

Sanou continued. 'You don't have much time. I know this magic - your stomach has already started to swell - that means you have only minutes until you die a very painful death. Only *I* can save you ... that is the truth, but everything in this world has a price. Mine is information. You tell me the real reason you came here and your connection to the shooting of a man at the royal farm, and I will save your life. Deal?'

'Save me first.'

'No, you can die here. Your life means nothing to me. It's up to you.'

Malik gave a great bellow of pain culminating in shallow rapid intakes of breath. Tomos was certain he had no option but to co-operate; he looked as though he was already most of the way towards an agonising death. Apart from his grossly enlarged stomach he appeared to be burning up, judging from the amount of sweat pouring off him.

Malik decided to talk. 'I came here with my employer, Rashid Al-Hazbar, to confront that cursed man beside you. An African helped us ... told us he was an ex-soldier. Instead of Morgan, he shot the old man. Nothing to do with me ... no idea why he did it, I think there was bad blood between them.'

'I see, and what's the name of this ex-soldier?'

'Help me ...'

'Name the ex-soldier.'

'Zongo. Jerome Zongo.'

'Where ...?'

'I don't know where he is, that's the truth. Now please help me!' Malik's voice rose in shrill desperation before being cut short by a convulsive fit of coughing and vomiting. He held his stomach with both hands as tears rolled down his grey cheeks.

Tomos could see the man's gut had ballooned to nearly double its size since their entry. Malik was staring death in the face.

Sanou looked on dispassionately. 'Your stomach is swelling fast ... not long left for you. Last question ... why did Al-Hazbar leave the country?'

'To avoid repercussions of course, but in truth we're both innocent I tell you!'

Tomos interrupted. 'So why are you still here? Did Al-Hazbar ask you to stay on and finish the job of killing me?'

Malik didn't answer. He lay back on his bed, eyes glazing over, staring fixedly at the ceiling.

He didn't need Malik to speak; it was obvious he must still be a target. Al-Hazbar had ordered his execution, but why had this Zongo shot Monique's father instead?

He fixed Sanou with a stare. 'You can't let him die. If you do, it'll be murder.'

'I have the name of the guilty man, that's all I came for.'

'Save him, or I go to the police.'

Sanou sighed. 'Don't worry. I never had the intention of killing him if he co-operated.'

Tomos watched fascinated as a small bottle of clear liquid was calmly produced from a pouch in the front of Sanou's smock, along with a package from his trouser pocket. Black powder from the package was poured into the bottle and vigorously shaken.

Sanou handed the bottle to their muscular aide and ordered him to ensure Malik drank it all. When the bottle was empty, he leaned over and shouted into the old man's ear.

'When you recover, make sure you leave the country by the end of the week, or else I promise you will never leave here alive. Understand?'

He looked over towards Tomos. 'C'mon, let's go. There's nothing more to learn here.'

Tomos was only too happy to leave the fetid smelling room. Neither of them spoke until they reached the street outside. The air was still warm with the gritty taste of suspended sand, but after the confines of Malik's room it felt fragrant and fresh. The short walk allowed him to clarify his thoughts.

'Would you mind explaining what happened back there? What's really wrong with him?'

'Later ... better we leave this place first.'

Sanou dropped a coin into the hands of the young messenger guarding his motorbike. He rode fast for the return trip back to his villa, pausing only for a red light. Later they sat on the veranda, and after his wife had brought them each a glass of chilled fresh pineapple juice, Tomos again challenged Sanou to explain events.

'It was all planned to get Malik to talk, to find out who shot Gaston.'

Tomos was grudgingly impressed. 'But how?'

'It's a secret potion known only to a very few. I arranged it. The recipe is ancient but if understood is very predictable. I know the symptoms and carry the cure. I have influence everywhere. It was easy to arrange for it to be added to his lunch.'

'You mean you deliberately poisoned this man? You could have killed him!'

Sanou shrugged. 'As I said, it's ancient tribal knowledge, as is the cure. He should survive.'

'Why did you mention *magic* to him instead of telling him the truth?'

'People all over the world have a deep fear of black magic. It was always more likely to get him to talk than either threats or direct violence. The voodoo doll on his door was part of the act, to get him thinking the worst as soon as possible. Voodoo is internationally recognised. When people fear black magic is being used against them, they always talk. Anyway, what's the problem? It worked, didn't it? Now we know a certain Jerome Zongo is the killer. Believe me, it's only a matter of time before I find him.'

He felt sick at hearing Sanou's words. Gaston's murder - now Malik's poisoning. Where would it all end?

Sanou must have sensed his anxiety. 'I'm not a bad man. It's my duty to discover the truth for the king. Don't feel sorry for Malik ... remember he came here to kill you. I know that now. He's fortunate I gave him the remedy.'

'I understand your reasons but don't like your methods; this was a police matter really. I'm going to move out tomorrow. I don't know where to, but I need to get away from all of this.'

'Fine with me, I'll inform the king. I'm sure it's not a problem after all that's happened. One thing - do not go to the police about what you have seen today. It won't help anyone if you do. Agreed?'

'Fine; I won't say anything. I don't really want to know anymore. This Jerome Zongo is your problem now, not mine.'

Sanou threw his head back and laughed loud enough to raise the dead. 'Ah Tomo, that is very funny! Very funny indeed! I rather think it is Mr Zongo who has the problem now that I know his name. A good day's business wouldn't you say?'

35

Tomos held true to his word and moved out the next day. Not even knowing where he was going to lodge next, he declined Sanou's offer of a lift, preferring to walk instead.

One thing was clear; he was determined to stick around to see the harvest through. There was also the quandry of Monique. Learning of her betrothal was a real shock and an even bigger disappointment. She had aroused feelings in him he was going to have to deny if there could not be a future for them together. He wasn't going to leave Africa until he knew for sure where they stood.

For the time being he needed somewhere to stay. He trudged in the general direction of the old town, his battered rucksack across his back. Despite all the recent upheavals he felt a certain sense of freedom at the idea of living alone, away from the watching eyes of the all-powerful Royal Advisor for Magic.

He bitterly resented his role in Monique losing her father. He should let her know what he'd learned, as well as telling her he was moving out. Circumstances still weren't right for a first visit. He thought of Sabine, he was assured of a friendly welcome there and she could let Monique know he needed to see her.

Despite the early hour, he arrived to find the whole household engaged in the laundry under the meagre shade of the lone mango tree. Sabine was standing next to a heap of clothes. Wielding a slab of soap she was furiously scrubbing away in a bucket of water. Her mother stood next to her busily rinsing in another bucket, the calloused knuckles of both women raw with the effort. Pascal had escaped with the lighter duty of hanging the washing to dry from a line stretched across the yard.

Tomos clapped his hands to announce his presence. Pausing in her work, Sabine called him to join them.

'I'm guessing you want Monique? Pascal, it must be your lucky day. I'm sure you'd rather go and find your sister than stay and work.'

Tomos grinned. 'Thanks Sabine. What can I do to help?'

'Nothing; wouldn't trust a man to do a woman's job!'

Tomos chuckled and pulled a face. 'OK ... I'll carry on with Pascal's work ... can't sit here doing nothing.'

By the time Pascal returned with Monique in tow, the laundry was done and both women had disappeared indoors.

Monique joined him under the mango tree, sharing their customary body hug. She stood back and looked at his rucksack on the ground. 'I see you've left then.'

'Yes, I've left ... wish I had earlier, but never mind that. How are you and your family holding up?'

'We're OK for the moment. I have to finalise plans for the funeral tomorrow, so can't stay long. It's at the cathedral starting at nine; you will come, won't you? I'd like to know you're there.'

'I will if you're sure, but I've been told to stop seeing you, and I don't want to make things harder for you than they already are.'

'Who said that? Sanou I suppose? Well, I want you there. You probably won't get a chance to see me anyway; I'll be sitting right at the front. First, though, we need to sort you out. Where are you planning on staying?'

'I don't know ... hotel I suppose.'

Monique bit her lip. 'No chance, let me check with Sabine. Wait here.'

Within minutes a beaming Sabine appeared at the doorway alongside Monique. Both re-joined him under the tree.

Monique gave one of her huge smiles, the first Tomos had seen in days. 'You can lodge here, better than wasting money in a hotel. Sabine and her Mama are only too pleased for you to stay.'

Tomos looked helplessly from one to the other. 'Are you sure Sabine? If so, I insist on paying my way.'

Monique interrupted. 'Good that's settled then. If you can pay a little, you'll be doing them a huge favour; money is always tight. I wish you could stay with me, but wounds are raw, and people talk.'

She took Tomos's hands in hers. 'There is something I have to ask you - and trust in God you'll help me.'

'Go on,' Tomos looked squarely into her eyes. 'I promise to help if I can, so whatever it is, don't worry.'

'OK, here goes. Yesterday I was summoned by the king. He's very upset about Papa, but said he still intends to take me as a bride to honour the memory of his friend.'

'So, that's it then. I was hoping he might have changed his mind.' Tomos took a deep breath. 'I take it you still don't have a say in the matter?'

'You know I don't want to marry him ... I want to be with *you*. This is what I want to ask you. Help me ... please. No-one else can.'

Tomos sat down. He needed to think. 'Oh God, I'm so sorry. What a mess all this is. You must know by now I want the same thing.'

'The wedding is to take place the week after the royal harvest,' she added in a small voice. 'That's only two months away.'

Tomos looked at her. She stood before him, a picture of defenceless beauty and so full of inner passion that his heart went out to her. He wanted her. He gently took her chin in his hand and tilted the sad lovely face towards his own. He brushed away the solitary tear on her cheek with his lips.

'It's OK. I've been waiting for the right moment to tell you just how strong my feelings are for you. It's true I've wanted you ever since I first saw you at the palace. Come back with me to Britain; I'll do whatever it takes to get you there, and help you start a new life.'

'I knew you'd help, you're a good man ... the best.' She drew in a big breath. 'I have a passport but no visa; will you help me get that?'

Tomos ran his hand through his hair. 'Of course, but I dont know if there's time. The nearest British Embassy is in the Ivory Coast, in Abidjan, and we would both have to go there. I'm not sure how these things work. Thinking about it, you won't even be allowed on the plane without a visa.'

'You're right,' Monique bit her lip. 'I'll probably need a visa to get into France first anyway as there's no direct flight to England.'

'Right, so here's the plan: You get a visa for France as soon as possible; you can do that here in Ouaga. Then straight after the harvest we go to Abidjan; get you a UK visa and fly back to Britain via Paris from there. How does that sound?'

'It sounds wonderful.' Monique flung her arms around his neck. 'My God ... Tomo, my aunt was right all along ... you really *are* my saviour.'

Tomos laughed. 'I don't know what you mean by that, but we'll have to keep this a secret. Having said that, will you say anything to your mam?'

'No, I shan't say a word to anyone. If I make it to England, I'll let her know what's happened; she'll stop me otherwise.'

Tomos hesitated. 'Fine, but we don't know how the king will react. I wish you could tell me there won't be any repercussions for your family.'

'No problem. Papa and the king were close. He might not be happy, but he'd never hurt any of us. In fact the opposite is true. Between the king and my other relatives, Mama and Nadine will be well looked after.'

'I hope you're right. Running away with me is definitely not going to please him; I reckon Sanou will go nuts as well.'

'Stuff them ... all of them!' Monique's eyes burned with anger. 'It's time these men caught up with the rest of the world. Tradition is one thing, but Africa needs democracy not subjugation of its people. Marriage should be about love, not some fancy whim on one side only. Don't you worry about the king; he's got plenty of wives already. He'll get himself more brides I'm sure, but I'll never be one - I'd rather die first!'

'It's alright, come here.' He took her in his arms, touched but not surprised by the strength of her spirit. Close up, he could feel the anger ebbing from her as she slowly relaxed, both taking comfort from the warmth of contact.

Eventually she broke free and smiled up at him. 'I have to go now, there's so much to do. I knew deep in my heart you'd support me; I'm sure we'll be fine.'

'Maybe I'll see you tomorrow at the cathedral.'

'Doubt it ... there'll be too many people. But please come, it'll be a big help knowing you are close by.'

'I'll go, I promise.'

He watched her leave. She looked so vulnerable as she sped off on her little moped. A wave of guilt washed over him as he reflected how he'd unwittingly brought so much suffering into her life. It was probably his fault her father was dead, so it was up to him to put things right. He was ready to do whatever it took. Poor Monique, why did the innocent always suffer the most?

• • •

He did as promised and attended the cathedral the next day, standing anonymously among the mourners behind the last row of chairs. The great church was already full to capacity by the time he arrived, the funeral having attracted a congregation of hundreds. Monique would be sitting somewhere at the front, but with every pew before him fully packed there was little chance of spotting her.

The service lasted all morning. Most of it was beyond his understanding; some texts were even read in Latin following the Roman Catholic liturgy. The regular worshippers were well used to long services and threw themselves into every hymn and prayer with gusto.

He stayed until the end. When he finally walked out, blinking in the strong midday sun, the sound of a thousand melodic voices from the final hymn continued to drum inside his head.

It had been a fitting tribute to Gaston. Now it was down to him to do something good for his daughter.

36

The day after the funeral Pascal dropped Tomos off at the royal farm where he was surprised to be greeted by a smiling Arzuma Sanou. The handshake he received was genuinely warm, making him wonder at the Advisor's continued good humour.

'Good news Mr Morgan, my contacts at the airport have confirmed the departure of Malik. You can relax now ... no more troubles, eh?'

Tomos allowed himself a sigh of relief. 'That *is* good news, and I sincerely hope that's the last I ever hear of him.'

Privately he remembered his vow to find Al-Hazbar once his work in Africa was complete; the promise never far from his mind.

'And the king wants to see you tomorrow morning. He has asked me to escort you to the palace.'

'Ah, OK. D'ya know why?'

Sanou shrugged. 'No, but you cannot refuse. Where do you want me to pick you up?'

Tomos described the nearest intersection to Sabine's. He wasn't keen to let Sanou know where he was staying just yet, even though it was more than likely he'd already discovered the fact for himself.

Walking his usual route through the fields of almost fully-ripened millet, he was aware of how previously friendly faces turned away to avoid catching his eye. It was to be expected. His association with a murder on their home patch and his relationship with one of the king's chosen women had branded him as 'dangerous'. His remaining time in Burkina was clearly not going to be easy. With some relief he completed his day's work and returned to Sabine's. There was no sign of Monique, so he guessed she was wrapped up with family affairs.

He spent the evening alone. In the morning Sanou took him to the palace and left him waiting in one of the small rooms at the rear of the building. Upon his return Tomos was led along a short corridor and up a flight of steps onto a balcony overlooking a tree-lined courtyard.

Leaning back against a plain wooden balustrade was the larger than life figure of His Highness. A bodyguard armed with a pistol tucked into a belt was standing discreetly to one side.

Sanou formally presented Tomos before standing back to guard the door to the stairs.

The king beckoned him over to a large wooden table supporting a bottle of whisky and several tumblers. He carefully filled two glasses; sipped from one and handed the other to Tomos.

'Good morning Mr Morgan, I trust you will enjoy my whisky. Sanou tells me the farm is going well and he's very pleased with your efforts. Well done for that.'

'Thank you, it's very kind of you to say so.'

'I am however very concerned to hear about the incident with Mr Tapsoba.' He looked straight at Tomos. 'It seems you knew the people who orchestrated this terrible crime. Do you have anything to say?'

Tomos shook his head with genuine regret. 'I had no idea such people were in Burkina Faso. It came as a total shock to me, and I would like to say that I am very, very sorry for the loss of your friend; he did seem like a good man.'

'Hmm, he *was* a good man, and as you say, my friend, too. The crime cannot go unpunished, so make sure you co-operate fully with Arzuma; no secrets, you understand? What do you think of the whisky?'

The sudden change of subject caught Tomos off-guard, 'Err ... very good,' he replied, taking an extra sip to emphasize the point.

'Excellent. I also want to talk to you about Gaston's eldest daughter, Monique, whom I'm aware you know very well.'

Tomos steeled himself for the worst. Was he going to be warned off again?

'You must know that Monique is due to become my wife.'

He held his breath and waited for the king's verdict.

'Times change,' the king conceded. 'Monique's behaviour and yours would never have been tolerated in the old days. Luckily for you Mr Morgan, the fact that she's lost her father persuades me to treat you both leniently.'

Tomos involuntarily took a gulp of whisky, barely feeling the burning in his throat. 'I don't know what to say. I'm very grateful and very happy to hear that.'

The king looked pleased. 'Very good; now hear this too ... and take note. Stay away from Monique. It seems to me that you are someone who attracts trouble, and I don't want any harm to come to her before the wedding or there will be repercussions. I hope I make myself clear?'

'Very clear, thank you; please believe me when I say I only have Monique's best interests at heart.'

'Time will tell Mr Morgan, time will tell. As I said earlier, Arzuma is pleased with your efforts on my farm so that's better news. I trust you still intend to stay until the harvest? It's a special time for us - one you shouldn't miss.'

'Certainly I'll stay. I'm looking forward to it very much.'

'Very good Mr Morgan; enjoy the rest of your drink.'

He put down his glass and, followed by his bodyguard, left without another glance at either Tomos or Sanou.

. . .

Time passed all too quickly. Monique explained that her Mama still found the loss of her husband too raw to welcome another man into her home, especially Tomos, given his connection to Gaston. And so he continued to lodge at Sabine's, where Monique visited him discreetly most evenings. Serious plans to flee the country and secret idle chats of a future life together in far-away Europe was a dream they shared and cherished.

37

One of the main duties of the Advisor for Agriculture was to set the date of the royal harvest. That responsibility now fell to the industrious Advisor for Magic, as the king had not yet inaugurated Gaston's successor. It happened one October morning. Acting on Adama's advice, Sanou agreed the time was right. Following tradition, the message was spread by word of mouth for all available labourers to convene at the royal farm in three days' time.

Tomos, along with the rest of the farming community, had long been waiting for Sanou's decision. For him especially, it meant so much more than just a gathering of crops; it marked the end of an era, and with God's blessing, the start of something better.

On the day he rose an hour before dawn. To avoid disturbing the rest of the household, he skipped breakfast and silently let himself into the street. A fifteen-minute jog took him to the palace to catch a lift to the farm. To help transport his workforce, Sanou had commandeered several vehicles across town, one of which was due to leave from the gates of the royal residence at dawn. As expected, the outline of a stationary truck loomed out of the semi-darkness as he turned the last corner. Slowing to a walk, he counted about a dozen men standing in the back, most of them peering at him with undisguised curiosity.

Someone in the passenger seat was furiously waving at him. Up close, Monique's familiar features took shape. She was beaming in welcome. 'I didn't know you were coming,'

Tomos sensed his own face breaking into a matching grin. 'Sorry, there wasn't time to tell you. I just *had* to come when I heard it was today, to do my bit for the king.'

She pointed to the back of the cab. 'You'd better jump in the back with the other boys ... avoid any gossip that way ... expect we can catch up later.'

'Yeah, that'd be good. Do you know any of 'em?'

'No, but I expect most of them are originally from villages around Ouaga, probably moved to the city in search of work. When Sanou needs help - well, he's got contacts everywhere and news travels fast.'

'Right, see you on the farm then,' Tomos replied, before hopping in the back.

Fully loaded, the pick-up clumsily rumbled its way through the streets of Ouagadougou. Morning twilight gingerly picked out the morning's first human activity: vendors preparing to open up street side stalls; Muslims on their way to the local mosque, prayer mats rolled under their arms; women fetching water for the day from communal taps, the inevitable bucket carried on each steady head.

They followed the main road out of town before enduring the hard bumps of the off-road tracks. As they bounced along, he watched the dawn's sullen-red tendrils of light battle past the treetrunks lining the eastern horizon. Brightening by the second they rose, flickering upwards through the branches to briefly capture each canopy in a golden halo. The initial warming of those first rays was welcome on the skin after the chill of the night; it wouldn't take long before the welcome would be outstayed.

Everyone disembarked at the great baobab. It was surprisingly busy, earlier arrivals already socialising, the air alive with chatter. Tomos noted two other trucks parked nearby, both with large woven grass screens erected in the rear, the purpose of which escaped him.

The place was alive with laughter, a great social gathering. To Tomos, it looked as though everyone within miles must have come. He estimated at least a hundred people in all, not even counting the numerous children; before getting down to work.

Detaching himself from the melee, Sanou appeared, raising a disapproving eyebrow when he saw Tomos and Monique standing together. He climbed into the empty back of their truck and called everyone to attention. The general hubbub faded to silence as the assembled workforce obediently shuffled into a respectful huddle in front of the Royal Advisor.

'What's he saying?' Tomos whispered to Monique, a few moments into Sanou's address.

'He's already thanked everyone for coming. Now he's asking the ancestors to bless the harvest and reward the workers for all the hard work they are about to do.'

Sanou stepped down. Adama took centre stage, and under his shouted instructions the adult men formed a line along one side of the closest field. Another shout, and they swept forward as one into the millet, hacking at the base of each plant and pulling it free to leave it lying on the ground.

Tomos watched as the millet stalks - he estimated them at almost ten feet tall - were mown down, the line of black muscle irresistibly advancing like a line of cavalry slashing at a helpless enemy. Beyond them lay an ugly great swathe of blackened scorched earth, a scar testifying to the destructive ravages of the bushfire, the same one where he'd first spoken to Monique.

Borrowing a machete, he took his place at the end of the line. It required little effort at first, the shallow rooted plants were easily reaped but as the sun rose higher and the temperature climbed the work became increasingly hard. Once the first field of red millet was cleared, the group moved on to the next; a larger plot of white millet. Most of the millet grown was white, the staple food diet. The red crop, being of lesser quality, was used mostly for brewing beer.

Children brought water for the men to drink, but the work never stopped. Most of the labourers had other fields to harvest and could not afford more than a day or two away from their own farms.

Harvesting was unending, hot and back breaking. It wasn't long before everyone was bathed in sweat and attracting the flies. The millet chaffed Tomos's bare arms and made them itch. Swinging the heavy-bladed tool blistered his hands, unused as he was to the unrelenting intensity of the labour. The workers couldn't avoid disturbing the dry friable soil, kicking it up into a fine red dust so that every time he bent down to swing his machete, he had to hold his breath to avoid choking. Tough work or not, he was able to struggle on, safe in the knowledge that unlike his fellow labourers he wouldn't be getting up the next day to do it all over again.

Sanou called a break at mid-day. Most, including Tomos, chose to congregate under the great baobab. Several tubs of millet beer were uncovered and freely served in wooden calabasas by the older women to anyone who wanted a drink of the strong pungent refreshment.

Few were overly-keen to get back to work after the stop; the heat was overpowering and the liqueur had dulled the will to work. The overseer reformed the line of men before breaking into song. It did the trick. Tomos had no idea what he was singing about, but Adama led with a chant which was picked up and repeated by the whole line of men, their strong voices reverberating through the savanna as they rediscovered their fighting spirit: a band of men bonded in song.

The blisters on Tomos's hands were bleeding, his arms ached and his back was sore, when late in the afternoon he felt a friendly pat on his back.

'I think that's enough for you, Mr Morgan. Go and get a bite to eat.'

He had never been so pleased to see Sanou.

Back under the baobab he relinquished his machete to its rightful owner and gratefully accepted a strip of dried meat to chew on. Looking around, he watched the women at work as they swept en masse through one of the cleared fields. The work they undertook looked even tougher than that of their menfolk. Armed with knives and bent over almost double, they inched forward cutting off the spiked heads of millet, collecting them in large wicker baskets as they went. They worked tirelessly; most were young, many carrying infants on their backs.

Tomos listened in wonder, for as they laboured they also sang, a cheerful tune with a faster rhythm that carried more clearly than the deeper tones of the men.

With baskets filled to the brim the women returned one by one to the pick-ups, where they handed over the precious spikes. Now he understood the purpose of the wicker screens which raised the sides of the trucks allowing a greater load to be carried, it was no wonder these vehicles always looked such wrecks.

With so many people to help, the harvest was completed an hour before sunset. After a final swig of beer, the labourers dispersed in various directions to eat and rest in preparation for identical work the next day on another farm.

Tomos watched Monique complete her last basket with the final group of women before joining him next to one of the crop-holding trucks. Sanou must have noticed them together for he too joined them, Obviously in high spirits the Advisor was keen to explain his good mood.

'This is the biggest harvest we've had for years, a great effort by everyone today. It means we can store some of the millet here on the farm for the locals benefit, although most will be transported back to the palace where it'll be used to feed the royal household and guests; anything in surplus is saved to help those in need. Every year there are villages and farms where crops have failed. Last year many places suffered a plague of beetles that ate many of the plants; the year before that was difficult as the rains arrived even later than this year. The trucks have been delivering all day.'

Tomos remembered seeing numerous stilted round mud huts with straw roofs in the palace grounds. They would now be used to store the millet spikes keeping them dry and generally safe from rats and disease.

Sanou thumped the side of the truck. 'Jump in you two, if you want to go home. This is the last load, so I'll be coming back with you.'

The rear of the truck was packed with the day's harvest. A couple of the labourers who'd accompanied Tomos on the outward journey had bravely squashed in among the mounds of spikes. He supposed the others had either left with earlier loads or perhaps were going on to work somewhere else, possibly even visiting their home villages.

Sanou seated himself in the front cab between Monique and Tomos. Little was spoken as everyone battled fatigue; it took a huge effort just to stay sitting upright as they were bumped and rattled back to the city. The descending night helped conceal Tomos's stealthy half glances at Monique at every opportunity. Work had prevented any dalliance between them, but the occasional flirty looks they shared were both exciting and full of promise.

Ouagadougou's familiar streets came as a welcome relief to tired eyes. Mindful of not being publicly alone with Tomos, Monique asked to be dropped off first. Tomos descended with the last of the labourers at the palace and wearily set off for the walk back to Sabine's.

• • •

Zongo followed the Britisher all the way home from the vantage point atop his motorbike. He knew the royal farm was to have its harvest that day, so it had been a simple matter to park near the palace gates. All he had to do was wait.

The vehicles returning with their cargoes of millet were easy enough to spot, although he'd had to stay alert to identify the occupants while keeping a low profile at the same time. Now that he knew where Tomos Morgan lived, he could plan his next move. He turned his bike around and with a twist of the throttle zoomed off to celebrate his good luck.

38

Zongo was anxious for the remainder of his promised reward. Getting paid depended on providing proof of Tomos's death to Al-Hazbar, but with the end of the harvest came the possibility his prize might leave the country. To attempt an attack at the farm a second time was out of the question; the labourers might already suspect him for Gaston's murder. On top of all that, he still faced charges for deserting the army if caught.

His problems were linked, as was the solution: eliminate Tomos and use Al-Hazbar's reward money to flee the country ... simple.

To start with, he needed to know more about Tomos. He began watching the street where he'd learned his quarry was lodging. After only a few hours he discovered Sabine also lived there, and that changed everything. He dared not risk loitering close-by, she could easily recognise him. A new approach was needed.

The hotel where he decided to rent a room for a couple of nights was respectable enough, quiet, and not too central. He invited Koné over, and together they finalised his new plan. Although Koné was a contemporary from Zongo's army days, he had been in a different division and both men were confident he wasn't known to Sabine.

Zongo rehired the same car, a Peugeot Estate, he'd used for Gaston's assassination, and bought the various items needed for the first part of his operation. Finally everything was in place. Seating himself in the hotel garden, he drank beer ... and waited.

Koné took the Peugeot, now clean and polished until it shone, and drove across town to park outside Sabine's house. It was noon, a time of day he was likely to catch her at home. The only soul in sight at this hour was a small urchin running while rolling a bicycle wheel along with a stick. Koné wound down the window.

'Hey boy - come here!'

The barefoot lad stopped and eyed the expensive-looking car before grabbing his wheel and running up to the door. 'Yes Sir?'

'Do you know the young woman living there?' he pointed at the house.

'You mean Sabine?'

'Yes, Sabine. Very good ... here ... take this,' Koné handed over a coin. 'You can have another if you go and tell her to come and see me right now. Tell her it's urgent, OK?'

The urchin ran off and promptly returned bringing a curious Sabine. The boy departed with his second coin, leaving Koné to greet his target with a charming smile.

'I know this might sound strange as I'm new to the area, but I noticed you the other day. Sabine, isn't it? Sabine, I must say you are a very beautiful woman, and I think we can help each other. You see I'm in the fashion business, and I would like you to model some new dress designs for me. I'm taking photographs for a magazine and you're a perfect choice; the right size and shape ... exactly what I'm looking for.'

'Seriously? I don't think I'm beautiful ... how do I know you're telling the truth?'

'Look, you can come with me now and see. I'm staying at the Hotel Faso. It won't take long; I only need a few photos. I promise to drop you back in an hour. It's well paid by the way. You'll get a hundred US dollars for an hour's work. What do you say?'

A hundred dollars was an enormous sum. Sabine's eyes bulged at the size of the offer. Ouagadougou by African standards was a very safe city; the hotel was a respectable one, and the photographer appeared genuine; driving a car implied he had money and responsibility. She could even see a new-looking dress spread out on the back seat.

'Hundred dollars - really? I'm not dressed nice, even my hair isn't done!'

'You look great! You see Sabine; the problem is that I must complete the photo shoot this morning. It's now or never I'm afraid. If you don't want the money, that's fine, I'll find another girl. It's your choice but I really want *you* ... you're perfect.'

'Promise it'll only take an hour?'

'Promise, I only need an hour. Get in ... you won't regret it.'

. . .

The plan was going well. Zongo smirked as he watched Sabine walk straight past him in Koné's company. He briefly removed his sunglasses and carefully looked round wanting to make sure she hadn't been followed. He needed her to be alone and vulnerable.

Koné had the room key, so Zongo tapped the door and waited for his accomplice to let him in. He entered to find his partner had completed his work perfectly. Sabine was already gagged and bound tightly to the single chair, her eyes rolling madly as they blinked away streaming tears.

He relished the moment as he planted his massive bulky frame in front of the young woman. The look of sheer horror that froze on her face as she recognised him was highly gratifying. He observed with satisfaction how the fear must be running through her, making her convulse and rock helplessly from side to side on the chair. The choking sobs muffled behind her gag completed his feeling of total control.

His natural impulse was to immediately strike her to get what he wanted. He forced himself to adopt a diplomatic approach; only if that failed would he resort to violence. He waited impatiently until fatigue calmed Sabine to the point where she sat still, panting heavily, her torso held rigid under her bonds.

'I see you remember me Sabine; nice to see you again after all this time.'

It took seconds for her to react. She slowly turned her head towards him.

'I don't want to hurt you, quite the opposite. I'm sorry you've been scared but this was the only way I could get to speak to you. You see ... all I want to do is talk ... understand?'

Sabine remained totally stiff, eyes wide and staring. Unperturbed, Zongo continued, his voice low and soft. 'Sabine ... listen to me, I'm a changed man. I'm now a man of God, and I want to atone for my past sins. I wronged you once but now I'm ready to make amends. I want you to forgive me. If you do, I promise to pay the hundred dollars my colleague offered earlier. Nod your head if you understand.'

Sabine nodded, her eyes never leaving the face of the man before her.

'Good. Like I say ... I only want to talk to you ... help you even ... by paying you.'

Zongo signalled Koné to release her.

Ungagged and untied, she remained seated, rubbing her wrists.

Koné retreated to stand guard in front of the closed door leading to the corridor.

Sabine peered around. Zongo knew she was looking for any possible routes of escape. There weren't any. There was one closed shuttered window, and the only internal doorway led to a shower cubicle - a dead end. She would have no choice but to appease her captors with whatever they wanted.

Zongo smiled in a failed attempt at charm. He produced his wallet with a flourish, counted out the promised dollars and handed it all to Sabine. The money was too good to refuse; it could be used for all sorts of things, not least supporting her mother and younger brother. She took it and tucked it away under her dress.

'I remember you well, Captain Zongo ... and the things you made me do. What do you want?' She made no effort to hide the loathing in her voice.

'I'm not a captain any more, in fact I'm no longer in the army. I'm guessing you already know why ... I'm a wanted man. I face a court martial and a life sentence, or worse. Which is why you're here; I need your help. I need you and Monique to ask for the charges against me to be dropped.'

'You deserve jail and worse for what you did. Why should you get away with it?'

Zongo shrugged. He was beginning to tire of the diplomatic approach already. 'I told you, I'm a changed man. From now on I want to do *good* in this world, not bad. Don't deny me this chance to redeem myself.'

'If I agree to drop the charges, you'll let me go?'

'Yes that's right, and you can take the money with you. That is apart from one other little thing.'

'Oh ... what?'

'I want *all* charges dropped, including those brought against me by your friend Monique Tapsoba.'

'I don't think Monique has made any allegations.'

'Don't play games; the charges have been made by her father on her behalf and yours. I know he's dead, but the charges still stand until you both withdraw them.'

'Alright, I can ask her after you've let me go.'

Zongo shook his head. 'No, I want her personal word.'

He walked to the solitary table in the room which also doubled as a desk. On it was a telephone, another reason he'd chosen this particular hotel; only a few in the city were furnished with telephones in individual rooms. He picked up the set and returned to stand in front of Sabine.

'I want you to call Monique and ask her to come here immediately. You will tell her that you need her to come alone - and you will explain *why*, when she's here. Don't mention me or she won't come.'

'And if I refuse?'

'Don't ask. Remember, you'll be doing both of you a favour since Monique will also get a hundred dollars if she agrees to drop the charges. If you do as I ask, I swear you'll both go free, never to see or hear from me again. I have Monique's number from the directory. Tell her she must come now: Hotel Faso, Room 10. Tell me, will you do as I ask?'

Sabine hesitated before whispering her consent, as he knew she would. His words were spoken so convincingly he almost believed them himself. Anyway, some weak people *did* mellow over time and find remorse for past wrongs. She couldn't know he wasn't one of them. His words made sense. If the charges were dropped, he'd be a free man.

Zongo dialled and Monique replied, her faintly insolent tone immediately recognisable. He handed over the phone.

'Hello, Monique ... it's me, Sabine. Listen ... please ... you have to come and see me immediately. I'm at the Hotel Faso, Room 10. Sorry I can't explain until you get here, but you must come alone ...'

Zongo smiled broadly and ended the call. 'So far so good. You'll wait here for Monique.'

'I thought you said I could go now I've done what you asked,' Sabine retorted angrily, getting to her feet.

Zongo didn't even look at her as he beckoned his colleague over. Koné shoved her roughly back down onto the chair. 'Just wait like you've been told. You better hope your friend turns up.'

Sabine tried to stand again only for Koné to raise his arm. The backhanded slap across the face was so hard it stunned her. Another slap and blood spurted from her mouth. Koné replaced the gag before binding her legs and arms so tightly to the chair she couldn't move.

'That's better, you just relax now,' her assailant cooed, gently stroking her hair, then her cheek. 'Perhaps we'll all have a little party when your friend turns up.'

The full horrible implications of his words sank home. Sabine struggled feebly, swallowing hard and snorting as she tried to breathe through a blood-filled nose.

Zongo was satisfied - for the moment. At last the stupid bitch must have realised what she'd done; put her own and Monique's life at risk for a hundred dollars. If she was praying for help, she'd left it far too late. He watched with ever growing pleasure as the tears rolled uncontrollably down her cheeks from tightly closed eyes.

39

Zongo resumed his earlier position in the garden where his vantage point gave a clear view of the entrance. As with Sabine, he needed to be sure Monique came alone.

He needn't have worried about her not rushing to her friend's aid. The silly fool came riding up alone on her moped within half an hour and dismounted only metres away from him.

From the corner of his eye he watched her enter the hotel lobby before returning to the outside bar. She called the barman over and engaged him in a short conversation before going back inside. He made himself stay seated for a few more minutes before casually sauntering after his quarry. Things were about to get interesting.

Not a sound emanated from within Room 10. The door was closed but would have been left slightly ajar for Monique. He and Koné had earlier concluded the best set-up was to leave the room dark inside with the blind shut. The glow from the weak ceiling lamp in the outside corridor would pass through the open door casting a patch of light just inside the room, enticing anyone to enter. Like an antelope seeking refuge in a lion's den.

He rapped on the door, eager to enjoy his dominance over a second victim. Inside he found Monique trussed, gagged and face-down on the bed. He watched dispassionately as he gave the struggling figure time to come to terms with her predicament. Being made to wait while not knowing what lay in store would maximise her fear factor and make his job easier.

The struggles subsided as Monique tired. It was time to act.

He walked over to the prostrate figure which kicked out at him as soon as he grabbed hold. Pulling her back and upwards by her long hair extensions, he forced her into a sitting position on the edge of the bed. From there he knew she would be able to see Sabine gagged and bound in the middle of the room.

She would also see Koné standing by the door from which she'd entered. Dressed in jeans and tight-fitting shirt, aged about thirty and physically fit, he cut a figure almost as intimidating as himself.

He gave Monique a few seconds to take it all in, before yanking her head round so she was facing him. He put his head up to hers so their foreheads touched, his foul breath enveloped them both.

'Remember me, bitch?'

He drew back, allowing Monique to discern his features; and he saw the glint of recognition flicker across her eyes.

'Nice of you to visit me Monique ... I see that you do remember me. I'd like to have a little chat with you ... but no shouting, otherwise my friend over there ... well if you don't want him to hurt Sabine, you'll behave ... understand?'

Zongo slowly dropped the gag. Monique took in air in short rasping gasps.

'Good, let's not waste time. You are going to do me a small favour. I want to meet your friend, Mr Morgan. The problem is, how are we to arrange a meeting where the two of us can be alone? Any ideas?'

Monique's stare turned from fear to anxiety-tinged hatred. 'What the hell are you doing? And why do you want see Tomo?'

'Let's just say he could be good for business.'

'What business do you want with him ... and Sabine ... or me? What do you want from any of us?'

'No more questions ... listen ... You're going to phone home and ask for someone to get a message to Morgan asking him to be at your place tonight at nine. You will then phone him again at nine to arrange a meeting somewhere - just him and me. After that, you and Sabine can go home. Easy, isn't it?'

'Is that how you got me here ...? Told Sabine a pack of lies to trick me? I'm not doing anything you want ... that's final.'

'That's disappointing for me - but not for my colleague.' Zongo turned towards his accomplice. 'Yousef, the Sabine woman is all yours.'

'Wait!' Don't ... we can work this ...' her voice trailed off, interrupted by a loud double knock at the door. 'Help!' she yelled, the first to react.

Zongo slipped the gag back across her mouth. The intrusion was unexpected and infuriating. Koné, standing again in front of the door, spun round to face it.

'Who is it? What do you want?'

'I've brought the two beers, as ordered by the young lady.'

'We don't want anything - take them away.'

'They were ordered by a young lady for Room 10. She insisted on them being delivered.'

'Well, we've changed our mind. You can take them back.'

'Is the young lady there? She did insist.'

'She's fine. Just take the beers back - I already told you, we don't want them.'

Koné put his ear to the door and listened to the retreating footsteps.

He turned to face Zongo who was standing with arms akimbo, fists clenching and unclenching in supressed anger.

'We should go. He suspects something's up ... too risky to stay ... it's not worth it.'

Zongo knew he was right. He could feel it. Everything had gone exactly according to plan up to then. Now he had some big decisions to make.

'You're right; it's time to end this once and for all. These two bitches need to die. I'll not have them hanging around to testify against me.'

'Don't be stupid - you're already in enough trouble. Adding murder to the list of charges against you isn't going to help.'

'Shut up Yousef! I'll do what the fuck I want. These two deserve it - especially this one!' He spat the words out and kicked Monique in the shins at the same time. All pretence was dropped; his bartering to get to Tomos or paying for the girls' silence.

A blood lust was rising in an unstoppable wave inside him - and he recognised it for what it was - an unwelcome gift borne of a career based on brutality in the army. There could be no going back now; the lust was too strong to fight.

He was vaguely aware of Koné watching him, working out for himself what was happening.

'Jerome, I'm going - you do what the hell you want. You know me - I'll say nothing. But I want no part of this.

Roughing up these girls is one thing, but I'm not committing murder.'

Smouldering with anger, Zongo cursed as Koné slipped out of the room. He was going to have to finish the business alone. The thirst for violence had taken hold and the fury inside him was burning uncontrollably, demanding satisfaction. Struggling through the primeval mists swirling inside his head, a grain of logic crystallized and grew: if the hotel staff really were suspicious they could return at any moment. He might not have much time.

He turned back and slapped Monique across the face as hard as he could. The bruising was instant, one eye immediately swelling shut.

'You know what Monique - your kind makes me sick. Rich and pampered - think you can get away with anything - do anything to anyone. Well it's all over for you now, just the same as it was for your father.' He saw the spark in Monique's remaining good eye at the mention of her father. 'Yes, it was me that killed your sweet Papa. Now I'm going to kill you and your friend. Without your father to press charges and you to testify, I'm a free man, and I've struck a blow against the privileged classes. Everybody wins.' He sneered maliciously, 'except you.'

He advanced on the struggling young woman and placed his big hands around her neck. 'Hope you're watching Sabine ... you're next. Can't have a witness to murder walking around, can I?'

He pressed his fingers against the fragile windpipe, almost caressing it as he gently applied pressure. The pulse weakened as he squeezed. He watched with thrilling exultation, enjoying every second of the ultimate feeling of power as he cut off the life-giving air. The neck pulse stopped altogether. He counted slowly to sixty before he was convinced the woman was dead. Only then did he release her. Monique's eyes rolled open, and he stepped to one side momentarily repulsed by the whites of the eyes staring back at him, as if condemning him for his sin.

Shaking and gasping in a state of ecstatic anguish, Zongo turned and glimpsed the shocked horror etched across Sabine's transfixed face. She screamed in muted silence, her gag dripping with saliva as she lost control of her senses.

The fog in his head thickened, blurring the image of the two women. Slowly it began to clear. As it thinned he became dimly aware of a knocking sound. A voice replaced the knocking, gently calling through the mist; a weak and ethereal whisper. It strengthened, dispersing the remnants of the fog as he struggled to focus.

Someone was outside the door. The voice condensed into separate words; a name was being called.

'Monsieur Traore ... are you well? Is everything alright in there? We're worried about you and the young lady.'

Traore? It took another second to complete the connection. Traore was the name he'd used when booking into the hotel, a very common West African name. The query demanded a reply.

'We're fine ... just enjoying some private time.'

The lie seemed to work - for the moment. The voice faded, and all went quiet outside the door.

He hadn't admitted it to Koné, but he'd always planned to kill Monique at some point; certain her high morals meant her silence could never be bought.

Ignoring Sabine, he dragged out one of two giant sports bags from under the bed and with difficulty stuffed the still-supple corpse inside one of them. There were droplets of deep crimson all over the bedding, and almost as an afterthought he stuffed the bloodied sheets into the bag as well. The second bag intended for Sabine would have to remain unused, it was too risky to return.

He heaved the heavy load over his shoulder. One last thing ... he stooped down to whisper in Sabine's ear as he left.

'If you don't want to die like this, tell no-one about me. You can say Monique left alive ... left with a man you didn't know. Do that and I won't come looking for you.'

He cautiously opened the door and checked left and right; luckily no-one was in sight. With the way clear, he left the building through the fire exit at the end of the corridor as fast as he was able. Panting with exertion, he steadily clumped to the Peugeot parked around the other side of the hotel, opened the boot and gratefully heaved the bag inside.

Just in time. A shout accosted him from behind. He jumped into the driver seat, started the engine and pressed down hard on the accelerator. As he sped into the street, he glanced in the mirror. A figure was running out of the hotel, arms waving frantically, the mouth opening and closing in unheard calls.

He drove carefully through the streets of Ouagadougou. It was a shame he had to let Sabine live, but there was a good chance she'd remain too scared to ever mention him by name. He smacked the steering wheel as remembered he'd left his money with the bitch. It was too late now to retrieve it; anyway, he had a more immediate problem than lost cash... how to dispose of the body in the boot of his car.

The city was hectic at this hour. Every street and every square had eyes a-plenty; a body couldn't be dumped just anywhere. He could simply park up and walk away, but tracing the vehicle to him was too easy.

He drove on through the city, hit the main road north and followed it. He knew where to go, and congratulated himself on his foresight. The road eventually took him through the outer suburbs. Houses and people became sparser and poorer with each passing kilometre. The city outskirts boasted few amenities, its only settlers the constant trickle of new immigrants from the country.

A few kilometres beyond the city limits but well before the first of the official roadblocks that surrounded it, he turned off the main road and followed a deeply rutted track for another kilometre. Despite the heat he wound up his window. The smell outside - a potent mix of stagnant water and decomposing flesh - was overpowering.

The long low buildings of a tannery came into view. He ignored them and doggedly bumped his way along the perimeter until he was able to circle around to the rear of the site. The stench from the working of hide and leather permeated the inside of the Peugeot despite the closed window. The smell hung in the air like a vast tenuous mist, offensive enough to keep all people away from the entire area apart from a handful of employees.

The rearmost building was a rarely-used slaughterhouse, most raw hides arriving from farms ready-skinned. He stopped at an open pit, the deserted slaughterhouse between him and any curious eyes that might be watching from the tannery. He checked no-one was about, dragged out the heavy sports bag, unzipped it and emptied the contents down the hole. He would burn the bag later, somewhere else.

The body slid down the gentle slope for a few metres before coming to a stop, nestled up against the maggot-ridden remains of a cow. A thick carpet of black flies rose then settled back down in a unified wave. The whole stinking pit was filled with the bones and rotting flesh of carcasses shorn of their hides, a dumping ground of slaughtered animals. The corpse of the young woman was welcomed by the scavenging bugs which crawled over and gnawed at the newcomer with greedy interest.

Gagging, Zongo drove away as fast as he dared. Checking his mirror he was pleased to see the first of the vultures arrive, keen to investigate this latest offering to the pit of the dead.

40

The London weather welcomed Tomos with bucket-loads of empathy. The leaden-grey skies that frequently dimmed to ash-black as bundles of rain-laden clouds raced overhead, perfectly complemented his own personal angst. The latent power that could be unleashed with the fury of a winter storm brooded menacingly all around him. Inside, his emotions seethed with unbridled anger. Was it only two weeks ago that Monique had been so callously murdered?

The unwanted memory of the exact moment Pascal had told him the awful truth thrust itself rudely into his mind. Walking into the yard at Sabine's and seeing his tattered rucksack sitting under the forlorn mango tree was his only warning that something was wrong. He would never forget being told of the unbelievable horrors witnessed by Sabine on that terrible day. He flinched as he recalled Pascal's words.

"My sister saw it all. Monique is dead; she was strangled by someone - an African. She can't or won't say who did it, but whoever it was took her body away in a bag. That's all she'd tell us, and I'm only telling you because I know how much she meant to you."

Pascal, defensive and apologetic at the same time, had handed him his rucksack. "Mama cannot face you; she asked that you leave - this minute. I'm sorry ..."

His world had imploded. Desperate to speak to Sabine he'd gone straight to the police station where Pascale said she was being held. Not being family, he hadn't been allowed to see her.

He looked up at the moisture sodden sky hovering above Heathrow airport. He'd never felt this way before, so angry and alone. It was Monique's dream to be here with him. It was his dream too. Why couldn't dreams ever come true - not even once?

The lump in his throat made him oblivious to the rain soaking through his clothing. It was almost impossible to believe, and too sickening to visualise what Pascal had told him. And for what reason? He couldn't even begin to think of an explanation.

He paused to look around. It seemed an age since he was last in England. Everything looked alien yet familiar at the same time. He'd been standing on the kerb outside the glass exit doors of the terminal building, and must have looked strange daydreaming in the downpour without coat or hat if the undisguised stare of the taxi driver opposite was anything to go by. A sign pointed to the bus terminal. Automatically he followed it.

The anger was simmering deep inside him, demanding an outlet. There was only one possible course of action: find and confront Al-Hazbar and exact his own revenge. Both the police and Pascal had told him the killer was African not Arab, but Tomos believed Al-Hazbar was behind the killing, even if someone else had committed murder on his behalf.

He had been desperate to leave Africa and start his mission, but there had been one unfinished job to attend to first. He'd booked his flight to London via Paris, before returning to Koutatenga. There he worked tirelessly helping to supervise the drilling and testing of the new village borehole. It's success provided a brief respite of satisfaction from the otherwise constant heartache.

After fond goodbyes to Isaac, his family, and Wendbenindo, he'd finally left for Ouagadougou airport. That had been two weeks after the murder of the woman he cared for more than any other - the first time he'd felt himself truly falling in love.

And so here he was, back in Britain. But now things had changed. No more running, no more hiding. This was his country and he intended to take control.

41

When Tomos called to say he wanted to return, his mother heard the dejection in his voice and had tried to cheer him by telling him about Saif's visit and the promise of his old job back in Oman. He'd been so glad she hadn't been able to see his face ... the nerve of those murdering bastards!

He didn't believe the Saif story. The visit could only mean one thing; Al-Hazbar had successfully tracked down his family. There just wasn't any other explanation. It must have been how he'd been traced to Burkina Faso. So what was next? Threats against his family? That would never happen - not if he could help it.

It was the morning of the first day of November. Waiting for the bus, Tomos sucked in the cold damp air. He welcomed it, relishing the sharpening of his senses. He had a job to do and needed to concentrate. The forty-five-minute journey to Victoria bus station in central London allowed him time to think.

The Saif character must be working for Al-Hazbar. That meant Al-Hazbar had contacts in Britain, most probably London where foreigners always congregated. He obviously had money to burn, that much he knew; it was possible he therefore owned or rented property somewhere in the city.

From the bus station he walked straight to the post office. It was a long shot, but a scroll through the phone directory of London residences revealed only one Al-Hazbar. It was an unusual name and seeing it in the directory's tiny print gave him a glimmer of hope. He carefully copied the address which meant nothing to him, before buying a street map.

Needing somewhere to sit for a moment, he bought a coffee from a streetside café. Sitting, he re-read the address: 7 Market Place. The map showed the address to be near Oxford Circus, only a couple of stops away on the tube. He could be there within minutes. He grabbed his rucksack and left, his coffee untouched.

From the outside, 7 Market Place was an uninspiring square-set block of flats, its bland grey concrete façade intuitively contradicting the sign facing the road that read "luxury suites for sale". Set in a panel to the side of the security door was a list of flat numbers with occupants' names. Al-Hazbar was listed against Flat 6. Tomos took a deep breath and pressed the buzzer.

Seconds passed before a female voice answered, her foreign accent made all the stranger by the tinny twang of the speaker.

'Yes please?'

'I'm here to see Al-Hazbar.'

A pause. 'You have business, sir?'

'Yes, important business - and I don't have all day.'

The door buzzed and he pushed it open. Flat 2 stared him in the face. A downward flight of steps presumably led to Flat 1 with the bigger numbers higher up. Ignoring the lift, he took the bare concrete steps two at a time until he reached Flat 6, the topmost one.

He rapped hard on the door which opened to reveal the frightened face of an older teenage girl who quietly beckoned him in. She was inexplicably dressed in a French maid's outfit, the kind sold in cheap costume shops.

'Please sir, this way.' The girl stepped back into a hallway as he strode in.

'Who is it?' a shrill male voice reverberated.

Tomos followed the maid towards the unseen voice, his eyes taking in the dark bruising on the side of her cheek as she turned away from him, her ridiculously skimpy outfit more pathetic than enticing.

She showed him into a living room at the end of the hall, before fleeing back up the corridor.

The room he entered was lavishly decorated, best described as erotically exotic. Plush deep rugs covered the floor; furs draped an expensive looking sofa with others spread across a chaise longue. Seated at a desk tapping away at a computer was a youngish man of olive complexion. Tomos guessed his age to be nearer twenty than thirty. He was smartly dressed in designer jeans, sweatshirt and bright new trainers.

'Yes?' The man spoke arrogantly without even looking up from the screen.

Tomos was in no mood for politeness. 'Are you Al-Hazbar?'

'I ... I'm Saif Al-Hazbar,' the reply was stammered, the man obviously taken aback by the directness of the question. He swivelled round in his seat and frowned. 'Do I know you? Are you here to see father?'

'I'm here to see Rashid Al-Hazbar.'

Saif looked again before slowly standing and grabbing the desk for support, as if he were about to faint. Tomos noticed the sudden change; the man was acting as if he knew him. He examined the face more closely from across the room, the features looked vaguely familiar.

His hesitation must have emboldened Saif. Visibly relaxing he proudly drew himself up. 'I'm the younger son of Rashid Al-Hazbar. Now you know who I am, you'd better get the hell out before father gets back.'

Saif's words struck home. Tomos tried not to show surprise; he had no idea Al-Hazbar had a second son.

'It was your brother that drowned in the wadi? Then you know who I am.'

'Yeah, I know. You're the infidel, my brother's murderer; what the fuck do you want?'

'What do I want? I'll tell you what I want - an explanation. I never harmed your brother - and you know it. I want to know exactly what the hell your father's been playing at these past two years.'

'Fuck you! You killed my brother! Now get out, before I call the police.'

Anger and frustration boiled over. Two years of pain and suffering had to end one way or another. He flew across the room giving Saif no time to defend himself. His punch jarred his whole arm as it connected with the man's face. He watched with grim satisfaction as the nose cracked, releasing a stream of blood. He threw a second punch before Saif could react, this time into the solar plexus. Already doubled over in agony, a third strike to the back of the head sent him to the floor where he cowered and writhed on a cream-coloured rug, smearing it with bright red stains.

Tomos knelt. With one knee in the small of the back, he gripped Saif's hair, pulling his head back; his other hand gripping the throat. Lowering his head he snarled into an exposed ear. 'Because of your damn family, someone I loved was killed - strangled in fact. I've been dying to do the same to one of you lot. So if you wanna live, tell me what the hell's going on. Why's your father keep trying so hard to kill me?'

The throat made a loud gurgling noise. Tomos relaxed his grip a little.

'OK ... let me breathe first. Please ... I'm so sorry ... just let me go I beg.'

'Stop the blubbing and tell me everything. Start from the day at the wadi.'

Saif's words escaped in a hoarse croak. 'I was there ... that day at the wadi. I was with Malik ... you know him ... the old man. We saw everything ... the drowning ... you trying to get to Ahmed. It was me that held you back when we pulled you from the car.'

'Go on.'

'We didn't even know Ahmed was travelling that day, but we did know that if father found out we were there and didn't save him, our lives wouldn't be worth living. We got scared. Ahmed was the first born and father's favourite ... he always preferred him to me.'

Despite Saif's fear, Tomos could sense anger creeping into the young man's voice. 'How very sad,' he replied sarcastically. 'Get to the point.'

'So we told father we did our best for Ahmed, but you got to him first and were alone with him for a while. We said you did nothing to help - no first aid - nothing. We told him that when we arrived we saw you trying to pilfer his body. I'm very, very sorry, but we had to do it - otherwise father would have blamed us for Ahmed's death. I would have lost all my inheritance for sure. Things were bad enough anyway after that. Father made me go with Malik to try and take revenge on you at Quriyat. You remember ... the day we chased you along the beach? Please ... I'm very sorry ... I had no idea father would go to these lengths to avenge Ahmed.'

The pieces added up. Now he remembered Saif's face from the folk festival at Quriyat, the young man unsheathing his dagger even as he walked towards him through the crowd. The scumbag was telling the truth. He'd lied to his father, deliberately endangering Tomos's life.

Saif continued, his voice rising in a shrill tone of desperation. 'Father already hated you, ever since the day you humiliated him over his wells. That became public knowledge, and in our world it made him a laughing stock. I guess he was only too willing to blame you for losing Ahmed after that. He's not the sort of man to allow things to happen to him without fighting back.'

Tomos tightened then loosened his grip on the windpipe. Saif obligingly wheezed and coughed.

'What about Wadi Al Khabourah? Did your father try to have me killed there, too?'

'I ... I don't know ... I think so. I know Malik went there some days before you did, to meet some people up there. I never asked him why. I swear that's the truth.'

'I see ... and what about Libya? Tell me the truth or I swear you'll die this minute.'

With tears rolling down his face to fall hot on Tomos's hand, Saif blurted out what he knew.

'I don't know about Libya, really I don't. I heard father on the phone to his contacts there; he knows people everywhere. When he drew a blank and realised you'd escaped, he was more furious than I've ever seen him. We all feared for our lives that day.'

'Yeah? Shame he didn't kill you – would've saved me the trouble. Tell me ... did you know that apart from trying to kill me, your father also had a young woman murdered in Africa? Maybe you've heard of her ... name of Monique? Why don't you ask me how she died?'

Saif trembled. 'Never heard of her.'

He sobbed as his head was yanked back hard.

Leaning forward Tomos rasped into the ear. 'I said ... ask me how she died!'

'H-how did she die?'

'She was strangled to death. Why shouldn't the same happen to you?'

He meant it. His hand started to tighten around Saif's throat, clamping down and shutting off the vital air supply.

The door clicked open and the frightened face of the maid looked in. It was all Tomos needed to bring him to his senses. He looked up and forced what he hoped was a reassuring smile.

'Dont worry - just giving a lesson in manners. You OK?'

The girl didn't move, transfixed by the sight of a man she probably hated being strangled by a stranger.

Tomos looked around. 'Get me something to tie him up with. The wires out of the back of the TV will do. Can you bring them here please?'

The girl did as she was asked, and he bound Saif's arms and legs with the intention of searching the flat undisturbed. Before starting he asked two more questions. 'Was it you that visited my family in Wales?'

'Yes,' Saif replied sullenly.

'And was it you that hit the girl?'

'No, it was father. Ask her.'

The girl nodded to indicate Saif was telling the truth. He knew it anyway; the man was far too scared to lie.

With Saif safely restrained, Tomos took stock. First, he needed to talk to the girl to reassure her of his good intentions.

'What happened to your face? Why the bruises?'

'I'm a prisoner here ... not allowed out. I'm locked in all day. I tried to escape two days ago and was beaten for it.'

Her eyes lowered in shame. 'I clean and cook but it's not enough. They make me dress like this and do whatever they want with me ... both of them.'

She cast a contemptuous look at the trussed-up Saif. 'He's bad, but his father's worse. I heard what you said; I wish you *had* killed him.'

'Don't worry, it's over now. I suggest you get changed, pack your things ... we'll leave together before anyone else arrives.'

His heart was beating fast. He needed to calm down and think straight. Speaking more gently, he continued.

'Who are you?'

'Sunita, I'm from Sri Lanka. I came here illegally and the gang that smuggled me into England sold me to this family.'

'Well, let's get you out of this place first; then figure out what to do next. Like I said, why dont you go and pack your things - we'll leave in five minutes. You OK with that?'

Sunita nodded dumbly. 'Yes, thank you; anywhere is better than here.'

While she went to change, he searched the flat. He didn't know what he was looking for; any evidence linking Al-Hazbar to Monique's murder would be ideal.

In the larger of two empty bedrooms was a small desk. He yanked open the top drawer. It was empty apart from a small bottle of perfume and a couple of fliers. Frustrated, he pulled out the lower drawer and was rewarded by a small gleaming revolver lying innocently in an open box, a smaller box of ammunition by its side.

He slammed the drawer shut. It was better than nothing. He would call the police as soon as he could; Saif would have some explaining to do. An idea occurred to him and he returned to the living room.

'You said I'd better leave before your father comes. That means he's in London. Tell me where he is and avoid yourself some pain.'

'I don't know. He's the boss ... does what he wants.'

'You'd better be telling the truth, you're not safe yet. I'm still minded to kill you.'

Saif's eyes, wide and staring, told Tomos he believed every word.

'I swear I don't know. But what I *do* know is that he's going to make you suffer when he catches you.'

'We'll see about that. You're going to have your own problems when you're found tied up like this.'

Ten minutes later he left the flat with a nervously excited Sunita. They hurried to the end of the street and turned into a busy thoroughfare. Only then did they stop. Both took a deep breath.

Sunita had done some quick thinking during her packing. 'I'm going to try to find my uncle, he's the only person I know and trust in London. I was supposed to meet him when I first arrived but ended up with the wrong people. I won't make the same mistake again.' She looked up at him with tear-filled eyes. 'How can I thank you?'

'Just stay safe. Look, I'll write my home telephone number down. Any problems get in touch. I don't suppose you know where I might find Rashid - Saif's father?'

He fumbled in his bag for pen and paper, his attention focused on her response.

'No, but I know he's got a boat somewhere ... I think on the river. I'm sorry I don't know *where* but he goes there very often. I've heard him talking about it many times.'

Tomos handed over his details. 'D'ya know anything about this boat? Type ... size ... name? ... Anything at all?'

Sunita shook her head. 'No ... nothing. If you do find him, be careful. He's a very nasty, bad man, but I think maybe you already know that.'

He was anxious to continue his hunt, driven by the anger still swirling through him. The business wasn't finished yet, but it felt like the tide was turning.

'OK, thanks Sunita. Good luck. Here ... take this.' He dipped his hand in his pocket and pressed a small number of notes into the young woman's hand. It wasn't much, but he guessed it would make her feel less vulnerable on London's big and hostile streets. Watching her leave he found himself hoping he'd done the right thing by not taking her to the police. If he had, she risked being deported, and he didn't want to be responsible for that. Also he didn't want the police getting involved. His relationship with Al-Hazbar was deeply personal, something that only *he* could end.

42

Tomos found a phone box and dialled *999*. Refusing to give his name, he warned of an unlicensed gun hidden in a bedroom. The police would need to hurry to recover it before the owner could dispose of it. He gave the address and replaced the receiver. Hopefully the gun would be recovered, Saif taken in for questioning, and the whole Al-Hazbar family investigated. With luck the police might even find further evidence of some other wrong-doing to get a conviction.

Right ... what should he do next? Walking the length of the Thames looking for a boat owned by a rich businessman wasn't much of a lead.

The association with a boat triggered a link far too obvious to ignore. He remembered the top flier in the drawer, in particular its title, The South Essex Yacht Club. It wasn't much, but it was all he had to go on.

He was exhausted but anger and adrenaline spurred him on. There was a new emotion too - anticipation. Despite the lack of hard evidence his gut feeling told him he was on the right track. His only other option would be to just wait and watch the flat, hoping Al-Hazbar would return. He didn't fancy that - and if Al-Hazbar learned the police were onto him he might never go back.

He hailed a cab and gave the name of the Yacht Club. The journey took longer than expected, a combination of the heavy evening traffic and distance travelled. He wasn't familiar with London and its suburbs, the roadside names meant nothing. All he knew was that the taxi carried him a long way east of the capital, all the way to the open flat landscape of Canvey Island.

The cab dropped him at nightfall, his ride having crawled the last two miles as the driver searched for the destination. The rain had stopped but the wind stayed damp as it gusted in chilly bursts. He walked towards the illuminated square of the clubhouse, its identity advertised by a small sign clamped discreetly to a lamp-post. Beyond, he could just make out the dark waters of the Thames as they merged into the twilight. Rucksack over one shoulder, he mounted the steps to the building and pushed open the door.

Inside was quiet. A wood plank floor supported a few tables, only one of which was occupied; two men in a deep conversation over a bottle of wine. At the far end of the room a long bar was flanked either end with pointed arrow signs for the ladies and gent toilets.

Ignoring the two white middle-aged drinkers, he walked up to the bar and ordered a coke. The barman moved to fill a glass.

'Haven't seen you here before ... you a member?'

'No, just passing through. To be honest, I'm looking for someone. Rashid Al-Hazbar. D'ya know him?'

The barman scowled as he placed the full glass on the bar. 'You mean Ash? ... You a friend of his? Two pounds.'

He detected the deliberate note of disdain in the man's voice.

'No ... not a friend. We need to have a little chat, that's all.'

The barman took his money and chuckled. 'If you want to catch him you'll have to be quick.' He pointed at a large clock behind the bar. 'It's high tide. When I arrived earlier, he was out on the quay looking like he was preparing to launch.'

‘Thanks.’ Tomos glanced at another unfinished drink- his second that day - before spinning on his heel and hurrying for the exit. Outside he ran to the rear of the clubhouse bringing the estuary into view, the full width of the river highlighted by tiny pinpoints of light on the far bank; the intervening space largely indistinguishable as the night stole in.

He slowed to a brisk walk through a maze of small craft and lifting derricks adorning the concrete-paved boatyard. If Al-Hazbar was about to set sail, he must already be on the river. Looking towards the bank he spotted a long wooden jetty running straight out into the murky estuary, at the end of which was a large motorised yacht. A figure on the lower deck was in the act of hauling in a mooring rope. It had to be him.

Without thinking, Tomos sprinted as silently as he could along the jetty’s planking, rucksack bouncing clumsily behind him. The slack water of a tide just on the turn was allowing the craft to drift very slowly away from its berth.

He estimated there was about four feet of open water to clear when he leapt, landing awkwardly against the stern ladder. His rucksack slipped down his arm and splashed into the sea as he fought to maintain grip. Looking down he glimpsed it disappearing into churning white foam as the boat’s engines fired into life.

He climbed up to the top rung and swung himself onto the deck. A face appeared, gaping down at him in open-mouthed astonishment, one hand still holding the free end of the mooring rope.

He recognised the man’s features even as he punched them as hard as he could. The shock from the impact ran up his arm, stinging already bruised knuckles. Caught off balance,

Malik fell backwards onto the deck, the sickening smack of his head on a metal ringbolt audible even above the hum of the engine. He was unconscious - but for how long?

He gathered in the rope and quickly bound the limp arms and legs in as many tight coils as it allowed. Malik didnt move, his eyes not even flickering. A moment of mild panic fluttered through Tomos, the sensation riding on the notion he may have just killed the man. Without time to dwell on past actions, he pulled the last knot taut, stood up straight and looked around.

A couple of long fishing poles were lashed upright to the side railings of the lower deck. This was suprising, he would never have imagined Al-Hazbar as a fisherman, especially on a cold night on the Thames. In front of him were steps leading to the small upper deck and the wheelhouse.

The yacht was accelerating, the hull bouncing over the dark waters, smashing the surface into linear streaks of white that disappeared astern almost as soon as they formed. The lights on both banks had receded; the width of the estuary was growing. It meant they were heading east, towards the open sea.

Tomos crept forward and cautiously climbed the steps until he reached the level of the wheelhouse. He stood swaying with the boats motion on the exposed deck, considering how best to make his next move. In front of him the door to the cabin was open. Inside he could just make out a shadowy figure holding the wheel silhouetted by an electrically-lit control panel.

The background hum stopped as the engine was killed and the pilot stepped forward. Wearing jeans and sweater Al-

Hazbar would have been otherwise unrecognisable he was so out of context. Tomos, heart thumping, could only stare at the pistol being pointed at him.

'I knew it had to be you. Move closer, infidel, where I can see you better.' There was no mistaking those harsh tones.

Tomos ventured as far as the door and stood in the frame, thinking fast. He was unarmed, the advantage wholly with his opponent. Why the hell hadn't he taken the gun from the flat? Stupid - stupid - stupid!

'I told you once before I was going to kill you ... justice will be done, filthy infidel. So glad *I* get to kill you; not some idiot desert nomad or an old soldier - the pleasure of seeing you die would be wasted on *them*.'

Time slowed. Did he only have seconds to live? The sense of losing so tamely to such a detestable character raced through him, renewing his anger, giving him strength. He looked around for divine hope - and found it. Being adrift with the engine cut, they were at the mercy of tide and current. Beyond Al-Hazbar's shoulder, through the salt-stained front window of the cabin, he could just make out the creamy white bow wave of another vessel. Low in the water, it had to be a barge. Their craft appeared to be swinging inexorably across its path. He had to stall for time. He needed about ten seconds.

'I've been talking to Saif,' he spoke trying to keep his voice steady. 'He admitted he lied to you about that day in the wadi.'

'Leave Saif out of this ... I know what you are ... and what you've done.'

'Don't you ever stop to think about all the pain and suffering you've caused? Whatever you believe, two wrongs never make a right.'

Five seconds.

'No-one's suffered more than me - and it's all been your fault.'

'Kill me if you want, it won't bring back your son. Go ahead - shoot. I'll be one more murdered soul condemning you to an eternity in hell.'

'Fuck you, infidel!'

In one move Al-Hazbar deliberately brought the pistol up to eye level. Everything seemed to happen at once.

As soon as he saw the pistol start to rise, he threw all his energy into one desperate lunge at his enemy. He was young, fit and very fast. He almost made it.

Al-Hazbar squeezed the trigger and stumbled at the same time - the shuddering impact of the yacht being rammed by the barge throwing him off balance. The stumble cost him his aim. The bullet missed Tomos by a whisker, passing through his sleeve before ending its flight the other side of the door, into the estuary beyond.

Tomos slammed into his adversary. They grappled; both desperately searching for a superior grip. Locked together, they were hurled out of the cabin and onto the open deck beyond; the yacht keeling over under the driving force of the barge's impact.

Tomos concentrated on the gun, trying to knock it out of Al-Hazbar's hand. He clawed his wrist, twisting it away. Without releasing the gun and with a grunted effort, Al-Hazbar tore himself away, just as the bows of the powerful barge finally pushed the yacht into clear water. With a savage lurch the yacht righted itself and rolled right over onto the opposite beam end.

Al-Hazbar staggered back under the twin forces of the unexpected roll and Tomos suddenly releasing his grip. Still holding the gun, he hit the side rail enclosing the tiny deck, and disappeared over the top.

Tomos heard the crunch of ribs against metal before Al-Hazbar vanished overboard. Staggering to the edge of the deck, he gripped the rail. Heart thumping, he looked over the side.

Nothing. Then a splash of white fading into the distance. The tide would be moving the yacht really fast downstream; a swimmer had no chance, especially an injured one.

He focused on the splash and glimpsed his man; the head bobbing, one arm raised in defiance, the fist clenched in fury. In a final act, first the head, then the arm sank out of view. The opaque waters closed, leaving not a trace to betray the passing of Al-Hazbar.

Tomos wrenched his mind back to his own predicament. He was still adrift, but a quick look around revealed no other shipping close by. He could just make out the barge continuing upriver as if nothing had happened, the wake from its powerful screw dimming as it ploughed the dark swell.

He made his way back into the cabin and fumbled with the unfamiliar controls, eventually managing to restart the engine. The sensation of the deep thrum and vibration through the deck restored some sense of purpose. He wasn't confident of being able to navigate to safety. He was sure they hadn't come far from the club's jetty but it was too dark to make out any detail on the banks. And there was Malik ... he ought to check he was OK.

Deciding it was safer to be adrift, he switched off the engine and hurried down to the lower deck. The old man was conscious but groggy - a large patch of slowly congealing blood matted the hair on the back of his scalp.

Tomos knelt beside the bound figure and spoke loudly into one ear. 'Can you hear me?'

Malik gave a slight inclination of the head.

'Good ... now listen carefully. Rashid Al-Hazbar is dead ... drowned in the river ... d'ya understand?'

'Yes, I saw him go over.' Malik's slurred reply convinced him the man was genuinely concussed.

'Right ... and you've hurt your head and need to see a doctor as soon as possible ... d'ya understand that too?'

'Yes.'

'You remember how I helped you before ... in Africa? I saved your life then, so you owe me. I can help you again, but first I want you to tell me what's going on here? Why are you and Al-Hazbar on this boat?'

Malik rolled his eyes to the heavens before they settled on Tomos.

'So, infidel, you win after all. It's all over now - for both of us.'

'What d'ya mean?'

'You've killed the boss so you're a free man. Me? I want to go home ... I want nothing to do with the boy Saif ... he's a nobody without his father anyway.'

'You still haven't answered my question. Why are you out on the river? Don't forget you owe me the truth.'

Malik stayed silent, his eyes flicked to stare vacantly out to sea.

'OK, you stay here. I'm going to ram the boat into the bank and leave you. You might bleed to death or you might be found by the police. They'd love to know how you got to be tied up, especially when Al-Hazbar's body gets washed ashore - good luck with that one.'

Malik groaned. 'No need for that. Untie me and I'll take us back. You go on your way and I'll go mine - and may our paths never cross again.'

'Fine with me ... Now, for the last time you gonna tell me what's going on?'

'Well infidel, you might as well know. The boss sells arms ... guns mostly ... all over the world. In your country it's only small stuff ... hand guns to criminal gangs here, and sometimes in Europe. Safer to do business out on the river, no-one's interested in people stupid enough to go fishing on a cold night.'

'C'mon, let's go.' Tomos untied Malik and helped him up to the wheelhouse. Standing behind the older man, he carefully watched him restart the engine and set course upriver.

Malik had obviously regained most of his wits, though he was clearly still in discomfort. Nothing more was said until they completed the short trip back. The tide was still on the ebb as they came alongside the jetty. Tomos climbed the few steps up to the walkway from the lower water level and tied the mooring rope.

'Infidel, before you go there's something you ought to know.' Malik's voice called down to him.

'What's that?'

'Don't think too badly of Rashid. He's gone now, and no threat to anyone.' Malik paused, as if weighing up the worth of his next words. 'He always thought you murdered Ahmed, it was Saif's idea to convince him of that. I see you are an honourable man and have suffered for it. I'm sorry now I went along with it.'

'How can he possibly have thought I murdered his son?'

'Saif told many lies ... that you spoke to Ahmed, encouraging him to cross the wadi. He said he saw you both talking and you waving him on.' Malik sadly shook his grey head. 'He told Rashid we both tried to stop Ahmed, but couldn't get to him in time ... that is what I wanted you to know.'

Tomos found himself staring at Malik as the old man's words sank in. Although scared, the liar Saif clearly hadn't revealed the whole truth to him. He fully believed Malik's version of events, it explained everything about Rashid's motives. With nothing more to say, he walked silently along the jetty to towards a new life. Malik was right when he said they would never meet again. It was over - it was finally all over. The sudden realisation swept through him with an overwhelming sense of relief.

He glanced back at the inky black of the Thames. Somewhere in its murky depths lay the body of Al-Hazbar, drowned like his first-born son.

Tomos turned away and looked ahead. It was time to go home.

43

With his rucksack gone, Tomos had lost all his money apart from a handful of coins, and had no possessions apart from the clothes he wore. He needed help. It was Simon who came to his aid. Simon, back in Britain on leave, drove straight to London from his flat in Bath as soon as Tomos called him.

On the journey to Tomos's home in Wales, Simon was initially quiet, concentrating on following the signs to the M4 as they threaded their way through the city traffic. The idle time afforded Tomos the luxury of considering the last forty-eight hours. Was this finally it? Was this the end of years of struggle, running and hiding?

He ought to be happy, but he wasn't. Instead he just felt empty; the loss of Monique still too raw to allow for anything else. One chapter of his life had closed. Right now, he didn't care what the next might bring.

Once they hit the motorway, Simon relaxed a little.

'I hate driving in London. So, tell me what's happened ... how have you ended up stuck here with no money? ... And what about Africa? You attract trouble like a magnet; it should've been the last place on earth you went to.'

'It's a long story, and you're right about Africa - it brought me nothing but trouble and heartache.'

'Hey, I was only kidding ... you wanna talk about it?'

Tomos found he *did* want to talk. He needed to offload, and Simon was the perfect person to confide in. He already knew much of it anyway.

'I'll give you the short version: see what you think.'

He explained how Al-Hazbar had followed him to Libya and then on to West Africa where he'd probably been responsible for two murders. He told Simon almost everything, omitting only that he and Monique had been lovers. Simon would probably guess that anyway, from his anguished narrative of how he'd been hurt by her loss. Speaking out loud made everything sound so coldly matter-of-fact. Explaining Monique's death seemed to unjustly downgrade her to a mere distraction, a minor side-issue of a bigger story.

Simon wanted to know more. He waited patiently until they reached Reading Services. There, over a coffee, Tomos completed his tale.

'Monique's friend Sabine witnessed her death - actually saw her being strangled. I spoke to Pascal, Sabine's younger brother afterwards, so there's no doubt about it. I guess it's all in the hands of the local police now.'

'Did this Sabine say if she knew the killer?'

'Pascal said no ... but I do wonder if she was just too scared to tell the truth. According to her brother, she initially stated to the police that Monique left with a stranger before breaking down and confessing to witnessing the actual murder. Incredibly, she claimed the killer put her body in a bag, I've no idea if it was ever recovered.'

Tomos could hear his voice quiver with emotion as he spoke, the past tense sounding so unnatural and wrong. 'Poor Monique - she didn't deserve any of this,' he murmured.

'What happened then? Why did you leave when you did?'

'Without Monique there was nothing to keep me there, I'd already fulfilled my agreement with the king. I wanted to go to the memorial service but one of the royal Advisors came to see me the day before and told me I wouldn't be welcomed by Monique's family - what's left of it. Apparently, the king didn't want me there either.'

'Oh ... why's that?'

Tomos shifted uncomfortably in his seat. 'Believe it or not, he once told me I had to look after Monique. I promised him I would.'

'... And now she's dead.' Simon whistled softly. 'Boy ... you do have a real talent for pissing people off.'

There was no answer to that, and the coffee was finished in silence.

Tomos eventually broke the impasse. 'Thanks for the lift by the way. I left most of my money in Africa; split it between Sabine's and Monique's family. I lost the rest the other night, so I was a bit stuck.'

Simon grunted his acknowledgement. 'Let's just be glad it's finally all over. Take my advice buddy; stay in Wales and keep your head down - at least for a while.'

'My thoughts exactly ... It's the simple home life for me from now on.'

During the remainder of the journey he filled Simon in with events in London, including the demise of Al-Hazbar. Simon was still shaking his head in disbelief when he parked outside the little terraced cottage in Pontyafon.

His homecoming was a blur. He'd only warned his parents he was on his way just before leaving London, so was surprised to find the house full of people. His parents were there of course; a huge hug and kiss from his mother and typically firm handshake from his father. There were also the old Jones' couple from next door, as well as his aunt and uncle from the other side of the village. Everyone talked at once, and Oscar his fat labrador pushed his way to the fore barking with the excitement of it all.

He hadn't expected quite such a welcome, and being surrounded by so many happy faces did more for his morale than he would ever have believed possible. The moment he walked through the door seemed to encapsulate the end of a journey of a lifetime as much as anything.

The pace slowed and he became aware of a concoction of interesting smells drifting in from the kitchen.

Gwyn noticed his son's interest. 'Tomos my boy, hope you're hungry. Your mam's hardly left the kitchen since you called.'

'Just as well - the poor boy looks half-starved.'

'Thanks mam. Can Simon stay over? It's too far to drive back tonight.'

'Course he can. Gwyn ... sort the boys out with some drinks while I bring the food.'

The Jones' went back next door, followed by his aunt and uncle. His father was right about the food: a full pork roast with all the trimmings and dessert to follow. Unused to big meals, Tomos was unable to empty his plate much to his mother's consternation, a concern only a little assuaged by the fact that Simon ate heartily.

'You need feeding up, my boy. You're all skin and bones,' she scolded.

. . .

After his meal Tomos slipped outside on his own. He needed to taste the fresh clean mountain air, and have a moment's privacy to remember Monique. He still couldn't bring himself to fully accept she was gone, but he did pray she'd found peace at last.

A biting wind was whistling down from the mountain top ... had been since nightfall his father said. It cut through the darkness in sharp blasts that slapped his face and stung his ears and nose making them feel raw. The cold air felt so good, it made him realise just how much he'd missed the old place.

The ragged edges of a scurrying cloud glowed briefly as it raced past a pale half-moon. More clouds were gathering and he felt the first spots of drizzle on his upturned face.

A car drove slowly up the street. The gentle purr of the engine was just loud enough to disrupt his quiet contemplation, causing him to watch it pass in annoyance. The car's headlights sparkled on the damp streets and glinted on something small and white stuck to the garden gate facing the road.

Curious, he walked over to investigate. Icy fingers - far colder than the bitter wind - gripped him in a chill embrace. He yanked the object off the top of the gate where it was suspended by a loop.

Returning to the front door he held the object up to the porch light. The voodoo doll dressed in suit and tie looked back at him, mocking him, Tomos Morgan - a mere pawn in life's fateful game. The wire noose around the neck from which it had been hanging, glistened silver in the bulb's harsh glow.

All around him the village lay dark in its protective cloak of a Welsh winter night. His own street was empty, there was no-one in sight. He looked at the false promise of warmth and light escaping through the curtains. The infidel pocketed the effigy and entered his home. This was where he lived. There was nowhere else to run.